D0962621

A Fatal First Night

Books by Kathleen Marple Kalb

A FATAL FINALE

A FATAL FIRST NIGHT

Published by Kensington Publishing Corp.

A Fatal First Night

Kathleen Marple Kalb

KENSINGTON
PUBLISHING CORP.

www.kensingtonbooks.com

KENSINGTON BOOKS are published by

Kensington Publishing Corp.
119 West 40th Street
New York, NY 10018

All Kensington titles, imprints and distributed lines are available at special quantity discounts for bulk purchases for sales promotion, premiums, fund-raising, educational or institutional use. Special book excerpts or customized printings can also be created to fit specific needs. For details, write or phone the office of the Kensington Special Sales Manager: Kensington Publishing Corp., 119 West 40th Street, New York, NY, 10018. Attn. Special Sales Department. Phone: 1-800-221-2647.

Library of Congress Control Number: 2020952368

ISBN-13: 978-1-4967-2724-4
ISBN-10: 1-4967-2724-X

First Kensington Hardcover Edition: May 2021

ISBN-13: 978-1-4967-2730-5 (ebook)
ISBN-10: 1-4967-2730-4 (ebook)

10 9 8 7 6 5 4 3 2 1

Printed in the United States of America

Acknowledgments

Well, that sure wasn't the debut year anyone expected.

And all I can say to everyone involved in bringing Ella Shane to the world is: THANK YOU.

To my agent Eric Myers and my editor John Scognamiglio, thank you for the chance, and the help, and the desperately needed reassurance as we faced a lockdown release.

To Larissa Ackerman, Lauren Jernigan, and the team at Kensington, thank you for your extraordinary efforts to get the word out in an amazingly tough environment.

To the reviewers, bloggers and podcasters who were so kind to a terrified new author showing up like a big sloppy puppy begging for attention, thank you for not telling me to go away . . . and for pointing me in the right direction. Special thanks to Robin Agnew of *Aunt Agatha's* and *Mystery Scene* magazine for all of the encouragement and advice.

To my 1010 WINS family, thank you for taking the time to care about my book while we were in the fight of our lives. I hope I'll be able to hug you by the time you read this.

And to my families of blood and affection, there just aren't enough words. We never expected to be there, but we were . . . and we came through.

Safe and well until next time,
Kathleen Marple Kalb

A Fatal
First Night

Chapter 1

In Which Premiere Night Does Not Go to Plan

Beware Premiere Night. The words conjure images of ovations and acclaim, artistic triumph, and extravagant tributes, floral and otherwise. In the event, though, openings bring first-show glitches, importunate stage-door Lotharios, and always, inevitably, some disaster we did not anticipate. That said, I must admit that Tuesday night in early October 1899 was the first time we had seen a murder in the dressing room.

The debut of *The Princes in the Tower* began as a sensation in entirely the right way: the unveiling of a brilliant score by composer Louis Abramovitz and lyrics by his wife and partner, Anna, with two appealing blond divas in the lead roles. Marie de l'Artois, tiny and angelically beautiful, renowned for her spectacular high register and Queen of the Night in the Met's production of *The Magic Flute*, played the younger brother, the Duke of York. She doubled as their lovely and vengeful mother, Queen Elizabeth Woodville.

The older brother, Edward V? That would be me. Ella Shane, internationally acclaimed, or at least paid in several different currencies, for my coloratura mezzo, usually

heard in trouser roles, like Bellini's Romeo or Handel's
Xerxes. Tall and strawberry blond, in contrast to Marie's
silvery delicacy. Not to mention the marquee name, company owner, and general smart aleck, if you ask my cousin, manager, and co-owner Tommy Hurley, and you
probably should. I doubled as the heroic king Henry
Tudor, in *The Princes*, ending the show in triumph by van-
quishing the evil basso Richard III. I do fancy a good van-
quishing.

We'd filled a medium-size Broadway theater, as we
would for the rest of the limited run. With the twentieth
century fast approaching, opera isn't quite the popular
form it once was, but our show was an event. A well-
attended one. A new work by an unknown composer
would not conflict with, or draw much attention from, the
august precincts of the Met, right up the street. But it certainly drew interest from opera fanciers and more plebian
theatergoers alike—at least in part because it featured the
aforementioned blond divas in doublets and hose.

More than one friend of the company, as well as Tommy,
had described it as a license to print money, and while I
wasn't prepared to go that far, we were certainly off to a
strong start.

Marie and I enjoyed our standing ovation and curtain
calls and made sure that our Richard III, a young singer in
his first lead, got his share of acclaim, as well. Then we
dragged Louis and Anna out of the orchestra pit to get
theirs.

As Marie and I took our final bows, hand in hand in
front of the ensemble, we exchanged smiles. I knew what
she was thinking, because I was thinking the same thing.
Not a bad night for Maisie Mazerosky of Poughkeepsie
and Ellen O'Shaughnessy of the Lower East Side. If we
hadn't had the gift of voices and the good fortune to find

teachers to train us, we'd be sewing shirtwaists or scrubbing floors. We know how lucky we are, and we don't forget it, even when people are tossing roses at our feet.

Not my favorite, by the way. More than once, I've taken a thorn in the heel when I stepped on a bouquet in my slippers. A simple "Brava, diva!" will do nicely.

When the cheers finally faded, we took our glow to our respective dressing rooms. I would have been happy to host everyone in mine, but Marie is entitled to her own orbit and used it mostly to accommodate her family, all of whom, except her youngest, tiny Joseph, had come to congratulate her. Even her husband Paul's parents, the Winslows of Boston, were there, pouring praise, now that they'd finally tumbled to the idea that having a diva in the family is a fairly prestigious thing.

At the next door down, it was a familial scene of a different sort. Tommy was having a happy play fight with his best friend, Father Michael Riley, sparring about whether the language of the blessing in the scene before the climactic battle was accurate and appropriate to the time. Rosa, Tommy's and my former housemaid, newly promoted to dresser as well as lady's maid because Anna was too busy with both lyrics and costumes, was carefully helping me out of my cape, and we were all waiting for the stage-door admirers to start knocking.

I sat down at my vanity, not to remove my makeup, since that could be more than an hour away still, but to have a suitable place to receive visitors. And also, I will admit, to take a moment to admire my floral tributes. Well, one floral tribute among them.

I'm sure that in our modern day, it is within the realm of possibility, if insanely elaborate, for someone in England to send an order of lilacs to a particular event here. But the fact that the Briton in question had troubled to do so was ridiculously pleasing to me. The card was simple enough: *I look forward to seeing* The Princes, *and you, in London. G.*

The greasepaint thankfully hid my blush, but I confess to looking at my eyes in the mirror and remembering lines from a recent letter about whether they are bluish green or greenish blue. His are unquestionably ice blue, terrifyingly cold when he's angry, and sparkly like a naughty little boy's when he smiles.

"Stop mooning over the lilacs, already, Heller," Toms teased.

"Your duke again, Miss Ella? Are you sure you don't want me to post the banns?" Father Michael added.

I glared at the boys, who snickered, as they always did at the occasional tokens of esteem from Gilbert Saint Aubyn, Duke of Leith, who had become a friend during our investigation of his cousin's unfortunate demise and might well become far more in the fullness of time. Not that I wanted to speculate at that exact moment.

Saved by the stage-door Lotharios. There was something unctuous and grubby about the very sound of the first knock, and much more so about the knocker.

I sighed and nodded to Tommy, who opened the door to Grover Duquesne, Captain of Industry, resplendent in white tie, a floral brocade waistcoat straining to contain his paunch, and a towering top hat covering his egg-bald head. Beneath his eruption of bushy whitish-brown whiskers, his pouty baby mouth contorted into an attempt at a smile, and he seemed to actually lick his lips at the sight of me. My stomach lurched as the tiny eyes fastened on me and did a filthy appraisal that reminded me of a cattle market, only much less nice.

"Miss Ella. Such a magnificent performance," he said, holding out a sizeable bouquet of red roses in hands with a distinct and disturbing resemblance to charcuterie. *Small* sausages. The Captain of Industry is from the earlier generation who collected chorus girls, and is incapable of understanding that I am a respectable lady, and an artist, not a candidate for his kept woman.

For myself alone, I am rather more blunt: I'm nobody's whore.

Toms tensed at the door and narrowed his blue-green eyes at Duquesne, with the expression New Yorkers generally reserve for outsize vermin, like the sewer rats of the Gowanus Canal.

"Thank you kindly, Mr. Duquesne," I said, doing my best to maintain demeanor as I held out my hand and let him bow over it, as diva protocol requires. It would not do to empty my stomach on his spats.

"Indeed, Miss Ella. Are you planning to adjourn to Delmonico's tonight?"

I had never yet adjourned to Delmonico's of a night, nor would I. As a Lower East Side orphan made good, I was perhaps excessively careful about even the appearance of impropriety. Nothing on offer at Delmonico's was worth the risk to my reputation. "I'm sorry, no."

"Ah, well. It's a delight to see you and the lovely Madame de l'Artois in such wonderful roles. And that death-scene aria of yours, 'Never Shall I Love.' You truly sing it like you mean it."

"Well, Mr. Duquesne, I do." I doubted that would discourage him, but one could hope.

"Indeed she does, Duquesne," an acerbic voice contributed from the door. "We don't have to have a word again, do we?"

Preston Dare, sports editor of the *Beacon*, dean of the gentleman writers' corps, and informal uncle to Tommy and me, filled the frame, managing to look simultaneously amiable and menacing. Even in black tie, with a red carnation at his lapel, his salt-and-pepper hair and mustache neatly groomed, Preston managed to project just a tiny bit of threat. He and Tommy had both been known to "have a word" with any admirer of mine they deemed insufficiently respectful.

While it might seem more threatening if the word came from Tommy, who'd been a boxing champ before he turned from managing his own career to mine, Preston was also quite effective against the depredations of stage-door admirers. Under the convivial chronicler's patter simmered the unmistakable message that this was a man you did not want to cross.

"Good to see you again, Dare." The Captain of Industry tried for joviality. "Great column on boxing rules last week."

"Thank you." He bowed.

Duquesne bowed. Tommy bowed.

Duquesne took one more vile run at it before he left. "If you and your protectors should find yourselves at Delmonico's . . ."

"Thank you very kindly, Mr. Duquesne."

Tommy took his cue and held the door, allowing the Captain of Industry to scuttle through it. Any resemblance to a cockroach was entirely unintentional.

"Great heavens, kid." Preston shook his head. "He gets worse every time."

"Someday, I am going to have to really teach him a lesson," Tommy said darkly.

"No, you're not, either of you," I chided them. "He's just looking and being repulsive, and that's not worth you risking his lawyers or worse."

They scowled like cranky little boys. Cranky large boys, actually, since both are well north of six feet.

Father Michael, no delicate flower himself despite the cassock, joined in. "I wanted to clock him one, too."

"Right?" Tommy growled. "Swine."

"Worse." Preston's scowl deepened. "At least you can make bacon with swine."

Father Michael just shook his head.

A knock at the door announced the next contender, saving us all from further discussion.

This swine was more like a piglet, actually, accompanied by his sow of a parent, and his uncle, who inspired no barnyard comparisons whatever.

Teddy Bridgewater—yes, *those* Bridgewaters—is barely a legal adult, and barely noticeable. His most remarkable feature is his mother. Mama Bridgewater inevitably reminds me of one of the lesser Valkyries, if they were in the habit of lurking about in bombazine dresses and mourning bonnets. She has never yet spoken to me, since as a performer, I am beneath her exceedingly respectable notice.

That, at any rate, is what she wants me to think. In fact, since these days all but the most narrow-minded acknowledge my profession as respectable and honorable, her antipathy for me is rather less noble. I suspect she's far more bothered by the fact that I am perhaps half a decade younger than she, while she looks at least twenty years older, never mind my being slim enough to convincingly play boys.

It would have truly enraged her to know that I feel a bit sorry for her.

As usual, Teddy handed me a bouquet of lilies of the valley, the scent of which nauseates me, and took my hand in his clammy paws to bow over it. He'd actually kissed it once, but it had clearly been an accident, so he was not the recipient of a "word."

Teddy bleated a few admiring sentences about the opera, and then his mother turned her eyes away from their attempt to set fire to my costume and gazed sharply at his face. "Yes, then, I need to go home to bed."

Mother and son turned to leave, and the third member

of the delegation made his way from an amiable chat with Tommy to me, his dark blue eyes sparkling with amusement at his ridiculous relatives. I am always amazed that the same family that spawned Teddy could have produced Cabot Bridgewater.

Cabot, the current ranking male in the storied Knickerbocker clan, has spent most of his life quietly working to improve the lot of his less fortunate neighbors. Better: in addition to building libraries, he's actually been known to read the books inside.

Tommy and I had crossed paths with him and Teddy at a baseball game a few months ago, and he's taken to coming over for the occasional tea and excellent conversation. Born to the Bridgewater prestige and fortune, he is so high in the social firmament that he has no need of pretension, and Tommy and I have both come to greatly enjoy his company.

"Well, Henry Tudor never looked so fair." Cabot produced a bouquet of violets and took my hand, then held it warmly instead of making any real, or pretended, move for a kiss.

"Thank you, Mr. Bridgewater." I did not pull my hand away. Yes, I've promised to allow Gilbert Saint Aubyn to pay court, but he's in England. Still, while Cabot is very much here, he is also very much not His Grace. I don't feel even the faintest trace of the odd electrical disturbances that happen when the duke is about.

It did not especially matter, really, since Cabot seemed quite happy sharing a cordial friendship with both Tommy and me at the moment and had so far given me no indication of a desire for anything more. For which I was secretly relieved, though I would not admit that to anyone.

Just then, though, I did not have to pursue that line of thought, because we heard shouting from King Richard's dressing room.

It was right across the hall, so Tommy and I were first in the door, to see our Richard, Albert Reuter, with blood all over his shirt and a knife in his hand. His brown eyes were wild, and his blond hair stood up in spikes. He looked more frightened than menacing, but the man at his feet might disagree.

The victim was blond, like Albert, young, and probably fairly tall. That was about all I could tell, because there was so much blood from the wound in his neck.

"Arterial slash. He's gone, kid," Preston said behind me, shaking his head.

"How do you . . . ?" I started.

"I was a drummer boy at Gettysburg. Don't ask me anything more, all right?"

Speechless, Tommy and I both stared back at Preston for a moment, thinking about what horrors he must have seen on those three burning days in July 1863. As we stood there, Father Michael walked in, took one look, and knelt by the victim to begin last rites.

"Albert," I asked finally, "are you all right?"

It was an insane question, but no more insane than what happened next.

"Oh, Miss Ella!" He dropped the knife and collapsed, sobbing, in my arms. "I didn't want him dead."

I was still holding him and patting his back, comforting him as if he were an upset child, when the police arrived.

Chapter 2

In Which Reviews Are Good, but the News Is Not

Even sans homicide, premiere nights are late and taxing to the voice. There may be some chorus girls who get away with staying out into the wee hours and carousing in any number of unspeakable ways with no diminution of their skills, whatever they may be. There are no successful opera singers who can sustain such behavior for any length of time.

No matter their swaggering boasts, even the most debauched among the tenors must rest to protect their instrument. Most singers actually lead quite disciplined, moderate lives because the instrument works far better in a healthy body, and no form of misbehavior is enjoyable enough to risk one's career.

All of that to say I went directly to bed when we finally returned from the theater. The police had not released us from the scene until well after the first round of papers and reviews had come in. Those, at least, were rapturous. The critics loved the opera, the cast, and the frisson of "two spectacularly beautiful and spectacularly talented blond divas in trousers singing their glorious best," as the

Republican Star put it. We were not to be missed, according to the *Spectator*. And the *News of the City* simply proclaimed its absolute adoration for us.

It all had come, of course, with the taste of ashes, considering what had happened even as the critics were writing those sensational reviews.

The police had been kind enough to question Marie and the Winslows first, so they could take their two wee ones home to bed, but that had made a longer night for the rest of us. By the time we got home, Tommy and I were both exhausted and heartsick. I washed away the blood Albert had left on my hands and face, drank a medicinal brandy, and collapsed on the pillows . . . and stayed there, quite appropriately asleep, until well into the midday, as was my habit. Not decadence, discipline.

When I finally emerged from my slumbers, I was hungry and headachy, and hoping that the whole thing was a bad dream, a fantasy immediately dispelled by the voices coming from the parlor as I padded down the stairs.

I had buttoned my purple plush wrapper over my nightclothes and stepped into matching slippers embellished with sweet pink flowers, leaving my hair still in its sleeping braid. At the sound of what seemed like a very serious conversation, I turned to go back upstairs and put on a suitable housedress, because of course I do not normally wear nightclothes around anyone but family.

But there would be no escape.

"Miss Ella!" called a familiar voice as a smallish, slightly pudgy redheaded man appeared from the parlor. Cousin Andrew the Detective. He's actually Father Michael's cousin, but everyone thinks of him that way.

His precinct is close to our town house, so he would not normally be involved in the theater murder, but Father Michael had called him, and he had talked his way into helping the inquiry, offering his special expertise with the witnesses. The actual detectives in charge didn't much care, assuming they had an open-and-shut case.

"Hello, Detective Riley." I bowed as graciously as I could manage. "You are not here merely to enjoy Mrs. G's baked goods, are you?"

"Sadly, no." His eyes twinkled despite the mournful tone of his voice. "But delightful baked goods they are— almost as good as your reviews this morning. Your cousin, Mr. Gosling, and Mr. Dare have been helping me in my inquiries."

"Ah. Well, then, lead on."

I drew myself up to my full height and tried to convince myself the wrapper was just an unusually thick and warm tea gown as I proceeded into the parlor. It might have worked if Tommy hadn't snickered at the sight of me.

"Well, Heller, you can't say you don't look like the morning after," he teased. He, of course, was perfect in a gray day suit, with not one strand of his dark auburn hair out of place, the wretch.

Henry Gosling, our booking agent, had the grace to put down his muffin and blush. Preston just laughed, but his eyes were wearier than usual.

Cousin Andrew gave me a courtly bow as I took a chair. While I'd woken hungry, the smell of actual food made my stomach lurch. Tommy poured a cup of coffee, and Preston offered it to me.

"Gret, um, Mrs. Grazich has made some very tasty graham gem muffins," Preston said.

I took the coffee gingerly and most carefully did not smile at the slip, or the tiny bit of color in his cheeks, which softened his worn look. Preston was very quietly and respectfully courting our lovely widowed cook, after decades of flirting with barmaids. "Perhaps later. My stomach's a bit dicey."

"Washing blood off in the wee hours will do that," Cousin Andrew said, shaking his head.

Tommy favored him with a glare. No matter whose cousin he was, he was not allowed to distress me.

"It's fine, Toms," I said quickly. "And nothing more than what actually happened."

"You shouldn't be drawn into this, Heller, and now, of all times."

Cousin Andrew shook his head. "I'm terribly sorry, Tom, but I'm afraid you're all in it already."

"It's our company, after all," I replied quietly. "I know. How is Mr. Reuter?"

"As well as can be expected. Michael is visiting him, but I doubt spiritual comfort will help much. He's likely to get the chair." Cousin Andrew did not sound happy about it. Like Father Michael, and many other enlightened people these days, he has moral concerns with capital punishment.

I wondered if there was more to it than that. Some detectives, and highly intelligent Andrew Riley might well be one of them, are very suspicious of overly easy cases.

I sipped my coffee gingerly as the others watched me with varying degrees of concern. Henry looked particularly distressed, his normally amiable round face drawn into sharper lines.

"Miss Ella, I am so sorry," the agent began. "You know we've been working to do a much better job at checking the bona fides—"

I shook my head at the reference to a very unpleasant tenor who'd slipped through his usually diligent vetting a few months ago. "I'm not blaming you, or your son-in-law."

"Thank you."

"You'll take some muffins back to the office, of course," I added as evidence of goodwill. He's powerfully fond of Mrs. G's efforts, especially since his own Mrs. G—Gosling—has banned most treats, in hopes of banishing his small paunch.

"Someday, we may lure Mrs. G away from you."

Preston's eyes narrowed ever so slightly at Henry, and the agent quickly became very interested in his coffee.

"Now, about last night, please?" Cousin Andrew is not unused to the rather scattershot conversation at our house, but it can be irritating to a commonsensical copper.

"Sorry," I said.

"Ah, I know what to expect anytime I come here." The detective put another muffin on his plate. "Let's start with how you came to hire Mr. Reuter."

Henry took that and restrained himself from another gem. "I auditioned several bassos and bass-baritones and narrowed it down to three, whom I presented to the company."

"And how did you choose, Miss Ella?"

"We actually hired all three. One, Eamon Morrissey, is very young and not really ready for a leading role, despite a magnificent voice. He's playing several small parts and understudying the male second lead, Neville."

Cousin Andrew took a thoughtful bite of his muffin and nodded.

"The second one, Ruben Avila, has tremendous presence and is really a better swordsman than Albert. He's playing Neville and understudying Richard, with the understanding that he'll go on a few times during the run."

"All the time now," the detective observed.

"He seemed quite happy with the opportunity as it was."

"All right. So why was Albert the choice for Richard?"

"The voice. He's just got that tiny bit more polish than Ruben . . . even though Ruben may eventually be the better performer."

Tommy smiled. "Can you tell she argued for Ruben and I convinced her we should give the part to Albert?"

"No?" Cousin Andrew twinkled. "All right. So none of your Richards knew each other before the show?"

"I don't think so," I said, "other than the vague way we all know each other in our world."

"Eamon and Albert may have been better acquainted," Tommy cut in. "I think they're from the same parish, so they would likely have had some connections."

"I'll check." The detective made a note. "Have you ever heard of Florian Lutz?"

"The victim?" I asked.

He nodded.

Tommy and I shook our heads. The name Lutz was vaguely familiar, for some reason, but I was certain that neither of us had ever known a Florian. Preston, though, put down his cup with a contemplative expression.

"What?" Cousin Andrew studied him closely.

"Played for the Brooklyn Superbas a season or two ago and got traded to Cleveland."

"Not the Spiders," I began. The Cleveland Spiders are universally acknowledged as the worst professional baseball team in the nation. Even by their own (dwindling) fans.

"Yes." Preston took another graham gem and just turned it in his fingers. "I'm afraid the poor boy had his hell on earth, and no need of your Richard to send him there."

"Rather a strong description of a season with the Spiders, Pres," Tommy reproved.

"Even if quite possibly true," I contributed.

Preston glared at us both. "Not playing for the Spiders, you two. His wife was murdered while the two of them were in Cleveland."

Tommy and I just shut up. Nothing to say to that. Especially since it quite likely reminded Preston of his own loss: his wife and child, who died in a cholera outbreak nearly thirty years ago.

Cousin Andrew nodded. "Hell on earth, indeed."

"I don't remember all the details. I'll look at the clips in the morgue."

"Thanks."

"Stop looking like bad kiddies." Preston shook his head at us. "You couldn't know."

"Still." I patted Preston's hand. "It was unkind. Even to the wretched Spiders."

"And you try so very hard never to be unkind," he replied, squeezing my hand for a second. "You're good kids, both of you."

"But sadly, not much help." Cousin Andrew bit back a smile at the description of Toms and me and our complaisant reaction to it. "I don't know what else I might glean from you at the moment. I'm sure I'll be back."

"Just helping the Broadway precinct make the case?" Tommy asked.

"Something like that."

He *did* have some misgivings about the apparently obvious killing. But he would never say anything to us, so we would do better to leave him to it.

"Well, when you return, Mrs. G will make you something nice," I promised.

"I can only hope. Someday, I must trouble to find myself a wife."

"Many people do just fine without one," Tommy pointed out.

"Maybe. But I'm pretty sure I'm the marrying kind. If only I could convince Miss Katie McTeer of that."

"Really?" I asked. Like many maiden ladies, I love a little matchmaking. "Does Miss McTeer enjoy the opera?"

Cousin Andrew colored a bit. "I believe she does."

"Well, tell me when she'd like to come, and we'll see to it that you have good seats and meet the cast backstage." Tommy just chuckled. "Of course we will."

"Thank you, Miss Ella. I probably should decline, being an officer of the law and all."

"What?" I asked, with wide, innocent eyes. "There's a problem with a close family friend coming to see us?"

Cousin Andrew twinkled again. "Not at all."

Preston laughed. "Kid, you take the cake."

"Cake." I sighed. "I always crave cake during a run. And nobody wants a Romeo who looks like Brünnhilde."

Tommy grinned. "Soon enough, we'll finish the New York run, and you can have your cake . . . and head to London, too."

"They do have very good cake in London." I remembered something involving whipped cream and gooseberries at a tearoom near the British Museum.

"It's not cake you're going to London for."

Henry and Cousin Andrew, thankfully, seemed merely puzzled by Tommy's comment.

Preston, who knew and approved, smiled wisely. "It doesn't matter where you find the cake, kid, as long as it's the right one."

Soon after, Cousin Andrew took his leave, and we flew into a whirlwind. There was no time to sit and discuss matters, with so much to do. Ruben had started his vocal rehearsal for the night while I was still asleep, and now we had to get down to the theater and walk him through.

But first, I had to spend a few minutes with the other important member of the family.

"Love the birdie!" I called as I stepped into the rehearsal studio, formerly the attic of our town house, carrying a generous bowl of seeds.

Montezuma, my Amazon parrot, glared down from the rafters at me. He was clearly feeling neglected between the late night and the morning upheaval. "Sing for birdie."

"All right, just a little. I'm singing tonight, and I can't risk a bad night for the paying customers to please you."

"Paying customers!" he mimicked, giving me another hard look. "Sing for birdie."

I complied with some simple scales, and that was all he wanted. The point was to make me do something for him, not whether it was anything exciting. As I started the second run, he flew down, and I held my hand out and let him light on my finger.

He joined in, and we sang through a little light vocalization, which I would have needed at some point in the day, anyway. After I finished, I stroked his bright green head and put the bowl of seeds down for him.

"I've got a long day, Montezuma, but I'll be home more tomorrow."

"Home tomorrow!" Montezuma replied, and from the look in his eyes, I knew he wasn't just mimicking.

"I'll do my best, birdie."

Montezuma had come with the house—the old importer who sold it to us had been unable to take him along to retirement in his daughter's home—and the bird had soon decided he liked both Tommy and me just fine. As long as we were generous with seeds, carrots and, most importantly, attention.

The bird even enjoyed the road or, more accurately, the train. He'd probably been the happiest member of the company during our recent stand in San Francisco, though he'd been easily soothed with grapes and a good lullaby. Tommy and I had required quite a bit more to compensate for missing our dear friends for weeks on end. Mostly long walks around the lovely Paris of the West for him and long baths in the hotel suite's deep claw-foot tub for me.

In any case, I was already running late because I'd daw-
dled with Montezuma, as if it weren't a serious and important day. I stopped in my bedroom on the floor below
the attic, and scrambled into some rehearsal clothes, with
a long coat to cover the breeches. As I dashed down to the
kitchen to grab something to eat, I heard the sounds of
Tommy rummaging in his office, probably looking for information to help Cousin Andrew.

While we share the town house, it's only one of several
properties we own together. We've invested the proceeds
of our tours wisely, including setting up his mother, who is
my aunt Ellen, and the youngest cousins in a brownstone
not far away. But the town house is much more than an in-
vestment. It's a happy home, and proof of how far we've
come from the tenements of the Lower East Side. In addition to the comfortable, book-filled downstairs rooms and
the studio on top, we each have a floor to ourselves. Unthinkable luxury to people who grew up living cheek by
jowl in tiny spaces.

Admittedly, we have mostly unused guest quarters on
each floor, but day by day we have privacy and space most
New Yorkers of any social class can only dream of. The
thought was a good reminder of how fortunate we truly
are, a fact too easy to forget when in the midst of life's
maelstrom.

Belowstairs in the kitchen, Mrs. G was packing a basket, with Preston sitting at the table, drinking coffee.

They both turned a little pink when I walked into the
room. Despite being a widow with two mostly grown children, Greta Grazich can't be much past forty, and she's
blessed with a smooth peaches-and-cream complexion and
the same ashy fair hair Marie has. She wears hers in a
crown of plaits around her head. "Miss Ella, you really
must take care of yourself."

"I do my best, Mrs. G."

She handed me the basket, tutting. "Some nice date-bread sandwiches and a hot bottle of good cinnamon-orange tea for your throat."

"I can vouch for that cake, er, bread," Preston said, cutting his eyes to Mrs. G.

"I don't doubt you can." I gave them as neutral a smile as I could manage, carefully ignoring the plate of lemon-curd tarts on the table, since we youngsters aren't permitted to acknowledge the doings of our betters until they want us to. "We've got to go walk Ruben through so he'll be ready for tonight."

"Long day and long night for you," Preston observed.

I chuckled. "I'm planning to spend tomorrow lying about the house."

"And good luck, Heller," Tommy said as he walked in and took the basket. "Marie and her family are coming over for tea tomorrow, remember?"

"Of course they are." I sighed. We'd planned the little family-only gathering long before last night's unpleasantness. Now, though, instead of relaxing together, we'd likely be reassuring each other.

Even with graver matters at hand, both Toms and I would enjoy seeing the junior Winslows, who are the sweetest small people ever invented, excepting only Anna and Louis's little boy, the Morsel.

"I'll make a nice batch of monkey faces," Mrs. G offered with a smile. "I know the small ones love cookies."

"So do the big ones." Preston shot Tommy a grin.

Tommy chuckled and nodded to me. "Well, next week it will be matinee Wednesday, and you can be early to bed and late to rise."

"Mr. Ben Franklin would not approve," Mrs. G, who'd been to a lecture on the American Revolution not long ago, put in, "but he never had to sing every night."

Preston smiled. "You've got that right."

I grabbed a tart from the plate in front of Preston. "Off to the Wars of the Roses."

"Have a good afternoon, you two," Tommy called as we swept out, giving me an impish smile and deliberately not giving Preston a chance to comment.

Chapter 3

Enter the Second Richard III, Stage Left

At the theater, Ruben Avila was already onstage, in cape and old breeches much like mine. He is Cuban and quite glorious to look at in that dark Spanish way, with a neatly trimmed beard and mustache framing his caramel face, and big, sweet brown eyes. That sweetness of personality is the other major reason I didn't fight Tommy to make him our first Richard; Ruben was still inexperienced enough that it takes a good bit of extra effort to radiate the appropriate degree of menace. He would get there with practice, but in the meantime I was not entirely certain I wanted to duel every night with an evil king who inspired nothing so much as a desire to feed him cookies.

Eamon Morrissey was onstage, too, taking his rehearsal for Neville. No one will ever mistake Eamon for anything but a big Irishman. He's an inch or so taller than Tommy and sturdier of build, with the flaming ginger hair people associate with our brethren. My father, who lived only long enough to give me his blessing and his name, was a redhead; and on the strength of my mother's stories of the man she adored, I have always had a soft spot for them.

Poor boy, Eamon needed the full benefit of my soft spot and Tommy's willingness to give a fellow Irishman from a tough part of town a chance. He had an utterly magnificent voice but not yet enough of the acting and movement skills to go with it. That would come with time, and a run of understudying Neville would be very good for him. Well, he'll either sink or swim now, I reflected, watching the two of them.

They were practicing the scene in which Neville notifies Richard of Gloucester that the princes are dead and he is king. Neville is a baritone role, purposely written so either a heavier-voiced tenor or the basso who understudies Richard could do it well, with a few adjustments. His announcement here is fairly short and simple. His big moment comes a little later, when he brings the same news to Queen Elizabeth Woodville, quavering in entirely justified fear and guilt, then flees in absolute terror before her devastating rage.

Louis's music is intricate, and Neville's feelings are complex, so it can be a real showcase. It had been for Ruben, and now, even though he was holding back so he would have a full voice tonight, it was proving to be for Eamon. The young singer's burly awkwardness read as ambivalence, and the sureness of his voice combined with the uncertainty of his body struck exactly the right balance.

I smiled at Tommy as we slipped in at the back. Eamon was going to be just fine.

Within a few measures, we learned that Ruben was going to be even better. One of the rare true bassos, he was comfortable with the deepest range of the role as written and quickly relaxed into Louis's glorious music. I could hear him trying to hold back for tonight and grinned at Tommy.

"We've got a winner."

"That we do." He cocked his head at me. "We were still right to go with Albert."

"I don't disagree. Ruben wasn't ready, but he seems to be stepping up now."

"No 'I told you sos,' Heller."

"Me? Never."

I noticed one of the hands in the wings, watching and glowering at Ruben as we walked up. I hadn't seen him before, and I wondered briefly why he was just standing there with a menacing stare.

"Who's that?"

"New hand. Drumm, I think. I'll tell Booth to keep him busy."

"Good idea." Booth, our New York stage manager, would work the glaring Mr. Drumm like a mule once he knew he'd been playing spectator. He is as hardworking as Tommy and me and has no tolerance for laziness.

"All right!" Louis called from the piano in the orchestra pit. "Very good. Madame Marie is not here, but let's have Ruben walk Eamon through the beginning of the vengeance scene."

Tommy and I walked to the front as the singers worked the scene. After, Eamon did a half-voice sing through of his big aria.

"Take a few moments, gentlemen. We'll work the death and duel scenes next, now that Miss Ella is here."

"Looks good to us," Tommy said as Louis stood up from the piano. "Are they ready?"

Louis pushed his glasses back up on his nose and smiled. "They're doing well. I'm actually quite impressed with them both."

"Excellent." I returned Louis's smile.

It faded almost immediately, though. "Any word on Albert?"

"Being held on a murder charge." Tommy took that.

"He knew the victim from his neighborhood, but we don't know much more right now."

Louis nodded thoughtfully. "Ah. That explains why Eamon seemed so much more rattled than Ruben. He's from the same part of town, isn't he?"

Tommy nodded. "Weird as it seems, the Germans and Irish share a parish in that part of the East Side."

"I'm sure it must make for interesting Sundays," I observed.

"Saturday nights are probably easier." Tommy grinned. "They all agree on beer."

"Not the same kind, though." Louis laughed.

"I'm told the German bock isn't so far from our fine red ale, but I've never gone to a bierstube to test the theory."

"Don't expect me to join you." Louis's amiable smile faded a bit. "A fair number of Germans aren't especially fond of us."

"I'd argue that there are ignoramuses in every nation," I cut in. My mother was Jewish, and if not from the same village as Louis's people, certainly a refugee from the same basic idea.

"Well, there you are right, Miss Ella. And I never sensed any prejudice from Albert."

"He would not have been here if we had," I assured him.

"I would not have let him within ten feet of her," Tommy growled. The Irish, in general, are not known for their enlightenment in matters of faith, but they are absolutely known for defending their own. And the minute my father, Frank O'Shaughnessy, fell in love with my mother, Malka, soon to be Molly, Steinmetz at Immigration, she was part of the tribe. So, too, their daughter.

"At any rate, we're waiting to see what becomes of him," I moved us along, "and we've got to prepare for tonight."

"We've run most of the vocals." Louis nodded. "But we should rehearse the blocking."

"Do we need to do the death scene?" I asked. "Eamon's simply staying in his usual spot as henchman, right?"

"Unless the murder gave Ellsworth a sudden growth spurt." Tommy chuckled wryly. "I don't think you want him trying to drag you offstage."

I had a good three inches on Ellsworth, a marvelous young tenor who had picked up several small parts in his first ever professional engagement. He was the henchman designated to kill tiny Marie, which was fine.

Eamon had charge of me, and that wasn't going to change with his promotion. Though slim, I am not a small girl, and we don't have any other males in the company who could reasonably murder me. The final duel at Bosworth Field was an entirely different art form; it had to look convincingly like single combat between men. Ruben is about the same height as poor Albert, an inch or two taller than me, which would work nicely.

As I'd told Cousin Andrew, Ruben was an excellent swordsman, almost as good as my fencing master, although like most men I've dueled, he took a while to get used to the idea of being at crossed swords with a woman. Albert had, too, and we'd spent extra time working on the scene, because it has to look real, and it is exceedingly difficult to get a properly brought-up man to come after me with the right look of blood in his eye.

Eamon actually had less trouble killing me on a nightly basis than either Ruben or Albert did fighting me. I did not ascribe this to any fault in his upbringing, but simply to the promise of better acting ability. Also, admittedly, there was the fact that attacking me with a pillow in half-light does not require nearly the same level of ferocity.

In any case, we ran the duel a couple of times, and Ruben settled in quite well, despite the stressful challenge of taking over for a colleague who was very likely a murderer. After the last time, I gave him a hand to his feet, and we walked to the edge of the stage together.

"How am I doing, Miss Ella?"

Think about the show, not why we're here. I understood completely.

"Wonderfully. You'll be magnificent tonight." I patted his arm. "Just remember, it's a fight. I'm there to kill you. I'm not your singing partner or even a woman. I'm your mortal enemy."

Ruben smiled sheepishly. "My mother taught me to treat women with nothing but respect."

"And I admire her for it. But her son has a job to do."

He nodded.

"Almost all men have a hard time fighting me at first. I'd be worried about you if you didn't."

"I don't have a problem fighting you," Tommy said as he walked up to us with a laugh. "But you usually throw in on my side, so I don't have to worry."

Tommy and I had never actually fought, beyond the usual chasing and hair pulling that all kids do when they grow up together. A few years older, and far smarter and kinder than the average boy, he'd been my adored protector when his parents took me in after my mother's death. A couple years later, when the neighborhood bullies came after him because he wasn't the kind of brute they were, I'd done my best to help him.

All I had to hear was one of those baboons snarling something like "Sissy," their favored opening, and I was right in the fray. Even if Tommy tried to stop me. There's more than one future Five Points gangster who ended up with a good bald spot thanks to my jumping on his back and yanking out a handful of hair when he tried to get a shot at Toms.

Within a couple of years, Tommy was half a foot taller

and the star of his boxing gym, I was the legendary soprano Madame Lentini's protégée, and our street-fighting days were over. So were the taunts. We in the family know that Tommy isn't the marrying kind, but most people just assume that he's chosen to take care of me and Aunt Ellen instead or that some girl broke his heart. No one would be fool enough to inquire further of the Champ, never mind use playground slurs. Really, it's none of their damned business, and people leave it that way.

For our part, Aunt Ellen and I are rather selfishly glad that we will never have to share him with another woman. We are both, though, also quite glad that he has many good friends and a full and happy life, as is entirely possible in our modern age for a person who does not marry, for whatever reason.

Street fighting is almost—almost—a fond memory these days. One of his old nemeses sometimes even comes to the opera when I'm in town and sends a bouquet to "the Champ's Spitfire Cousin." Connor Coughlan is bad news to most of the world, but he looks at Toms and me with affection. Which is fine—and safe—from a distance.

"Hopefully, we won't be fighting our way out of anything for a while." I joined in Toms's laugh.

Ruben, who'd lived in his own tough part of town until his last role, grinned. "I knew about the Champ, of course, but I didn't know you mixed it up, too."

"Not since before I started singing seriously." I chuckled as I quoted my mentor, Madame Lentini. "Bloody noses are bad for the instrument."

"Of course."

"Not as bad as you think," Eamon contributed, emerging from the wings as we got close to the stage edge. "Every once in a while, I still have to explain to someone that singing opera doesn't make you a sissy."

Tommy tensed beside me, and his eyes narrowed a little at Eamon. "People are who they are, singing or not."

Eamon backed right off, the usual reaction to that look from the Champ. "Sure thing. I do get sick of what people think about opera singers, though."

I intervened before tensions could rise any further. "Imagine how bored I am with what people think of a woman who dresses up as a man to sing for a living."

"It must be awful."

"Eventually, you decide that the people who matter know who you are . . ." I started Tommy's favorite line.

"And the hell with everyone else." He finished it as we took the stairs down into the pit.

Louis smiled at us all. "Acquainting the crew with Mr. Tommy's maxim, I see."

"I'd embroider it on a sampler if I did fancy work." I returned the smile. "What do you think, Mr. Composer and Conductor? Are we ready for tonight?"

"As ready as you'll ever be."

Tommy, Louis, and I exchanged glances. We knew, as our young singers did not, that you never really know until you're in front of the audience. But there was every reason to hope for a good night, if not a good night's sleep.

As it turned out, both of them were wonderful onstage that night, entirely justifying our faith in their skills, and the extra hours of preparation. Ruben even managed to seem almost menacing in the final duel, no doubt to the horror of his mother, who, he told me with a shy smile at curtain call, was in the audience. I was glad she got to see him receive such thunderous applause for his first lead.

I expected him to bring her backstage after the show, but he didn't. Perhaps just overwhelmed by the excitement of his debut. Perhaps he simply wanted to be home, so he could drop the cool façade after being so professional in the face of a dreadful situation. I could certainly understand that.

Eamon acquitted himself well also, other than a bit of awkwardness at curtain call because he'd never before had a role that allowed him an individual bow. Marie and I had to shove him in front of the audience, and everyone shared his laugh and cheered. A delight to be there for a fellow singer's first big moment.

Still glowing with a share of their fresh triumph, Tommy and I returned to the town house with much lighter hearts that night, not least because our immediate worry for the future of the show had been lifted. Moreover, after the hours of extra rehearsal, with another performance night coming up fast, neither of us had the energy to lose sleep over our myriad other worries.

They would return soon enough.

Chapter 4

In Which Our Divas Prepare

By Friday, things were starting to settle into a routine. With three smooth shows to our credit, and Ruben's and Eamon's strong transition into their new roles, we had put the ugly beginning of the run firmly behind us. At least on the stage.

Not as much backstage. Marie had been especially troubled, since the murder took place just a few doors down from her, with two of her wee ones right in the theater, never mind the in-laws. Tommy and I had allayed most of her concerns at our tea Wednesday midday, during a long conversation with her and Paul while the young Winslows did their best to demolish the drawing room and, not incidentally, a large batch of Mrs. G's monkey faces.

I didn't blame her for being worried; I was quite unnerved with no maternal instinct in play. But as unhappy as we were about Albert's arrest, it rather settled the matter and made it quite clear that there was no wider threat. Especially when Preston swung by to bounce the baby and inform us that Florian's late wife was Albert's sister.

Motive, opportunity, and a bloody knife in hand. Damning indeed.

That was enough for Marie and Paul, and the rest of us, too, though we still had a very difficult time believing our colleague as a killer. Not to mention Cousin Andrew's clear, if unsaid, doubts.

The alternative, though, was far more frightening.

In any case, when I wandered in a bit early Friday, a stop at a nearby bookshop having proved less than satisfying, the theater was humming. Booth, the stage manager, and the prop master were laughing at some kind of joke that left them blushing like bad little boys at the sight of me, as stagehands circulated about to check the set pieces, and the place was filling with that wonderful buzzy feeling that comes as the clock moves closer to curtain time.

Rosa was already in my dressing room, brushing my black velvet doublet and fussing over the brocade Henry Tudor cloak. It was one of Anna's lovelier creations, but it never draped to Rosa's satisfaction.

"Miss Ella. Running a bit early today."

"Yes." I shrugged out of my good purple coat and hung it on the rack. "Some days it's nice to have extra time. Think I will read on the settee, if I won't be in your way."

"Not at all, miss. Would you like the Lorgnette? There's another item on the show—but this time nothing on the murder."

I shook my head. Rosa loves her yellow papers, and the Lorgnette is the gossip column in the *Illustrated News*. I do not share her affection, but I'm glad to see her reading to improve her English. She came here as a babe in arms, but her family still speaks Italian at home, and her father takes only the Italian paper. "You should read the *Beacon*."

"It's there. Nothing on us today. I already finished Miss Hetty's piece on that murder trial that's starting next week."

I took the papers and scanned the fronts. The dressing-room murder had naturally drawn its share of headlines the first day, but a new indiscretion by the Prince of Wales had thrown us, and many other matters in the City, off the front pages. We were not disappointed by this, even though I did not wish to devote much thought to misbehavior among the British ruling classes.

Today it appeared the Prince of Wales was still up to no good, which did at least suggest an impressive level of energy in a man his age. With a little smile to Rosa, I dropped the Lorgnette on my dressing table and kept the *Beacon.* "What did you think?"

Rosa sighed. "I think I envy Miss Hetty."

"Really?" I doubted my good friend Henrietta Mac-Naughten, one of two women reporters at the leading paper, considered her lot so desirable.

"Oh, yes. To go to the courthouse and see such an exciting case? And then write about it, with thousands of people waiting to read my words?" Her face went dreamy. "What a wonderful job."

"Hetty would agree with you on this one, but not most days." I sat down on the settee, grabbed the mulberry-colored afghan Aunt Ellen had knit for me years ago, and curled up with my paper. "Her editor usually makes her write about hats."

"I could write about hats," Rosa said, looking over the velvet cap I wore as Henry Tudor.

"I don't doubt it. But Hetty is every bit the writer the men are, and her editor generally won't let her write serious things."

"Not fair." Rosa sat down in the vanity chair. "So how did she get to write about a murder trial?"

"It's a woman accused of killing her husband, so she convinced her editor that she has a special insight, being a female."

"Makes sense to me. But Miss Hetty isn't married."

"No."

Her brown eyes took on a naughty gleam. "I bet every married woman wants to kill her husband once in a while, but most don't. How would Miss Hetty know if this one did?"

"I think Miss Hetty wants to kill the men in the news office once in a while. Close enough."

We smiled together.

"But she wouldn't stab them fourteen times," Rosa said, getting up as she fussed with the feather on the cap.

"He was stabbed fourteen times?"

"At least, they say."

How did I miss that? I remembered the stabbing, but not the fourteen times. Distracted by the show, no doubt. I blinked and folded the paper to read as I sat on the settee. The trial was set to start next week, and the article summed up the case to date, so readers could be prepared to follow developments. Hetty was at her usual standard, outlining the case against poor Amelie Van Vleet in her vivid prose, sharp and smart, rather than the slipshod stuff that the sensational writers produce.

When officers arrived at the Fifth Avenue mansion that fatal afternoon, they found Mrs. Van Vleet in the drawing room, wearing only an embroidered batiste nightgown, kneeling and sobbing in a pool of blood by her husband's prone form. Suspicion immediately rested on her because she was the only family member in the house.

My eyes widened. This was a corker of a case, as our sports writer friend (and Hetty's oft argumentative colleague) Yardley Stern would put it. I read on, mentally checking off the boxes for a thrilling tale: husband gruesomely murdered, beautiful younger wife found by his body, wearing only a nightgown—a sheer, fancy one at that!—in broad daylight, relatives and neighbors raising questions about the couple's marriage and, not incidentally, Mrs. Van Vleet's fidelity. Oh, my.

Hetty handled it all with aplomb, making sure the reader understood exactly what was going on without ever crossing the line into matters unsuitable for a family newspaper.

"It's really starting to feel like a run," observed my leading lady as she knocked on the door and walked in. Marie was doing much the same thing I was, relaxing in the dressing rooms a little earlier than necessary, if for entirely different reasons.

At home in Brooklyn, she is Mrs. Winslow, the respectable, though unusually lovely, wife of a successful lawyer and mother of three small children. In a theater, she is one of the best coloratura sopranos of her generation, known for her utterly transcendent performances in the incredibly difficult role of the Queen of the Night, in Mozart's *The Magic Flute*. Her unusual skill enables her to work when and where she wishes, mostly the Met, but sometimes in prestigious regional productions. But, in my dressing room, she's just a good friend, the former Maisie Mazerosky of Poughkeepsie, another poor girl who struggled and made the best of her chances.

Marie often arrived at the theater early because she needed the time away from her family to think herself into the role and put her life as a busy mother firmly offstage. She certainly did not look like a Brooklyn matron at the moment, in a simple sky-blue floral wool dress that set off her sparkly cornflower eyes, with her silver-blond hair in a loose knot. Anyone who didn't know her might think she'd already begun applying stage makeup, because her lashes were dark and her lips pink, but I knew that was just one extra gift from nature.

"Are we as much fun as the Met?" I asked impishly.

"More. The Met is a bit too dignified for fun."

"See?" I gave her a triumphant grin.

"Dignified or not, you know they'd love to have you."

"And offer me only one or two roles a year. No thank you."

She sat down on the other end of the settee, sighing. This was not a new conversation. We had indeed had emissaries from the Met, but like some other personages who've recently appeared in my happy life, they had seemed to want commitments and limits that I was not prepared to give. And Marie well knew it. She took the *Beacon* from me, a safe change of subject. "Hetty's got some hot type this time."

"Hot type, indeed."

"Her editor must be thrilled that he gave her a chance."

"I hope so. We've both been so busy that we haven't had any time to talk."

"Why do I have the feeling that a velocipede ride is coming on Sunday?"

I shook my head. "Too cold. I'll probably just go for a walk with her after Mass and return home for a late breakfast or early luncheon."

"I know your Mrs. G doesn't hold with late breakfast any more than my Coralie does."

"No, but she will make compromises during a run. Won't Coralie?" I did not think it fair to Preston to mention that I strongly suspected she would not be *my* Mrs. G indefinitely.

"Grudgingly." Marie smiled. "I do enjoy being in a real production again. I'd forgotten how wonderful it is to be onstage every night."

"It is." I returned the smile. "Best feeling in the world."

"There are a few better. Or at least as good. But for those you need a husband." Her mouth dropped open a little as she realized what she'd said, and she blushed, before we both burst into giggles like schoolgirls.

"I wouldn't know," I said finally, playing stern maiden lady.

"I *meant*, of course, the joy of tending my little ones."

"Of course you did."

Her eyes drifted past me to the lilacs, which were well past their prime and really should have made way for other floral tokens of esteem. Except that I could not quite bear to toss them. "So why have you kept those lilacs so long? Does Cabot Bridgewater finally know you well enough to send lilacs?"

My turn to blush.

"Ah. Someone across the pond managed to send an order for lilacs. Quite resourceful." Her eyes narrowed a bit as she appraised me. "Well, now I know why you haven't given poor Mr. Bridgewater much encouragement. You're waiting for London."

"I don't know what I'll find in London," I replied with perfect truth, leaving aside the fact that Mr. Bridgewater didn't seem to want much encouragement.

"A duke who's been sending you letters for months, and now lilacs, if nothing else." She patted my arm. "I saw you two together back then, remember. He's dead gone on you, too. If it's just a matter of working out the singing and the geography, well, surely that's a great deal easier at his end of the social spectrum than ours."

"I don't know. He may have expectations I can't meet. And I—" I broke off, uncertain how to explain the strange complex of feelings that came up whenever I thought of Gilbert Saint Aubyn. Attraction, surely; enjoyment of his company in person, and as much of his colorful, witty letters; but something less pleasant, too.

"You're afraid."

"I'm not."

"Not of him, which would indeed be a good reason to leave him in London, but of what he may do to your nice comfortable life."

"Perhaps."

"I remember when Paul and I were courting. He swore on all he holds holy that he would not stand in the way of my singing and that he loved all of me, including the music. But I couldn't believe him."

"You couldn't?"

"Not really." She sighed. "I had to learn to trust him."

"How did you?"

"Mostly time. And seeing him do what he said he would do. Yes, there are a lot of men who want to shut us in a bandbox and keep us for their eyes alone. But there are also some wonderful men who enjoy standing beside, or even behind, their women. Paul is one. Your duke might be, too."

"I don't know."

"You don't have to know yet." She smiled. "You're probably also a bit afraid of all those feelings you have about him."

I shrugged.

"If he's a good man, and worthy of you, he won't take advantage. But I wouldn't make any plans for breakfast the morning after the wedding."

I could feel my eyes widening. "Marie!"

"As my Irish grandmother used to say, there's no reason to marry unless you're going to have someone to keep you warm in bed."

"She didn't."

"She did. And she made sure to give me the talk before the wedding, because she didn't want to leave that to my mother, who she described as a cold Polish fish."

I laughed.

"I'm glad she did." Marie gave me a very mysterious

smile. "And one of these days, I hope I get to pour you some whisky and pass on her wisdom."

"I don't drink whisky."

"You will for this."

We laughed.

"Two-hour call, Madame de l'Artois, Miss Shane!" Booth called, knocking on the open door with a long bony hand, his spare face warming with a smile at the sight of us. "You ladies make it easy for me."

"Anything we can do for the crew," I said, only half joking. "It's almost candle-lighting time, anyway."

Booth's smile widened. "I'll be back."

Marie nodded. "I'll just stay, then."

I pulled my mother's small pewter Sabbath candleholders, the only thing I have of hers, from the spot behind my mirror, where they'd been waiting for tonight. While I usually attend Mass at Holy Innocents with Tommy, I haven't lost track of Mama's Jewish faith, either. I light candles on Friday evenings whenever I'm at home. During a run, I host the company's little observance in my dressing room. Lighting candles alone at home often leaves me melancholy, but welcoming the Sabbath with my colleagues is far closer to the joyful intent of the observance.

We are anything but doctrinaire about it, though. Everyone in the company is welcome, Jewish or not, and many do come. Booth, who grew up in a fire-and-brimstone family, will not darken the door of a church but rarely misses candle lighting.

Marie, raised Catholic, as I ultimately was, also often joins us. She, like me, enjoys the warmth of the ritual and the joy of celebrating with our fellows.

Louis and Anna walked in with their small son, Morrie, otherwise known as the Morsel—for "small morsel of humanity." He looks like a golden-haired cherub from a carte de visite and is astonishingly well behaved besides.

Tommy was just behind them, and as soon as the Morsel sighted him, he marched right up to him and put his arms up.

"Sure thing, fella." Tommy bent down and helped him into place on his shoulders. Like all small, vulnerable creatures, the Morsel loves Tommy, and for him, it takes the form of demanding a ride at any opportunity.

While Tommy settled in with his new driver, making sure the little one wouldn't scrape his head on the ceiling, I set the candles in the holders. A few supernumeraries and stagehands filtered in the door, and then it was time.

I handed the matches to Anna. Her Hebrew is far better than mine, and while I can and do manage it at home, I also enjoy deferring to her. I'm sure we're violating any number of rabbinical laws by lighting candles to welcome the Sabbath, only to go out and perform, but this is not a traditional observance.

What it is, more than anything, is a chance to feel God in the room and share a special moment with our closest friends and family. Not even remotely orthodox, but it gives us joy and reminds us who we are. Any God I want to worship, never mind spend eternity singing for, would not be troubled by that.

Tommy took my hand as Anna finished the prayers, and we exchanged a little smile. He's as good a Catholic as any I know, but even when we were children growing up, he would often stay and watch while I lit the candles on Fridays, with Aunt Ellen's cautious but still amazing permission. "No different than lighting a candle at the church, after all," she'd said after seeing me light them the first time. "Just another way to talk to the Lord."

She did not share any of that with her priest, who was not nearly as progressive as Father Michael, considering it to be a matter inside the house and therefore none of his business.

Once the blessings over the candles were done, Louis reached up to bless the Morsel, who giggled at being so high above his daddy, and we all exchanged a hearty *Shabbat Shalom*.

"Well, now that we've taken care of our souls, it's time to look to our voices," Louis said with a wry smile. "Vocalization in ten minutes, ensemble."

And so back to the life of the theater.

Chapter 5

Intermission at Washington Square

The first week of the run ended as a sparkling success. No further untoward incidents marred our performances, and while we surely did not forget the murder, neither did we dwell much on it. Tommy was pleased with the sold-out houses, Marie and I were glad for the appreciative audiences, and all were amazed by the good reviews for quite literally everyone involved. One newspaper (the lowly *Brooklyn Lighthouse*) even praised the stagehands for the smoothness of the scene changes. And well-deserved praise it was, if somewhat unexpected.

The worst of the stage-door Lotharios stayed away, a small mercy we knew could not continue, though the dressing room was filled with society matrons happy to enjoy the cachet of a backstage visit while looking down on me. There's an expression, unfortunately, that I see too often on the sleek, well-fed faces of these women: envy for my talent and what they perceive as my freedom, held back by a great satisfaction that they are so far above me as respectable married socialites.

Most of the time, I simply do not take delivery on the insult.

And so, we came to our first intermission. Even performers who love their art and the particular piece they're presenting at the moment look forward to dark day. Most of the popular theaters observe similar schedules, whether they have some sort of extravaganza involving chorus girls, an operetta, or a truly serious work of art like *The Princes in the Tower*. And everyone, from the newest stagehand to the marquee attraction, rejoices in the rest.

For opera singers, of course, the physical strain is much higher than with lighter kinds of music, and the need for recovery far greater. So with that need, and Marie's family responsibilities in mind, we set up a rather unusual performance week. After the premiere week, Sunday and Monday were our dark days, with a regular night show Tuesday. Wednesday we offered only a matinee, allowing us extra rest before the most important performances at the end of the week. Not to mention giving Marie a nice long late afternoon and evening with her children, because her older son has only a half-day on Wednesdays. It worked well for us, and ticket sales suggested audiences agreed.

Despite the demands of performing, and all the extra drama of premiere night, what I needed most by the time we finished the first week of the run was not more rest but an ordinary day with my friends and family.

Sunday began with Mass at Holy Innocents, Tommy and I having both decided that spiritual comfort, and Father Michael's latest homily, outweighed extra sleep. That would change as the run wore on, at least for me, so it was wise to get to church while I could.

Soul tended and a candle lit for my father, I left Tommy to his own plans and headed out for another of my great joys.

Hetty MacNaughten, *Beacon* reporter and my best friend outside the opera world, was meeting me for a long midday walk in Washington Square Park, followed by a luxurious tea and gossip, before she headed off to the news office. It was our last chance for a girls' afternoon for some time, and we cheerfully seized it.

We were, of course, well aware that the boys might horn in on the party, and that was quite all right, too.

I took off with a smile and a spring in my step, humming something I'd heard Montezuma singing that morning. Just before the triumphal marble arch at the main entrance to the park, I saw a familiar bent figure crouched on a bench.

"A penny for a poor widow?" asked a raspy voice as I reached in my pocket for the coins I'd picked up earlier.

The plea came from a bundle of rusty black clothes, ragged layers piled one on top of the other, all unrelieved deep mourning. Mrs. Early was indeed a poor widow, one who spent most of the time she was not begging for her keep praying for her lost babies and husband at Holy Innocents. Father Michael did what he could to help her, as well, but it's not a kind world for people who've suffered so much that they can't do any sort of gainful work and don't have family to care for them.

Whenever I go to the park, I make sure to take some money for her, enough that it will buy her a few good meals or whatever she might need. I am all too aware that any one of us could be in her position if life were cruel.

"Here, Mrs. Early." I put the coins into her gnarled hand.

"God bless you." Her light green eyes, once beautiful, now full of untold sorrow, held mine for a moment.

She doesn't know my name or anything about me, other than that I give often and generously. I know her name and that she prays for her family at Holy Innocents only because Father Michael told me once when we both stopped to give to her.

"God bless you," I said and meant it. I patted her hand

and moved on, thinking as I always did how lucky some of us are and how unlucky others.

Hetty was waiting at the entrance to the park, and she smiled when she saw me. "Doing what you can."

"Don't look at me like that. I know you do the same for a beggar outside the *Beacon*."

"Well, of course I do."

"I won't tell anyone you have a heart if you don't tattle on me."

"Fair enough."

We shared a smile as we started down a path. Even though Washington Square Park was quite busy with walkers of all sorts taking their constitutionals or enjoying a more social promenade, there was still plenty of space and time, so we could prowl as we wished.

Late autumn in New York goes one of two ways, either unseasonably warm or bone-chillingly cold. We'd been cursed with the cold this year, so Hetty and I had skipped the sports costumes and bundled up in wool dresses and long coats, mine midnight blue, hers a sensible gray that set off her red hair and milky skin. I had left my furs, best coat, and fancy millinery at home—no need for diva airs here—and wore my simple dark blue velvet hat with a big satin rose, instead of any plumes. It was clearly better made and more fashionable than Hetty's simpler bow-topped green one, but not dramatically so.

"So, are you ready for the start of the trial tomorrow?" I asked as we circled the fountain.

"I can't wait. Morrison's finally given me my chance, and I don't plan to miss it."

"Well, your investigative piece on patent medicines last spring didn't hurt."

"*Our* investigative piece."

"Anyway, if your article is any indication, the trial's going to be quite the sensation."

"So will the conviction." She gave a grim nod. "She's putting on a good defense, so there'll be days and days above the fold, but I don't have much doubt how this is going to end."

"Poor lady."

"Poor lady, indeed." Hetty sniffed. "She married Hosmer Van Vleet for his money, broke her vows, and then killed him."

"That's quite an indictment." I chuckled a little at her disapproving scowl. "Are you sure she was unfaithful?"

"Well, she certainly seemed to have much too close a connection with Anatole Lescaut."

"That Frenchman who was doing business with Van Vleet?"

"Yes. I suppose some people would find him appealing, but I think he's too smooth by half."

"I haven't seen him. Tell." I was not, generally, a fancier of *les hommes français*, but one never knew.

"It's all the hand-kissing and, oh, '*Vous êtes très belle, Mademoiselle.*'" She wrinkled her nose. "Ugh."

"You met him." I swallowed a smile. "Perhaps he's one of those men who fancies *les rousses*."

"Right, he is. He fancies good headlines, Ells."

"I wouldn't doubt it. The Frenchmen I've known do tend to underestimate one's intelligence."

"Exactly." She shook her head. "And you know how well I react to that."

We grinned at each other. "Yes, but that wouldn't stop you from seizing an exclusive."

"It didn't. It'll run tomorrow morning, as the trial begins."

"Very good."

"Just barely worth sitting in his nasty little office, listening to him jaw about himself." Her face crinkled at the memory.

"What does he do?"

"His office is near the exchange. I believe an investor of some sort, who'd done some work with Hosmer."

"No chance that he had something to do with this?"

"It's a locked room mystery, remember? No one else was in the house at the time."

"That we know of."

"What are you thinking, Ells?"

"I don't know what I'm thinking. I know only that you have a very bad feeling about this man, and he's very close to a nasty killing."

Hetty scowled. "Close to the woman in the nasty killing, anyhow."

"Obviously, you find him vile. But what about her? Does he seem like the sort of man who could convince a woman to give up her principles?"

At that, she gave a bitter laugh. "I don't think Amelie Van Vleet has much in the way of principles. You assume everyone's like us."

"I don't. But flirting with a man and actually breaking your marriage vows are two very different things. Even if she didn't have our elevated principles, surely she wouldn't want to risk that."

"Maybe she figured she'd get away with it. People do."

"I don't know."

"You know, you are such a romantic."

"Romantic? Take that back!" I snapped, only half joking.

"Oh, you are, at least a little. After all you've seen—all we've seen—you still think that a woman can't take adultery lightly."

"How could she? It's a terrible risk—and a rotten thing to do besides."

"Absolutely," she agreed. "And nothing either of us would ever do, assuming we manage to find a man we can stand."

"There are men we can stand. They can't necessarily stand our work."

"Much too true." Hetty shook her head, and I suspected she was thinking about sports writer Yardley Stern, her colleague and frequent sparring and sometime reporting partner, not to mention a friend to Tommy, Preston and me. "Anyhow, Mrs. Van Vleet is absolutely not the kind of woman you are or I am, if only because neither of us would marry for money."

"Are you sure—"

Hetty reached up and knocked on the top of my head. "Anyone home there? Ella, most women wouldn't turn down a man who wasn't quite right if he came with plenty of scratch."

"I suppose." I shrugged. "And we don't get to judge, after all. Who knows what her life was before."

"Not bad enough to justify murder."

"Good point."

"Speaking of murder, will your first Richard get the chair?"

"It surely doesn't look good, standing there, holding the murder weapon and covered in blood," I said bluntly. If Cousin Andrew could not voice whatever his concerns were, I certainly could not bring up any doubts with Hetty. At least not now.

"Sad."

"Sadder still. The victim was a baseball player, apparently traded away from New York to Cleveland."

"Not . . ." Hetty knew her sports as well as I did.

"Yes, the Spiders . . . And then his wife was murdered there."

"Terribly sad, indeed . . . and a great story. Much better than some deadly little dispute in a dressing room." Her eyes lit up. "You'll keep me informed?"

"Of course."

She smiled as we turned down a path close to the side-walk. "How are you and Marie doing?"

"We're mostly wonderful." I shrugged. "The new Richard is excellent, as well."

"Any word from London?" she asked. "Speaking of men we can stand."

She had interviewed Gilbert Saint Aubyn during our collective investigation of his cousin's demise, and he'd passed muster, no easy task for a British toff, as she had dryly put it.

"Letters, as always. Some lilacs on opening night." I couldn't say it without a grin.

"Poor Cabot Bridgewater."

I laughed. "He's a friend. So, for that matter, is the duke."

"Right. Tell me you don't believe that, all right?"

"I don't know what I believe, except that I can't imagine any man being willing to share me with the music, no matter who he is or how much he loves me."

"And isn't that the problem." She nodded sadly. "Yardley walks me back to my house some nights, and once he even took my hand . . . but he also talks about wanting to come home to a wife."

"You'd probably like to come home to one, too," I teased. "Someone to cook your dinner and bring your slippers."

We laughed.

"Well, nobody's bringing me my slippers," I admitted, "but Mrs. G does make a magnificent tea. And I, for one, am getting chilled."

"Let's go."

Hetty and I were soon ensconced in the parlor with our jasmine tea and plates of little sandwiches, tarts, and cookies. Mrs. G had laid on her usual admirable company tea, but I suspected an ulterior motive. The tarts were lemon curd, which are nice enough but not a favorite of

Tommy and me . . . and Preston's absolute downfall. I hoped Mrs. G had social plans of her own.

While the lemon tarts made me smile, I did not, of course, mention them to Hetty. News offices are utterly merciless, and even my dear sweet friend would not be able to resist some teasing, never mind what her colleagues would do if they knew. Eventually, our world would know about Preston and Mrs. G—I hoped when they announced their engagement—but in the meantime, I wasn't going to spread the word.

Hetty and I had just returned to our discussion of the Van Vleet trial when we heard the door slam.

"Do I see a dainty wrap in the foyer?" a familiar voice called.

"Too dainty for Heller."

"Oh, just come in here, boys!" I responded needlessly as Yardley bounded in, followed by Tommy.

"Well, two lovely ladies," Yardley said, bowing to us with exaggerated formality, which looked even more comical on his skinny frame. Once upon a time he'd nursed a mild crush on me, but in recent months, he'd clearly been growing very fond of Hetty. She'd always been a little sweet on him, carefully hiding it with sparky comments, so they might one day become more than colleagues. Well, if they could stop sparring, and if Yards would back off that "Angel in the House" nonsense. Perhaps not.

"And two big boys," Hetty shot back with a smile. "How was the boxing gym?"

"The usual," Tommy said, with something that was absolutely not the usual in his face. "Always good to see old friends. Even if it's a reminder that I'm well out of the life."

I poured a cup of tea for Yardley, and Hetty handed it to him as he perused the treats with a glow in his brown eyes that would not have been out of place on a tenement child. "Mmm. Cookies."

"Have some snickerdoodles, Yards," I said, passing the plate.

He took two and turned to Tommy. "You really are lucky to be out of the life. Do they know what happened to Jamie Eagger?"

Tommy narrowed his eyes. "We haven't—"

"Sorry," Yardley said quickly, guiltily.

"Who is Jamie Eagger?" Hetty asked. I didn't need to.

"Sorry, Heller," Tommy said, sitting down on the arm of the settee and patting my shoulder. Jamie Eagger had been his close friend in the old neighborhood. About my age, Jamie had taken up boxing roughly the same time as Tommy. Not nearly as good, but good enough to make more money for his widowed mother and sisters than he would have any other way.

They'd been friends and comrades during the hard early years of their careers, which had created a special bond at the time, but over the years they'd lost touch, as people will when their lives go in different directions. Though there was no estrangement, I could not remember the last time Jamie had joined a boys' evening or come to dinner.

"Hurt?" I asked, hoping that was all.

Tommy shook his head. "He was training some new prospect, and the fool wasn't watching what he was doing. Hit him hard, and he fell backward into a stool. No saving him."

Tommy and I looked at each other for a long moment. It could have been him.

I took his hand and squeezed it. "How are his mother and sisters?"

"Terrible, as you'd think."

"We'll do a benefit."

Tommy nodded. "That'll help."

"Best we can do." I hoped it would give him some solace, too.

Hetty and Yardley shook their heads in unison.

"You two, always taking care of someone," Hetty said.

"What's wrong with that?" Tommy asked with a tiny edge in his voice.

They smiled.

"Nothing at all," Yardley said, grabbing a couple of tarts. "Not one thing."

Chapter 6

Messages from Far and Near

The next morning found me resting at home and Tommy heading out to the Eaggers. While the Irish don't follow the Jewish custom of sitting shiva, staying home for a week and receiving visitors while mourning a death, relatives and friends do gather around to support the grieving in their time of need. Toms was far closer to the Eaggers than I was, and the women Jamie had left behind might find my presence more intimidating than soothing, so I sent a small bouquet and my sympathies instead of paying a call.

Most of the girls I grew up with are in an entirely different stage of life than I am at this point; almost all who have survived are wives and mothers, often ground down from years of struggling to make ends meet or, even if they've been fortunate, just the daily toil of raising a family. Very few of them want to see me, well past thirty and still rather fresh looking, trim, and elegantly dressed, with the smooth hands of a woman who doesn't sew or wash for her living. No matter how humble my demeanor, and I hope, dear reader, that you know by now I am a diva who is not a *diva*, the simple sight of me would be a reminder

of how much better life could be outside the neighborhood.

Tommy's kind and respectful presence, even though he,
too, is far better off than anyone in the Eaggers' circle,
would be a comfort. Mine might well be an insult. I didn't
think it fair to a family in grief to find out.

Despite all of that, I would, of course, attend the funeral
with Toms. He would want me at his side, and that outweighed all other considerations.

That day, Tommy told me he might be late, and I knew
exactly what that meant. He and the boxers would likely
be going out to mourn in their own way, with a bit of "the
creature," as we Irish like to say. Whisky, beyond a small
medicinal drop, is not something he would indulge in on a
performance night, so this was really his only chance to
pay tribute with his fellows.

I understood completely. Men have their rituals. A smart
woman, whether Irish or any other persuasion, leaves them
to it when she can.

Once Toms was off, I took a short walk up to the
apothecary to order a new supply of cold cream and rose-
petal lip salve. When I got back, a pleasant surprise awaited
me: a letter from overseas.

Rosa's eyes twinkled, and she watched my face as she
handed it to me. Of course she'd seen the return address,
Leith House, and the bold hand in midnight-blue ink.

"Ah, how nice," I said coolly. "I will enjoy this after
luncheon."

She swallowed a giggle as I carefully placed the letter in
my book on the chaise. I am not a silly schoolgirl. I do not
swoon over missives from my swain.

If I happened to glance down at my silver charm
bracelet and notice a recent addition with crossed swords
and the legend *Until We Duel Again*, that was entirely my
own business. Likewise if I wished I were planning to take

my next fencing practice with His Grace. While not nearly as skilled as I am, and certainly not in the league of my fencing master, he brings other compensations to a match.

The charm, presented explicitly as a memento of friendship and not as jewelry, which would, of course, be presumptuous and insulting, had accompanied our agreement to exchange correspondence. Far more significantly, it was also followed by the formal request to call on Tommy and me when we came to London. That request, gladly granted, could be understood as only one thing: the official beginning of a courtship with honorable intent.

Not to mention a conundrum with no good answer for me, unwilling to give up my happy and interesting life for a man who offered things I didn't know I wanted or needed until he appeared. I would never admit it to Marie, but I was indeed afraid of what all of this might mean.

Thanks to my career, and my lifelong habit of educating myself about all things, I naturally understood that in our modern day, a progressive-minded British aristocrat who had already taken care of his dynastic responsibilities (see the two adult sons listed below him in *Debrett's*) might well be free to marry the woman of his choice. Perhaps even if that woman practiced an unconventional profession and occupied an unusual place between faiths. And yet, if the simplest clerk expects his bride to give up her work to tend his home, what more would a duke expect? No matter how modern of mind, a man is still a man.

So I had perfectly concrete reasons for my fears.

Admittedly, though, I was also quite curious about what might happen should the duke and I somehow find a resolution. What if I did need Marie's talk over whisky, and what might I do with that knowledge? As for every good Irish girl, my education in this one area of life consisted of a single sentence: your man will tell you what you need to know on your wedding night.

Until very recently, I had seen no reason to pursue the matter further. Still didn't, really.

In any case, these were thoughts I had absolutely no need to entertain just then. I collected my library books, stacking them in the usual spot so I could find them easily when it came time to return them, returned the checkerboard to good order from Tommy and the Father's last grudge match, and bustled through several other little tasks that I would never notice or care about on a performance day.

After a simple luncheon of Mrs. G's admirable mulligatawny and equally esteemed steamed brown bread, I went upstairs to the studio for a light vocalization session with Montezuma, who likely got more out of it than I did, because I was being careful of my voice. On dark days, the point is merely to move the muscles and keep everything in working order. And, of course, to please Montezuma with a few scales.

Only as teatime approached did I finally retire to the chaise and take up my letter. Montezuma perched on a shelf behind me, occasionally squawking to remind me of his presence.

Gil, as I've come to think of him, is an excellent correspondent, sending regular letters with vivid and amusing descriptions of his life in London and the North of England, accounts of events and happenings on his side of the ocean, and always, lists of interesting and improving books he's reading, often new works of history. Tommy and I are great admirers of Lincoln, and so, too, is Gil.

Today's letter followed the usual pattern, with an adorably oblique discussion of the uproar over the Prince of Wales's latest indiscretion, of which he took a very dim view. He had a much better opinion of one of Hetty's earlier articles on the Van Vleet case, which I'd included in my last letter, and very good things indeed to say about a new volume of Lincoln's legal correspondence.

Since he trained as a barrister, or trial lawyer, before several relatives in the line of ducal succession obligingly died, he no doubt took a far greater interest in legal letters than I did. But since it was Lincoln, after all, I thought I might see if my library had a copy.

All interesting enough, of course, but a man does not trouble to send transatlantic letters to a woman he plans to court merely to share thoughts on newspaper articles and improving books. The last paragraph of the letter was always where he allowed himself a hint of the sweet talk one might expect and, I admit, I'd come to appreciate.

He did not disappoint.

> *The moon is very bright tonight, and I find myself thinking that it is shining on you, as well, if very far away. Perhaps casting a silver gleam on your lovely eyes. I am still uncertain if they are greenish blue or bluish green, and have come to the conclusion that the matter will require much close study when you come to London. One hopes you will have matters of your own to study, as well.*
>
> *Yours, with much esteem,*
> *G*

British aristocratic reserve being what it is, I knew that was actually a passionate and rather lyrical way of saying what I was feeling, too. I wanted to stare into his eyes and see if what I'd seen before was still there, and if it meant what I thought it did. At that exact moment, I wasn't especially concerned about the consequences.

There is something to be said for having your swain an ocean away. If he had been there right then, I would not have been thinking about my happy and settled life, but of my unsettling and rather amazing feelings for him.

"A letter from abroad?" asked an amused voice.

I looked up to see Father Michael standing at the pocket doors.

"Miss! The priest is here!" Sophia, Rosa's little sister, announced, scrambling in behind him, her tawny hair slipping out of her cap, and her hazel eyes a little wild. Rosa was busily training her to take over as housemaid, and she seemed to be adopting Rosa's habit of announcing everyone, necessary or not.

"Hello, Father."

"Holy Father!" Montezuma greeted him, at least cheekily if not actively blasphemously.

Father Michael rolled his eyes and nodded to the missive. "You know, you probably should just put that poor man out of his misery and marry him."

"Only if he'll move over here and pitch in with the company."

"He certainly looked like he'd sign on to be your loyal second." The priest laughed as he sat down.

I shook my head. "That one is no supernumerary."

"A supporting player isn't worthy of you, anyway, Miss Ella. And you two will find a way."

"I wish I shared your optimism."

He shrugged. "What God has brought together . . ."

A line, of course, from the wedding service. I looked sharply at him.

"You know a little Hebrew, I think."

"Just enough to light my candles and pray for my mother's soul."

"Do you know the word *bashert*?"

For a moment, I just stared at him, barely breathing. I did know the word. It means "meant" or "fated."

My mother always used it to describe her meeting with and marriage to my father. Frank O'Shaughnessy's ship came in the same day as hers, and they were both at Immigration together. His Irish accent made his English almost unintelligible. Her English was almost nonexistent. But when their eyes met, the world changed.

My mother wasn't the only Malka to leave Immigration as Molly, but she might have been the only one named by her future husband. She was laying out her papers and trying to explain that she was Malka Steinmetz, coming to live with her cousin, and the overwhelmed official, for some reason, got stuck on the name Malka.

As he struggled to pronounce it, a friendly, teasing voice rang out, offering a solution. "Just call her Molly."

The comment, coupled with a smile I'm told was a lot like Tommy's, broke the tension and made everyone chuckle.

Malka Steinmetz smiled back at him, suddenly pretty and happy enough to charm the functionary, having already stolen Frank O'Shaughnessy's heart, and nodded. "Molly is good."

They wouldn't see each other again for months, when they passed on a street on the Lower East Side, both rushing to work. That was when they actually began courting . . . but everything started that day at Immigration.

Bashert.

"You know what it means," Father Michael said.

"I do."

"Well, I think it may apply to you and your duke."

I took a breath. He couldn't know how large and important that word was to me. I never talk about my parents, not even with Tommy or him, and they understand why.

My father died of typhoid when I was just weeks old. My mother lasted until I was almost eight, doing piecework and whatever else she could manage with the consumption that ultimately killed her. I took up some of the piecework as she faded, but it was never enough. The poorhouse was a real possibility before she died, and the orphanage a certainty if Aunt Ellen hadn't taken me in.

Tommy and the Father both had hard times, but they shared their struggles with large, warm families. I spent most of my first eight years alone with my mother in a tiny, cold tenement room, except for the time at the public primary school she made sure I attended.

"You're an American girl, Ellen," she would say in her still-accented soft voice. "You're going to be educated like one."

My eyes were suddenly damp. How proud she'd be of my book-filled home.

Father Michael touched my hand. "Are you all right?"

"*Bashert.*" I took a breath. "It's the word my mother used for her marriage to my father."

"Oh." He nodded. "I'm sorry. I didn't mean to bring back sad memories."

"It's all right. You couldn't know."

"I still think you and your duke are meant to be together. If you can find a way to stay on the same side of the ocean."

I smiled a little. "And if he doesn't mind my singing when we are."

"You're not giving him enough credit."

"Perhaps." I put down the letter and tried to shake off

my sadness. "Did you come here to help me with my Hebrew?"

He chuckled wryly as he shook his head. "I wish I had."

"Oh?"

"Albert Reuter wants to see you."

"Me? In the Tombs?"

"Yes." He had the tight, small smile I knew meant he wished he could tell a soothing lie instead of the uncomfortable truth. "You probably shouldn't—"

"Of course I'll go." Perhaps seeing him in jail would make it easier to believe him as a killer. Or at least make me stop wondering why Cousin Andrew seemed to have doubts.

"Are you sure?"

"When are visiting hours?"

"Saturday for anyone other than clergy."

I cringed at the exhausting thought of dragging myself down to the Tombs at the end of a performance week, but there was nothing for it. "Saturday it is."

"I know that's a difficult day for you, but I am sure Albert will be grateful."

"It's what we can do." I shrugged.

"Is Thomas about?"

"Paying respects at the Eaggers'."

Father Michael's eyes narrowed in concern. "Are the boxers having a bit of the creature in memory of Jamie Eagger?"

"I believe they are."

He nodded. "It's likely what they need."

"The Irish grieve as they do."

"Too true. He will not be happy about you going to the Tombs."

"I'll tell him, in a very quiet tone of voice, in the morning. He'll accept anything to get me to leave him to his headache powders."

The priest and I shared a smile, but then his handsome face turned troubled.

"Is Tom all right?"

"This is a hard loss. He thinks it could've been him."

"If you hadn't brought him into your career, it could have."

"But it's not." I sighed. "He's feeling guilty that he's so lucky when Jamie wasn't."

Father Michael nodded. "It isn't always easy to be the person who escaped when so many did not. Nothing new to you, or me, either."

"True. We'll just have to give Toms some extra care and feeding for a while."

The priest's serious mien melted to a boyish grin. "I hope that means I'll get some feeding too . . ."

"Trust you to bring it back to dinner."

"Mrs. G's meals are the greatest pleasure available to a man who's taken holy orders, Miss Ella."

We laughed together. "Well, since Tommy's out, perhaps you'd like to stay . . ."

"Really?" His face lit up.

"Really. But I'm going to throw you out after dessert because I have to wash my hair."

"Entirely fair."

Chapter 7

In Which We Make a Visit to the Afflicted

The performance week was uneventful, at least at the theater. That turned out to be a bit of a gift, since there was fair cause for concern at home. Jamie Eagger's funeral came on Thursday, and Tommy spent much of the week uncharacteristically quiet and thoughtful.

The service itself was wrenching. It's said that Catholics mark death well, and I suppose that is true. But this was not the celebration of a long life well lived. It was the cold comfort offered for a young man gone too soon in a senseless and inexplicable accident.

No one to blame. No one to help. No real consolation for his mother and sisters.

I stayed unobtrusively at Tommy's side, in a simple dull black dress and veil, like those of every other Irish woman in the church. Tommy held my hand for most of the Mass, jaw tight, throat working as he choked back tears, which I suspected were as much for the guilt that he wasn't the one in the coffin as for the man who actually was. Neither of us is unfamiliar with loss, but Tommy seemed to be taking this one harder than I would have expected.

As painful as it all was, I had one small blessing: unlike Tommy, who was grown when Uncle Fred died, I have no memory of my father's funeral, since I was just weeks old. My mother, of course, was buried by a rabbi, so a Catholic service holds no memories of either loss. At least I could concentrate on comforting Tommy without fighting my own demons.

Finally, it was over, and Tommy returned to the Eagger house for the funeral luncheon. I lit a candle for my father and went home alone. There I stretched out on my chaise, hoping to find a bit of rest before another arduous night. Of course, with the funeral hymns still echoing in my head, it was impossible.

The next day, on my way to the theater, I stopped off to see Aunt Ellen and the youngest cousins. She was worried about Toms, too, and we agreed among ourselves to give him as much extra care and feeding as he would let us.

She was, as always, a little concerned about me, too, but that was more easily handled with a promise that I was eating enough and doing my best to rest in my off hours. As for her other usual worry, that I was, as she put it, "really too solitary, acushla," I reminded her that I had a very acceptable beau waiting for me in London, and thanked my lucky stars that I could leave it there for now. Aunt Ellen, like most smart Irish ladies, believes that a woman should not marry until she's good and ready . . . but she also thinks I should have been good and ready at least five years ago.

I never argue. I love her too much to hurt her feelings. After the previous wrenching day, too, it was very comforting to have the usual light back-and-forth about my future and her desire to see beautiful babies with my father's smile.

That night I was very glad indeed to set up my mother's little pewter candlesticks to bring in some love and joy. Before we lit the Shabbat candles, I lit a small yahrzeit votive for her. It's traditional to light them only on the anniversary of a death, but I often do so when I need to feel closer to Mama.

The visit to Aunt Ellen and the candle lighting went a long way to lifting the darkness that night, but Saturday morning, the darkness was, of course, back in force as we made our visit to the afflicted. Naturally, if I was to go see Albert in such a horrible place as the Tombs, I was not to be allowed to go alone.

The men had planned to go as a delegation, but Preston was prevented from accompanying us by the need to discipline a junior sports writer who had distinguished himself in entirely the wrong way by challenging a bantamweight contender to a fight in a pub. Since the writer was promising and quite contrite, not to mention bruised, Preston planned only to terrify him into behaving well in the future. The chastisement, however, was both early and time-consuming, so he had bowed out of our trip downtown.

I was more than adequately defended by Tommy and Father Michael, neither of whom really approved of my meeting with Albert. Tommy was also noticeably annoyed with his best friend, apparently believing that he should not have passed on the message from Albert or, at the very least, should have lied and informed me that female visitors were not allowed.

"When have I ever lied to anyone about anything, Thomas?"

"Never. And it's one of the finest things about you," Tommy growled as we paid off our uneasy cabbie. "But this would have been a very good time to start."

"We're here now, boys," I said with a calm I didn't feel, straightening my simple dark blue hat and smoothing down my midnight-blue wool coat. I had worn the plainest and least remarkable things I own, hoping to be unobtrusive. What I did not realize until I walked inside the forbidding stone fortress was that the simple fact of my sex made me stand out more dramatically than even on the stage.

Tommy and Father Michael planted themselves on either side of me, and one or the other had a hand on my back or arm the entire time we were in the prison. Later, I would chuckle about that, but it was deeply appreciated reassurance during our visit.

The prison was everything I'd imagined, only worse. The books that describe such places are unable to capture the chill, the loudness, the cavernous stone echoing with the howls of inmates. And out of delicacy, they make no reference to the smell. It's probably best I leave that to your imagination.

The guards who let us in and guided us toward the visiting chamber were gruff but polite, but the man in charge of the room itself was less so. Perhaps not used to respectable ladies visiting his charges, or just not raised properly, he started to leer at me. Tommy cleared his throat. I don't think the guard recognized him as the former champ, but it didn't matter. He recognized that it would be very bad for his health to continue the leer, and he merely nodded.

"Here for Albert Reuter, then?"

"Yes," Father Michael replied. "His employers wish to speak with him."

"You're his employers? What's he do?"

"He's a bass-baritone," I said.

Not surprisingly, the guard gave me a blank look.

"A singer, sir," Father Michael explained. "They run an opera company."

The guard's gruff glare melted into a smile. "Opera? My wife loves the opera. Are you singers, too?"

"I am."

"Would she know you?"

"Perhaps. I'm Ella Shane."

Another blank stare. So much for international acclaim. "I'll tell her I saw you."

I smiled politely.

"How is Albert doing?" Father Michael asked.

"Hasn't been any trouble. That's all I know."

We nodded and walked into the ugly little room. It wasn't a cell; it was larger, with a table and three chairs, but the small window was barred, and the walls were the same blackish stone as the cells. I took a deep breath, immediately realized that was a bad idea, and forced down a shudder, keeping my face calm. Toms and Father Michael, I was absolutely sure, were watching for any sign of upset.

A door at the other end of the room opened, and a guard led Albert to the single chair on that side of the table.

"Miss Ella!"

He started to take a step toward me, but the guard, a younger, tougher-looking fellow, put a hand on his shoulder, and he stopped immediately, with a clank. I realized he had shackles on his ankles. Poor man.

Albert slowly sat. The guard gave a grim nod and stepped back to the door, where he stood with his arms folded. He glanced at Tommy and Father Michael and then glared at all three of us.

"You can sit if you want," the guard tossed out.

"I'll stand," Father Michael said.

"So will I," Tommy agreed but pulled out a chair for me. "You should sit so he doesn't have to look up at you."

I took the seat gingerly, knowing I would be handing off every article of clothing I was wearing for a thorough cleaning the second I got home.

Albert looked absolutely awful. He seemed to have lost weight in less than two weeks in jail, going from wiry to almost slight. A brown-eyed blond, he'd always been pale, but now he was almost transparent, with large purplish shadows under his eyes. I was relieved to see there were no bruises or other obvious evidence of abuse; even though I'm not supposed to know about such things, I was sure a singer would be all too easy a target in this place.

I reached over to pat his hand. The guard bristled a little, but as soon as he realized that I really was just resting my gloved fingers on Albert's bony ones, he backed off.

"How are you?" I asked, probably the single most foolish question ever posed in the history of conversation.

"I'm alive, Miss Ella." He shook his head. "I didn't do it. I swear to God, I didn't do it."

I nodded, acknowledging, not agreeing. And yet . . .

"I hadn't seen Florian in months, not since the memorial for a year since my sister . . ."

"You didn't invite him to the show?"

"Why would I? He was my friend once, but after Berthe, no more."

"So . . ."

"I didn't know he was there until I walked back to my dressing room after returning my props and found the door open and him on the floor like . . . like that."

I stared. Either he was lying or I had a killer on the loose in my company. I took a deep breath then, miasma or not, as I gathered my thoughts. It was an improbable story, the sort of thing a man would say to save his neck.

But if it was true? I glanced up at Tommy. He didn't

seem particularly swayed by Albert's protestations, and he's generally a better judge of character than I am, if only because a few years of having to decide where the next punch is coming from teaches a man an awful lot.

Best stick to the practicalities, I thought. "Have you hired a lawyer?"

"No. I don't know where to—" He broke off, once again seeming panicked by the enormity of it all.

"Well, luckily, we have a lawyer's wife in the company," I said briskly, glad to have something simple and straightforward to do. "I'll ask Marie to see if Paul can have someone from his firm help you."

"Thank you, Miss Ella."

"I'd do the same for anyone in trouble. I don't know what happened that night, Albert, but you're innocent until they prove you guilty."

He looked like he might cry. "I really am innocent."

"Then just keep your head, be quiet, and do what your lawyer tells you, once you have one," I told him, the same advice any intelligent person would give a friend in such terrible straits. I reached over to pat his arm, and he took my hand in an almost painful grip.

"I didn't do it." He looked to Father Michael. "As God's my witness, I didn't."

Tommy and the guard cleared their throats simultaneously, and Albert quickly let go my hand.

"Try to stay calm," I said finally. "Do you have books to read?"

"They allow only the Bible in here."

"Then I guess you'll become very familiar with the good old King James," I replied dryly. "Anything you can do to keep yourself quiet and your mind clear will do."

Albert almost smiled. "Typical Miss Ella. Books cure everything."

"They can't hurt, at least."

"Time's up," the guard cut in, not unkindly.

I stood and shook hands with Albert, who hung on to my hand a bit longer than he should have, but not so much as to get a glare this time.

"Thank you for coming, Miss Ella. You really are an angel."

"Far from that." I shook my head. "Take care and keep calm."

Outside, we all took deep breaths of the air, even though no one would consider the miasma near the Tombs to be fresh and clean. It was beyond prison walls, which made it quite good enough.

"What do you think, Father?" I asked. "Is he telling the truth?"

"How could he be?" Tommy shook his head.

"There's more under heaven than we understand," the priest said contemplatively. "He certainly believes what he's saying. Whether that means it's true is for someone well above me."

That night, after the show, sleep eluded me. After trying to fall asleep for an hour or so, I wandered downstairs for a medicinal sherry, since I could not afford to lose the night's rest.

I knew I'd done everything within my power: Marie had sent word to Paul from the theater, and a junior attorney from his firm would be visiting Albert as soon as possible. But it was all terribly troubling.

I could cast aside Albert's declaration or my own doubts or even Cousin Andrew's odd behavior. But all of them together meant something.

Tommy was on the parlor settee with his own medicinal libation, whisky, staring at the fire, his latest book face-down on his lap, where he'd abandoned it for the moment.

He looked up at me and shook his head. "You should sleep."

"That's what this is for." I poured my sherry and sat down on the other end of the settee. "You should sleep, too."

"I know."

"Albert?" I asked. "Or Jamie Eagger?"

"I could just as easily have been him."

"You chose to help me instead."

Tommy smiled. "I suppose you would put it like that. I think you probably saved me from the life."

"You saved me from scrounging from company to company, looking for work. And made us both a passel of money."

"Well, I can't argue with money." He sipped his whisky. "And we have a very happy and comfortable life these days."

"That we do." I raised my glass to him a little, and we fell back into amiable silence for a while.

"You believed Albert, didn't you?" Tommy finally asked.

"Almost. I don't know how it could have happened that way, but . . ."

"I almost believed him, too." He let out a small, bitter laugh. "My mother, God love her, is convinced he's innocent. Says the second sight told her so, and we should give him the benefit of the doubt."

She had not mentioned this when I saw her, because she knew I would not listen. Aunt Ellen is convinced she has the *gift*. In fact, her gift is a family that tolerates her occasional predictions and prophecies, not to mention her own exceedingly kind heart. "Your mother gives the benefit of the doubt the way temperance ladies hand out pamphlets."

Tommy grinned. "So do you."

"No pamphlets. No temperance, either," I said wryly, lifting my glass. "But it doesn't have to be a cold-blooded killing. Maybe it was one of those brain frenzies we've read about, where he just pounced on him and killed him without knowing what he was doing, then came back to himself afterward."

Tommy took a contemplative sip of his drink. "I wasn't thinking that."

"No?"

"I was thinking that if he is telling the truth, someone really put a fair amount of work into setting him up."

"True," I agreed. "They would have had to know about Florian and Albert's sister, lure Florian backstage, and kill him. That would take a pretty serious grudge."

"And a lot of effort."

I took a slow sip of the sherry and let it melt down my throat. I'd had enough now that I was starting to relax, which was a very good thing. "So either Albert is lying in hopes of saving his skin or there's someone out there working very hard for his downfall."

"Or ours."

"Ours?"

"Trying to make us look bad, perhaps. Harm the company, ruin Louis's premiere?"

"Maybe. Pretty roundabout way to do it, Toms."

"I suppose."

"And it would have to be someone who doesn't know much about the way the papers work around here. You'd know better than I, but I suspect all of this has actually been good for business."

He smiled ruefully. "We've almost sold out the extra week."

We had gone into the run with the plan that we would

add an additional week if sales were good. That, at least, had been one question with a quick and easy answer.

"I thought perhaps." I took a little more sherry. "I'm glad Marie and Paul were willing."

"Willing and thrilled, I think. Both of them."

"He's happy when she's happy."

"Good man, Paul."

I nodded. "Not many like him."

"I think perhaps that duke of yours is a contender."

"I'm not sure I want to give up my happy life to find out."

Tommy shook his head. "Heller, sweetheart, if it's right, it's supposed to add to your life, not take away from it. Marie still has everything she had before she married, as well as Paul . . . and the little ones."

"True." I couldn't help smiling at the thought of wee Joseph climbing up his mother's skirts.

"You want one."

"I want a lot of things, starting with a very generous slice of Mrs. G's opera torte. That doesn't mean I'm going to have them."

"I saw the way he looked at you. He'd marry you in a second."

"If it were just about him and me, and perhaps baby makes three, well, that would be one thing," I admitted. "And probably a very good one at that."

Tommy watched the fire. "I suppose it could be, if you both want it enough."

"But I can't give up everything I have and everything I am for him. I won't."

"Are you sure he'd expect you to?"

"No. But I'm not sure what he does expect."

Tommy took another drink and turned to me. "Then you'd best find out before you reject him, don't you think?"

I sighed. "I hate when you're right."

He grinned. "You must hate a lot."

"Aren't you adorable."

"Modest too."

I yawned.

"Go to bed, Heller. Everything will look different, if not necessarily better, in the morning."

No argument to that.

Chapter 8

We Duel Again

That Sunday I slept very late and woke only with enough time to brush my teeth, straggle into my breeches, and grab a sip of coffee from the tray Rosa had left at my door before I ran upstairs to the studio to prepare for my fencing lesson with the Comte du Bois. I do not hold with breakfast in bed; unless one is truly sick, properly brought-up people eat meals at a table. But a single cup of black coffee in the late morning after a show is not a meal.

Tommy, maddeningly superior being that he was, had already risen, gone to Mass, and headed off to a no doubt full day of virtuous activities, despite the fact that he had stayed up later than I. Naturally, I felt guilty for my sniping when I found his note on the studio door.

Visiting Jamie's mother. See you at teatime.

Poor family. Poor Toms.

Once again, I vowed to make sure he got some extra rest and care over the next few weeks. I knew he had a very bad case of "there but for the grace of God go I," and I was beginning to wonder if there was more than that.

Whatever was happening here, he was also wearing himself a bit thin at an already busy time. Hopefully, once the benefit was over and the Eagger family provided for, he'd be able to take some ease.

Right. He's no happier with ease than I.

"*Allez-y*, Monsieur le Comte," I called when I heard the knock at the door. I was in the far corner of the studio, taking my foil out of the cabinet, and didn't turn for a moment.

When I did, I wasn't squaring off with my little gargoyle of a pretend count, better known as Mr. Mark Woods of the Bronx. No, this was a much larger, and genuinely aristocratic, opponent.

Gilbert Saint Aubyn stood just inside the room. His ice-blue eyes closed on my face, studying my aspect, as I considered his. For a second, we just stood there, staring at each other, months of time and distance vanishing like so much smoke, the current crackling between us as strong as ever.

Bashert.

The word, in my mother's voice, slipped, unbidden, into my mind. Not now. Not yet.

"*Alba gu Bràth*!" Montezuma crowed from his perch, breaking the spell with the greeting Gil had taught him. "Scotland forever!" in Scottish Gaelic, for his Highland Scots mother.

We both laughed.

"Love the birdie," Gil said.

Montezuma preened. I shook my head.

"A rematch, Shane?" he asked as a smirking *comte* slipped into the room behind him, covering the social forms as chaperone.

"Certainly." I turned back to the cabinet to get another foil, allowing him a moment to prepare.

When I turned back, he had doffed his coat and jacket

and was standing there in shirtsleeves and waistcoat, looking like every maiden's dream of a wicked duke. I had somehow managed to forget that in addition to being an intelligent, well-read person and an excellent correspondent, the tall and dark Gil was also—

"Fine figure of a man!" crowed Montezuma.

Until that exact instant, I had no idea it was possible to blush and laugh at the same time.

"One wonders what you've been saying in that bird's presence," Gil observed, his own amused smile somewhat diluted by a sharp expression of assessment in his eyes.

Did he really think I'd said that of someone else? Not my lookout to correct him if he's that much of a fool. I tossed him a foil, and he caught it, not cleanly.

"Seems I still throw better than I catch."

My blush intensified as I remembered when I'd said that to him, soon after he'd rather awkwardly thrown me a much-needed dagger . . . and I'd thrown an entirely unexpected embrace at him. "I seem to remember you catching rather nicely not so long ago."

"The game is all in a good partner, isn't it?"

"We shall see." Fencing was likely safer than that line of conversation. I stepped into position with a smile. "What makes you think you will prevail this time?"

He grinned, the naughty little boy expression that melts my heart. "Nothing at all. But one must try."

"En garde, then."

Gil can hold his own, but he's nowhere near my level, and as usual, he took a few moments to acclimate to dueling a woman. I didn't start at the top of my form, either, with the attraction rushing back, but I quickly recovered my balance.

"You seem to have stayed rather sharp," he said as I blocked a thrust and attacked.

"Fairly."

"Fencing with the comte?" At that question, the intensity in his eyes matched the sound of steel on steel.

"And Richard III, of course."

"Ah, yes. Henry Tudor prevails. What's this I hear about a murderous Richard?"

"Not murderous toward me, thankfully."

He almost missed the parry at that, and I knew he was remembering my last misadventure, which had ended with me swashbuckling to safety from a man bent on killing. "Glad to hear it."

"Mostly," I said, pursuing the attack, "I have been researching my roles and learning the score."

"No tea dances?"

"I am persona non grata with Mrs. Corbyn at the moment." Aline Corbyn had tried to throw her last unmarried daughter at his head and had failed.

"Ah, yes. Miss Pamela. Did I hear she made a more congenial match? If somewhat enraging to her formidable mama?"

Pamela Corbyn had since run off with a livery driver. And much joy to both of them. "I did not sing at Miss Pamela's wedding."

"Elopement, did I hear?"

"Yes. She's apparently ridiculously happy in a small garden apartment in the borough of Queens."

"Better love in an apartment than none in a castle."

I looked too long in his eyes then and almost missed his advance. "Oh, well played." I parried, regrouped and started back in.

"And you?"

"What of me?"

"No elopements?"

I laughed as I attacked, then met his eyes again. We both froze for a moment. I decided he'd earned what he so clearly wanted. "No time for such nonsense, thank you. And, anyway, I wouldn't elope."

"You're right." Even as he played right past it, I could see his face relaxing at the acknowledgment. "You'd expect your man to stand before God and the world and make his vows."

I began a new attack. "The man who wins me will have to do it right."

Gil smiled and parried. "And a lucky man he'll be."

"At any rate, we have little romantic drama offstage here."

"I am still, however, considering the appropriate response to that assault upon my honor, Miss Shane."

"Really." I almost missed the parry again at his direct reference to my pulling him into a kiss after I swung to safety. I still don't know what came over me, other than playing the swashbuckling hero in the moment. Which, I guess, would make him the fair maiden. "Well, it was a truly terrible offense, Your Grace."

"Indeed. So awful an insult I haven't been able to forget it."

His voice was light and teasing, but his eyes burned into mine. The kiss, my first and only, had been entirely inappropriate and wrong, of course. But amazing.

"Ah." I smiled a little and backed him off. "Well, I suppose I shall have to pay the price for my rash actions."

"You could be facing a life sentence."

"I'm not sure I want clemency." Parry.

"What do you want, Shane?" Attack.

"What do you?"

I could have launched one more attack and cornered him, and he knew it. But the duel was now beside the point.

"Draw?" I offered.

"Someday, I will prevail."

"Perhaps."

We bowed and stood there for a long moment, eyes locked. My braid had come loose during the match, and he reached over and gently touched the falling curls, carefully pushing back a stray bit. His thumb rested on my cheekbone, the warmth of his skin soaking into mine, the electricity between us practically a wall of crackling blue fire.

"Bluish green, I believe," he said, his voice low and liquid. "But much more study is required."

"Yes." My reply sounded like I was agreeing to far, far more, and I probably was.

"Monsieur le Duc." The comte coughed.

"What?" Gil didn't move his hand or his eyes, and I didn't want him to.

"You are not affianced to Mademoiselle Ella, are you?"

"Oh, quite right, Monsieur le Comte." He pulled back, nodding to me. "Very sorry, Shane."

"What is this Shane business?" asked the comte, glaring suspiciously up at Gil.

"Miss Shane and I are old friends and address each other as such. Mr. Hurley has given his permission."

The comte nodded wisely. "Ah, well, if Monsieur Tommy approves, then it is all right. He is most careful of Mademoiselle's *honneur*."

"And quite right of him." Gil turned away from the comte and studied me again. It was the sort of look that coming from the right man makes you feel like a work of art. "It's the first time I've seen you with your hair down. It looks like honey . . ."

As he trailed off awkwardly, I blushed and quickly started pulling my hair back and rummaging in my pocket for a few pins. That was when I realized he was holding the ribbon, a somewhat fancy piece of lavender silk with a floral pattern. "You may keep it if you like."

I'd never been the lady offering her swain a memento before. It was rather nice.

"I would." He gave me a warm smile as he twined it between his fingers. "The scent of your hair, is it roses and . . . cinnamon?"

"My apothecary's daughter says roses alone are too insipid for a lady of years and discretion, and I require a bit of spice."

"Indeed you do." Gil tucked the ribbon into his waistcoat pocket.

"I'm sure you know it's one of our dark days."

"Only after trying to buy a ticket for tonight's performance, but yes." He looked a bit sheepish. "I lost track of days on the voyage, and somehow thought today was Saturday."

"It has happened to me before." I smiled. "Well, we generally have a late tea with friends so we can enjoy a little social time while still getting a good night's rest. Would you care to join us?"

"I would be delighted."

We smiled foolishly at each other for a moment, until the comte cleared his throat.

"You are, of course, welcome, too, Monsieur," I said quickly.

"*Merci*, but no. I have another engagement." His wicked gargoyle grin left no doubt as to the type of assignation.

Gil gave him just a tinge of a dirty look for hinting at such matters around a lady and left it.

"Tommy is probably back from his errands by now and would no doubt entertain you while I neaten myself a bit," I suggested.

"Did someone take my name in vain?" The man himself strode in smiling, only a faint shadow at his eyes suggesting that he'd just come back from consoling the family of a late friend.

"Winner and still champ-een!" Montezuma crowed.

"Well, who have we here? Good to see you again."

"Likewise."

They shook hands and exchanged smiles with the same easy friendship they'd had the last time. For a moment, Gil looked closely at Tommy, and it was clear that he'd picked up something. Tommy quickly brushed it off with a glance.

"He's staying to tea. Can you let Mrs. G know and amuse each other while I change?"

"Glad to." Tommy grinned. "Of course she's got to pretty up so you'll see her to full advantage."

"She's quite amazing as she is," Gil said with a glance my way, "but a smart man never argues with a lady's need to primp."

"Too true. So, Barrister, can I interest you in a game of checkers?"

"Why not?"

Chapter 9

In Which the Barrister Offers
a Lesson in Criminology

This dark Sunday, Marie and the Abramovitzes were enjoying their respective family nights, but most of our other close friends were about, as I discovered when I came downstairs after taking far too long to change into a lovely blue-violet cashmere afternoon dress with frothy lace trim, to twist my hair into a puffy Psyche knot, and to add a dab of rose-petal lip salve. If I'd been the sort of lady who used rouge, I would not have needed it. From the fencing, of course.

Gil, who had ceded his place at the checkerboard to Yardley and was leaning on the mantel with a teacup, looked up and smiled when I appeared in the doorway.

"You are lovely indeed when you trouble to wear clothes."

That earned him a laugh from Tommy, who knew it was a reference to what he'd said the first time he'd seen me in female attire, a nervous chuckle from Yardley, and a growl from Preston. Father Michael just shrugged.

The friends of the company filled the parlor, ranging around the chairs and settees. I took a space on a settee by

Hetty as everyone moved into place around the coffee table and Mrs. G's feast of dainties, which seemed to be rather more elaborately decorated than those at the usual Sunday tea. I suspected she was expressing approval of Gil's return and smiled to myself.

Hetty handed me a cup of tea, which turned out to be Earl Grey. Definitely a comment on our visitor.

Tommy took a couple of his favorite snickerdoodles and settled into his usual big chair as Yardley picked up the entire plate of jam tarts and took the arm of the settee by Hetty.

"So how goes the trial, Hetty?" Preston asked, moving a copy of the morning's *Beacon* off his settee to make room for Gil. "You're doing some really good work."

Hetty colored a little but took the compliment with a graceful nod. "Good for me, not so much for Mrs. Amelie Van Vleet."

"Do you really think she did it?" Tommy asked.

"Stabbed her husband in the drawing room, really?" Yardley added.

She glared at them. "I do, and I think she'll hang for it."

"Perhaps," Gil said, with a small troubled scowl. "I don't think you Americans have hanged a woman since Mrs. Surratt, and she gave you rather a lot of provocation."

He may or may not have known that New York disposed of the occasional lady murderess by electricity these days, but that was not the point for our duke. Tommy, Father Michael, and I knew, but the rest of the company probably didn't, that he held quite progressive views on capital punishment—absolutely opposed. Not to mention as a fellow Lincoln admirer, he had quite a negative opinion of the only female conspirator in the sixteenth president's assassination, Mrs. Surratt.

"Well, her lawyer's brought in some kind of criminologist, who claims she couldn't have done it. It's a lot of bosh."

Gil focused sharply on her. "Really? Tell me more."

Hetty gave him a funny look and a shrug.

I cut in. "He trained as a barrister, Hets. What we call a trial lawyer."

"It's rather more than that, Miss Shane." He smiled. "I've kept up a bit. My old friend Joshua is a barrister and is known as an excellent defender these days. If one is charged with murder in England, one wants Joshua."

"Really?" Hetty said. "So is there anything to this criminology stuff?"

"Quite possibly. Tell me what he's arguing."

"Well, the criminologist says Mrs. Van Vleet is too short to have killed Mr. Van Vleet. Something to do with the stab wounds."

"Not to mention getting him to just let her stab him," Yardley added.

"I imagine he never saw it coming," Preston offered.

"Or she distracted him," Yardley suggested, drawing a glare from the other gentlemen, as he had ventured perilously close to some imaginary line. He blushed a little and nodded into the jam tarts. "Never saw her."

Gil, Tommy, and Preston all returned the nod. Father Michael just smiled faintly, amused at their overprotectiveness.

"Right then," Gil said, standing up. "If it's height, there is something to the theory. Join me for a little experiment, Miss Shane?"

"All right." I stood, too, as he picked up a pen from my lap desk.

"Here. This will do nicely for a knife." He handed me the pen. "You'll note that even though our diva is quite tall for a woman, she's still noticeably shorter than I am."

We all nodded.

"Now, let's suppose I've made one comment too many about why woman suffrage may improve the world but not the ladies who wish to run it, and you've decided to end the debate in blood." He cut his eyes to me with an impish smile.

"Unlikely, but not impossible," I teased.

"Indeed. So you stab me, going, like any smart murderer, for the surest and fastest kill, the big veins in the neck."

For a moment, I thought of poor Florian Lutz. But I knew Gil would never deliberately remind us that we'd been there when a man died that way not long ago, and I shook off the memory as I mimed a move toward him, which forced me to reach up.

"Note how the stabbing moves in an upward direction?"

The others nodded, fascinated.

"That's going to show in the wound, and any decently observant coroner would be able to see it." Gil explained. "All right, my turn."

I handed him the pen and gave him a small wicked smile. "Let's say you are quite sick and tired of my defeating you on the field of honor and try for something more direct."

Gil chuckled and nodded to me as he held the pen like a knife but did not come even remotely close. "You see, this time the knife and the wounds would point down."

He handed the pen back, and our fingers touched, with another of those weird electrical disturbances. We both marked it but quickly moved past and returned to our spots.

As I did, I thought again of Florian Lutz and Albert. Could the wounds give a definitive answer in that case? I resolved to ask Gil later.

"And so, Miss MacNaughten, however much you don't

like this Mrs. Van Vleet, you may not get to watch her hang," Gil finished in an apologetic tone.

"It makes sense," she admitted with a frown. But since she didn't also point out that Mrs. Van Vleet was more likely destined for the electric chair, not the hangman, despite the common usage, I assumed we'd closed the topic.

"Anyway, the method is wrong," Yardley said. "Women don't stab people to death like that."

"What?" Hetty wheeled on him. "A woman can't kill?"

"Not at all." Preston smiled wryly. "They do every day. But women like poison. Knives are messy. Especially stabbing fourteen times."

"Fourteen times?" Gil asked. "I lean toward the gentlemen's views on this. Very rare for a woman to kill in such a grisly fashion."

"See?" Yardley crowed. "You tell 'em, Barrister."

It was clear by now that the nickname Tommy had started was going to stick, since it was, after all, appropriate, respectful, and a good deal easier in company than "Your Grace." If we're going to have a duke in the house, we have to call him something.

"Well, no insult intended to present company," Gil began with a chuckle, "but women aren't really made for killing."

"What?" I asked. Speaking of bosh.

"You are the mothers of the race, after all, whether or not you ever actually raise children." His eyes met mine with a terrifying intensity. "You are made for caring for others, protecting them. Made for love, if you will."

For a measure or more, it was no longer a discussion of crime and politics in company. It had become a private moment between the two of us, each watching the other's reaction, barely breathing.

"What absolute old-fashioned hogwash!" Hetty snapped. The spell broke almost audibly, and I managed a little laugh. "Not entirely. What he's saying is the same argument women make at the suffrage rallies, if much more elegantly."

Gil's eyes hadn't moved from my face.

Hetty snorted quite inelegantly herself. "Certainly not."

"It surely is," Tommy cut in. "Women deserve the vote because the hand that rocks the cradle civilizes the world." He smiled. "I'm not saying it isn't hogwash, but you're all talking the same hogwash."

"God made men and women differently," Father Michael observed. "Not that one is better, but each has gifts that complement the other." He shook his head with a sheepish smile. "That probably doesn't help."

Yardley laughed. "I'm with the barrister on this one. I don't think Mrs. Van Vleet did it."

"I did not say she didn't do it," Gil corrected him, briskly moving on. "I said only that it's highly unlikely that she stabbed him fourteen times. There is always the one case where the apparently impossible actually happens."

"Well, I agree with Yards," Preston said. "Maybe I'm just an old stick, but I don't believe a woman stabbing a man fourteen times. Even our Ella, who's comfortable with swords, probably couldn't do it, never mind a society matron like that."

"I bet I could, if I was mad enough," I said rather defensively.

Preston shook his head. "Kid, you couldn't kill a fly unless someone's life was on the line. You're just too kind, and we love you for it."

I was never sure how it happened, but just then Gil caught my eye and smiled. It felt like some kind of declaration.

Having quite exhaustively explored crime for the day, we moved on to other topics, with Yardley and Preston amiably play fighting over the Giants' latest off-season trade, and the rest of the ensemble weighing in with various thoughts on baseball's place in the sports pantheon. Gil even managed to hold his own; he'd clearly been reading up.

As teatime wound toward evening, Yardley offered to squire Hetty to the news office, and they took off, bickering cheerfully about what might make the front page. Preston simply disappeared; we knew, but didn't dare acknowledge, that he'd gone downstairs to see Mrs. G before he also had to go to work. Tommy and Father Michael made for the checkerboard, leaving me to walk Gil to the door.

"A lovely tea, Shane."

"Our pleasure to host you."

We bowed.

"Would you care to come to the show Tuesday night?" I asked. "It's a benefit for an old friend from the neighborhood, but you will still get to see the same performance."

"I should enjoy that."

"Of course, as a friend of the company, you're welcome to join us backstage after."

"I'll look forward to it. Will the other friends of the company be along, as well?"

"Tommy and Father Michael likely will, and Preston may, to cover the benefit. But not Hetty and Yards. They do have actual jobs to attend to."

"I'm quite certain they do." Gil smiled a bit. "Do Mr. Stern and Miss MacNaughten have some kind of understanding?"

I chuckled at that. Understanding to be at each other's throats most of the time, perhaps. "Understanding?"

"Well, somewhat like we do."

"We have an understanding?"

"I rather thought we did." He shrugged, suddenly looking almost shy. "That we are courting, with honorable intent, as we navigate matters of careers and geography and whatnot."

"Oh." I found myself smiling like a silly little girl with a crush. "Yes. *That* understanding. Hetty and Yardley most certainly do not have the kind of understanding we do."

Fortunately, he was giving me almost the same smile back. "Good."

I waited. It was far from his first awkward comment.

"I mean for us, of course."

"Of course."

We exchanged another smile and then stood there for a moment, just looking at one another, with the attraction between us once again striking sparks. Neither of us seemed to have the vaguest idea what to do about it, and really, there weren't many appropriate options available. Even, perhaps especially, with an "understanding," a courting couple must, of course, strictly observe the proprieties.

"Good day, Your Grace," Tommy called from the parlor door as he *just happened* to walk past with the box of checkers.

"Right, then. Good day, Thomas, Shane."

He took my hand and kissed it, finally settling on that perfectly proper gesture, which didn't feel remotely proper at all. Neither did the way we held hands after, unwilling to break the contact.

"Good day," I managed finally.

"A very good day, indeed."

Chapter 10

In Which We Consider
Vexing Questions

Soon after His Grace took his leave, I took to my bed with an improving book. I do not remember what it was or how much of it I read, and what or whom I dreamt of that night are no one's business but my own. Suffice to say that I was awake and dressed at what Mrs. G considers civilized breakfast time and walked into the dining room with a smile and a spring in my step. Because I was tagging along with Hetty for the closing arguments at the Van Vleet trial, of course.

Tommy looked up from his bacon and eggs and shook his head. "What was all that talk about not wanting to upend your happy life?"

"Nothing has changed."

"Except that he's here. Do we know why?"

To my utter shame and horror, I realized I hadn't asked. "Well . . ."

"So we are going on the assumption that he came just to see you?" The smile he was carefully smothering told me that he wasn't operating on that idea at all, and that he'd gotten there long before I did.

"I'm quite sure he has other things to do here." I poured

myself a cup of black coffee and buried my face in the rich steam for a moment, hoping to hide my embarrassment. How could I have neglected to ask why he had come? It wasn't, after all, as if he'd just taken the train down from the Bronx. He'd crossed the Atlantic, for heaven's sake, which generally takes more than a week. What could possibly be worth leaving his world behind for the better part of a month or more?

Certainly not me.

After his appearance yesterday, I had no doubt that he shared many of the same strong feelings. But we had already agreed by letter to address all of that when I arrived in London, now only about three months hence. More to the point, we were merely at the beginning of a courtship. It defied logic that he'd waste a trip across the sea to see me sooner.

His behavior didn't fit with it, either. A man who'd sailed the ocean to claim his beloved, assuming I even *was* his beloved, wouldn't coolly fence with her, then share a relaxing late-afternoon tea with her friends.

Not a bit of it.

After such a long trip, he would presumably be ready to march in and claim his prize. He would make his declaration, sweep his fair maiden into his arms, and probably drag her right to the nearest priest or judge to make it official. Or make sure she had no chance of escape. Win her and tie her right down.

None of that was in character for Gil, and good thing, too.

On the whole, I wasn't entirely displeased that I was not the motive for the journey. If I was already concerned about what he might expect, what on earth would he have wanted or hoped for if he'd made such a dramatic gesture? And what kind of man would he be if he tried it?

Insane, for a beginning. And very definitely not the man for me.

"What are you thinking, Heller?"

"That I am quite certain His Grace is not here just to see me."

Tommy, who had probably been entertaining many of the same thoughts, nodded. "I agree. Which makes one wonder."

"It does." I took a sip of coffee. "But not in a bad way."

"No?"

"That 'Rush in and sweep the lady off her feet' gambit happens only in books. A man who actually thought it might work—"

"Would be a fool or worse, and absolutely not the one for you."

"So whatever brought him here, it was not the pleasure of my company."

"I'm sure seeing you is part of the game, though," he added quickly. "He does care for you, and he is going to ask for your hand one of these days, you know."

I sailed past that one with a little more coffee. "But there is something else going on here."

"I'm sure of it."

"So am I."

"Which shouldn't stop you from enjoying the visit." Tommy smiled. "You know . . ."

"What?"

"If he's up to something, it will be that much harder for him to complain about your career."

"What do you think he's up to?"

"No idea. But the empire on which the sun never sets has a lot of interests. It's not impossible that he's bringing a message to a friend or working on some mission you'll never need or want to know about."

"While playing my adoring swain."

Tommy took another muffin and buttered it as he contemplated. "He's not just *playing* your adoring swain. But there's more."

"Of course." I turned my cup in my hands. "Though I'm not sure how that helps matters."

"Look at it this way. You're concerned about him upending your life, right?"

"Right."

"Well, if he has some other important vocation, you can demand room for your own work."

"Makes sense." I drank a little coffee. "There is absolutely no way this is all about me."

"Sorry, Heller. No way at all." Tommy took a bite of his muffin. "What do you think he'd expect if he'd come all this way just for you? Not a little duel in the studio, for sure. Things you aren't prepared to give."

"I know. You're right." I considered a muffin and decided my stomach wasn't quite up to it. "And yes, whatever this is may improve my negotiating position, if I decide I want to negotiate."

He laughed. "You two are already at Appomattox Court House. It's now just about working out the terms of surrender."

I tossed my napkin at him. "Does that make me Lee or Grant?"

"Never. You're still Henry Tudor, the hero of Bosworth."

"And don't you forget it."

We laughed together.

"So how am I going to find out what he's up to?" I asked.

"Surely you haven't been a female for thirty-odd years without gaining some persuasive skills."

"Perhaps."

"And he's clearly susceptible to your charms . . ."

"Are you suggesting I—"

"Nothing improper, of course. Take your suitor for a walk in the park and some sweet talk. Whatever did you think I meant?"

Tommy grinned at me and returned to his bacon and eggs.

I poured more coffee. I was going to need it.

"Miss! Mr. Tommy!" Sophia called. "Something in the mailbox."

"Perhaps Madame Lentini magically knows I need her guidance again," I said as Toms took the envelope from the girl. I could have used some encouragement from my teacher and mentor just then.

"Not Madame. Too early for the post. And no return address."

We exchanged glances. Every once in a while, we have been known to get the occasional nasty letter. Tommy, as a former champ, and I, as a woman who very publicly practices a rather unconventional profession, do draw a certain amount of ire, in addition to the entirely deserved admiration.

He got up from the table and took the cheap plain white envelope into the parlor. I followed and watched as he carefully slit it open, and then I read over his shoulder.

To the Ella Shane Opera Company:

> *You should know the sort of man you have hired. Ruben Avila is not what he seems. He is harboring a terrible secret that will bring disrepute upon himself and the entire company. You should send him away at once.*

Of course it was unsigned. The hand was very careful cursive and perhaps a bit feminine, or perhaps just overly precise. Not to mention, the letter was an ugly echo of the past; the imprecation against Ruben inevitably reminded me of the trouble we'd had with a previous member of the company with a bad background and worse intentions. Tommy was watching me.

"Henry checked all his bona fides." He scowled.

"I know. So did you."

"Drank two terrible pints at the singer's bar. Ruben's as clean as they come, and a good man besides. As far as the boys know."

I nodded. "Lives with his widowed mother, doesn't he?"

"Yes. Very quiet, by all accounts. Engaged a few years ago, but the young lady decided to become a nun instead."

I winced. "Well, losing out to God is probably a little less painful than losing out to another man."

"Perhaps." Tommy didn't seem convinced. "Problem is, there's no way to compete with God."

"And He always wins." I nodded. "Funny that it all comes so soon after he took over the male lead, though."

"Jealousy?" His eyes narrowed. "A lot of that going around in opera companies."

"Inside and outside."

"Someone we didn't hire, perhaps. I'll talk to Henry later today."

"And I'll sniff around at the theater. I think Marie knows him a bit better."

Tommy nodded. "Let's hope it's just some foolishness that we can easily resolve."

"When has that ever been the case for us?" I asked, not unkindly.

"Well, there's a first time for everything."

We returned to the dining room and drank our coffee quietly for a few moments, contemplating the possibilities, none good. I wondered if it might somehow have something to do with Albert, though it was hard to imagine how.

"Well, while you play reporter, I shall play detective and see what I can see about this latest development," Tommy said.

"Reconvene at dinner."

"Father Michael is coming over. His usual housekeeper has been down with the gout, and there's been a great deal of boiled dinner."

"Poor thing. Let Mrs. G know, and we'll all feast tonight."

Tommy's eyes gleamed. "Exactly my plan, Heller."

Chapter 11

On Trial for Her Life

Considering all the various dramas of the moment, I would have far preferred to rest on this particular dark Monday, but it was closing arguments and really my last chance to join Hetty at the trial. The unfortunate Mrs. Van Vleet would no doubt know her fate by our next break. Even though I was attending to support Hetty in her work, and not for the sensation, I couldn't repress a tiny frisson of excitement as I buttoned my serviceable midnight-blue coat over my very plain dark blue suit and white shirtwaist and topped the outfit with the same unremarkable hat I'd worn to the Tombs a week ago.

On the way out, I caught a rather depressing glimpse of myself in the mirror. *Just a boring, respectable lady past her first youth*, I thought irritably, vowing to bring out my splashy purple coat with the nutria fur trim and my new broad-brimmed violet velvet hat topped with a huge bow, plumes, and a glittery pin as soon as ever I could.

My sartorial sulk ended as soon as I met Hetty outside the courthouse. She was every drop as respectable and dull as I in dark gray plaid, but it did nothing to diminish the sparkle in her eyes. I recognized it immediately as the same feeling I had at curtain time. When will men realize that we're capable of loving our work as much as they are?

"Ready for closings?" she asked, holding up her tools. "You did bring a notebook?"

I pulled a similar one and a pencil out of my sturdy bag. "I have my props."

She grinned and took my arm. "Then on to the show."

At the door, Hetty showed her *Beacon* press card to a guard, who seemed only a little bemused, having had a couple of weeks of trial to get used to her. Then he looked at me. "Bringing a friend?"

"An assistant."

"Probably need it today." He nodded to me. "Good luck, ladies."

We bowed and went to take our seats in the press gallery. Unsurprisingly, we were the only females. The gents tended to be older and far more serious of mien than the sports writers. Probably not surprising, considering that this story could well end in an execution, however richly deserved.

The press gallery was really just a couple of rows of seats at the back of the packed courtroom. Once the reporters were in place, they started letting in the ordinary spectators, who apparently were on some sort of first-come-first-served basis. While Hetty made some initial notes and chatted with a few of her peers, I studied the audience, which was my own area of expertise, after all.

The crowd was mostly male and mostly older gentlemen. Younger folk would be working. A few ladies appeared in knots, apparently huddling together for the safety of numbers. All of them had dressed carefully and soberly, as Hetty and I had done. No one really wanted to stand out while doing something as unladylike as attending a murder trial.

Speaking of standing out, though, I found myself staring in shock when I saw the next to last gentleman allowed into the spectators' benches. Gilbert Saint Aubyn owned any room he entered, whether he intended to or not, and he seemed to be cultivating an unobtrusive air as he strode to his seat.

"Isn't that—" Hetty began.

"It surely is."

"Maybe we piqued his interest at tea yesterday."

"Maybe."

Gil took a carefully casual glance around the room, and his eyes landed on us. For a second, he looked puzzled. Then he grinned, entirely inappropriately for the venue, and bowed.

I couldn't avoid a blush as I nodded.

"Heaven help us," Hetty whispered. "That smile's a dangerous weapon."

"Aren't you here to work?"

"You should get to work on that courtship, Miss Diva." She chuckled. "That is some very fine real estate."

I just shook my head, since the matron was bringing in the defendant.

Amelie Van Vleet seemed to be quite appealing, at least from this distance. Naturally, after a lifetime onstage, I am well aware that all you really need to give the impression of loveliness from a few dozen yards away is large eyes with strong brows, a regularly shaped face, and a noticeable mouth. All easily accomplished with makeup. Probably not an option for the woman in the dock, but she was in a simple black dress rather than a prison uniform, so she definitely did have some chance to see to her toilette.

Her hair and brows were dark, and I couldn't be certain about the eyes, but she definitely had dark lashes. She was very pale and seemed to be leaning on her lawyer's arm. Rowan Alteiss is one of the best defenders in the City, a tall, spare man with rumpled salt-and-pepper hair and a kind aspect.

As he guided her gently to the defense table, she smiled at him, and I caught a flash of something between them, but I couldn't be sure precisely what. I didn't doubt that I'd be awfully fond of the man who was keeping me from the electric chair, after all, and she must be a charming woman, Hetty's reservations notwithstanding.

"All rise!"

As everyone complied with the bailiff's cry, I noticed Gil watching Mrs. Van Vleet and Alteiss very closely. Well, his friend Joshua *is* a top barrister in Britain.

"Be seated." The judge, a tiny little man of considerable years, discretion still to be determined, looked over the courtroom. "I will issue my usual admonishment to our spectators of the weaker sex. We shall have no fainting . . ."

"Or emotional outbursts of any kind," Hetty hissed irritably in my ear. I bit back a smile.

"Approach the bench?" asked Alteiss.

"You may."

Alteiss exchanged a few words with the judge, who then motioned the prosecutor over. They all talked for a few moments, and the judge finally nodded.

"I'll allow it. Defense may call one more witness."

"Call Mrs. Herman Naylor."

The name was vaguely familiar, and as soon as I saw her, I knew why. She and her husband kept a small florist's shop just off Fifth Avenue, not far from the Ladies' Mile— or the Van Vleet manse.

Under normal circumstances, Mrs. Naylor was a cheerful and friendly blond lady of a certain age, with a bit of extra avoirdupois from a prosperous life, well hidden by a voluminous florist's smock always tied with a bright bow that gave color to her ivory face. For court, though, she was in a very serious black merino dress and coat. No doubt it was the outfit she wore for funerals or other important events, but the grim fabric washed her out, and the close fit made her look stouter than she was.

Worse, her usually bright smile was replaced by a determined scowl. I hoped she'd be back to her usual self the next time I dropped by for a few flowers for the drawing room.

She walked to the box, carrying herself with the stiffness of one afraid of doing something wrong, and who could blame her? Most people never find themselves in the witness box at all, never mind in a murder trial.

After she was sworn, Rowan Alteiss greeted her and thanked her extravagantly for coming, clearly in an effort to put her at ease a bit. It did have some minimal effect.

"Now, Mrs. Naylor, can you tell me what you do?"

"My husband and I own the florist's shop on Washington Terrace, just off Fifth Avenue." She spoke clearly and with pride.

"Where is that in relation to the Van Vleet home?"

"Less than a block. I can see the servants' door of their home from my window."

"Ah. May I take you back to the day of April fourteenth?"

"A pretty day, even though it wasn't an especially good spring this year."

"Very true, ma'am. Why do you remember it?"

"Well, I remember the afternoon, when there was all the commotion at the Van Vleet mansion, of course."

"Did anything else unusual happen that day?"

"I didn't think it unusual at the time, but knowing what happened, I remembered it."

"And what was that?"

"Well, a Frenchman came in and bought a large bouquet."

"Was that unusual?"

She smiled a little. "Mostly, we see New Yorkers, sir. Frenchmen stand out."

"Did he stand out enough that you would recognize him if you saw him again?"

She pointed to the bench behind the defense table, where Anatole Lescaut was trying to look unobtrusive. "Him. That's the one. I'd recognize that oily look anywhere."

Hetty choked back a snicker, and she wasn't the only one. The judge raked the room with a glare.

"What did he buy?"

"A big bouquet of pink peonies. Not my favorite flower, especially in spring. So showy and not much scent. But some people like them."

"I imagine they do. And then?"

"He had me wrap them all up with a nice shiny pink ribbon and headed off with them, proud as punch."

"Did you see where he went?"

"Last I saw, he was going up the back drive at the Van Vleets'."

A murmur in the courtroom. Another judicial glare.

"And did you see him after that?"

"I didn't. Another customer came in to buy violets—a much better choice in April, ask me—and I didn't think of it again until much later."

"Why are you coming forward now?"

"Well, the poor thing shouldn't hang for him, even if she was up to no good."

That brought the house down. The judge pounded his gavel once, to no avail, and then a second time, while yelling, "Order!"

That accomplished the purpose.

"I will remind the jury that we established yesterday

that the scullery maid could not remember locking the back door," Mrs. Van Vleet's lawyer said.

"That's for your closing argument, Alteiss," snapped the judge.

"I move for immediate dismissal on grounds of reasonable doubt," countered the lawyer.

I saw Gil wince a little. So did Hetty and I. We were no barristers, of course, but we'd followed enough trials to know it was a premature move.

"Not on your tintype, Counselor. Prosecution may cross-examine the witness, and you'll all make your closing arguments as planned. The jury will decide this case. Not me, not you, and not our lovely flower seller."

Mrs. Naylor blushed just a bit as the judge gave her an actual smile. "Why, thank you, Your Honor."

"I prefer violets in April, too, ma'am." The judge turned his face and glare back to the lawyers. "Get to it. We still have a trial to finish."

Finish they did. The judge, no gentle taskmaster, drove the lawyers right through luncheon, with the plan of turning the case over to the jury by early afternoon. At least in this courtroom, the wheels of justice were not going to grind slowly if he had anything to say about it.

They ground quickly, indeed. The jury adjourned for their luncheon at about two, with deliberations to follow, leaving the rest of us to return to our lives while Amelie Van Vleet waited to learn her fate.

Chapter 12

While Awaiting the Verdict

Outside the courthouse, it was a relief to be in the clean fall air. Hetty planned to go back to the news office and file her story, then return for what would likely be a long evening of deliberations. Since I was back onstage the next night, I was glad of my quiet plans with Tommy, Montezuma, and poor starving Father Michael. A few days of boiled dinner would drive anyone to distraction, religious calling or no.

"Shall we share a hansom, ladies?"

Gil was standing behind us. Hetty, the reporter on duty, bristled a little, and she was clearly ready to tell him she didn't need any male protector. But I was quite curious about what game he was playing here. I shot Hetty a quick, squashing glance and bowed to him.

"That would be lovely. We'll go to the *Beacon*, and you can walk me home after Hetty returns to the newspaper office."

"As good a plan as one could wish for."

Once we were properly handed up into the cab, the conversation turned on the obvious topic.

"Do you think they've proven the case?" Hetty asked him.

"I know you'd love to see her at the end of a rope, but I'm sorry, no."

"Actually, the electric chair these days," she corrected him with a scowl. "But I have to agree with you."

"Even before the last witness, it was a weak case, and with that good lady's help, and her lawyer pointing to the evidence that the killer had to be taller, then looking at Lescaut every second, it'll be hard for the jury to convict her."

"They don't like her," Hetty said. "*I* don't like her."

"Fortunately, we are not permitted to condemn people because we don't like them," Gil reminded her.

"It's rather more than that. She almost certainly broke her vows with that nasty lizard Lescaut."

"Don't insult lizards." When she didn't smile at my comment, I shook my head. "I don't think anyone's been stoned for adultery in the past few centuries. At least not here."

"Well," Hetty replied irritably, "if you're going to trouble to marry a man, you should at least be faithful to him."

"Of course." I very carefully kept my gaze on Hetty and not Gil.

"Oh, I know people in those fancy circles hand spouses around like we do books, but it doesn't make it right."

"It may be wrong, but if her husband didn't mind, there was no reason to kill him," I pointed out very sensibly.

"Of course he minded. All men mind." She turned to Gil, who had been diplomatically silent during the exchange. "You wouldn't want your wife running about with some slithery Frenchman, would you?"

"Ladies, while this is a most fascinating discussion," he began, with what certainly looked like a trace of a blush, "you may wish to look more to the facts of the case."

"No doubt we should," I put in quickly, hiding my amusement at his discomfort. "Her lawyer proved that someone could easily have gotten into the house to kill Mr. Van Vleet, and even gave them a viable suspect."

"Exactly. People will believe the impossible when it's the only option left, with a nod to Mr. Holmes." Gil smiled slightly, clearly relieved to return to criminology. "But if they have any other theory, they'll take it before believing that their sweet wives would stab them fourteen times."

"Isn't that the truth." Hetty shook her head. "I don't know what to believe."

"You aren't really required to believe anything, Miss Hetty. If she's acquitted, she'll walk away with the legal presumption of innocence, as any of us would—no less . . . and no more."

"There's that."

"And I suspect the social sanctions for this will be rather severe."

"No doubt," I agreed.

After we left Hetty at the *Beacon*, Gil offered his arm, and we walked the few blocks back to the town house.

"So did you get some good insight into the American judicial system?"

He didn't look at me. "Some, for certain."

"Perhaps you'd like a bit more." Time to put my expert to work.

"How so?"

"Albert's lawyer is a junior partner at Paul's firm and well out of his depth. Your expertise could help." The thought that skill might make a life-and-death difference had occurred to me while watching Alteiss argue for his client.

"You are *not* defending that man." Gil's arm tensed beneath my fingers.

"He's a member of my company. And everyone is entitled to a defense, Barrister."

"That is true." He gazed down at me with something that might just be protective concern. "But he slashed a man's throat in his dressing room. A few doors down from you, and at your premiere night, Shane."

"He swears he didn't."

"And you believe him?" He studied me with a searching gaze.

"I'm not sure."

We walked in silence for a few moments, before he finally let out an exasperated breath. "What would you like me to do?"

"Look at the autopsy report."

A muscle flicked in his jaw. "All right. For you, Shane."

"Thank you most kindly. I'll have it sent to you. It will be a good use of those criminology principles you demonstrated last night."

"Ah. That's what gave you the idea."

"You did. So it's your own fault." Rather than trouble him with my doubts, I gave him a teasing smile. "If you'd kept the conversation to books and the weather, I wouldn't be asking you to pitch in."

The tension in his face eased a little, and he chuckled. "All right."

"Well, your own fault and that of my aunt Ellen."

One of his perfect brows arched. I had told him about my aunt's prediction that a tall dark man would bring me trouble during his last visit to our shores. "The second sight again?"

"What else? She says Albert is innocent and deserves the benefit of the doubt."

Gil sighed. "Well, I'm not a great believer in the second sight, but your aunt has rather nicely summed up the legal ethics in play."

"Don't forget, she raised ten, plus me. She's spent her life as judge and jury in sibling disputes."

He smiled. "My mother had only my sister and me, but we kept her docket full, as well."

As we continued on, enjoying the mutual warmth of our conversation, I remembered Tommy's advice about a walk and some persuasion. No time like the present. "I am aware that you did not cross the ocean merely to sit at my feet and discuss stab-wound angles."

I felt his arm tense beneath my fingers again, and he turned sharply to look down at me. "What do you think—"

"I don't *think* anything." I gave him a reassuring smile. "I just know that you would never cross the ocean for the purpose of seeing me, when I am going to be in London three months hence."

"True. Not that I hadn't considered it . . ."

"You've never fed me pretty lies before. Don't start now."

He stopped walking and took my hands. "Shane, I will never lie to you. There will be times, and this is one, that I can't tell you things, but I will never lie to you."

"Nor I to you. I assume I have the same right to leave out matters you don't need to know?" Of which there could well be many.

"Of course." To his credit, he didn't even hesitate.

"So you can't tell me why you're here."

"All is can say is I am doing a favor for a friend. And I will admit I seized on the chance to see you."

"I'm glad you did."

"As am I." He gazed down at me again, and his eyes lingered on my face, then briefly on my lips. It did not take a barrister's understanding of evidence to know he was remembering our kiss. He took a breath and spoke briskly. "And I had best get you home safely to your cousin."

We started walking again.

"Seized on the chance to come here?" I asked once his eyes were safely on the sidewalk once more.

"With both hands, sweetheart."

It was the first time he'd used an endearment for me, and it was probably at least a mild violation of protocol. But I didn't mind, even if I should have. "I'm glad you did."

We were at the town house, and the gaslights were starting to come on. In the window, I could see the sizeable shapes of Father Michael and Tommy at the checkerboard. "You are welcome to stay to dinner if you like."

"I would, actually."

"I warn you, you'll likely have to referee a dispute between the boys."

"Not impossible."

"But there will be compensations."

"Oh?" A faint note in his voice hinted of compensations entirely forbidden to couples with a mere "understanding."

He almost certainly couldn't see my blush in the fading daylight. "Father Michael's been living on boiled dinner, and Mrs. G will be feeding him up."

"That bodes well for us all."

"My thought exactly."

While I do not believe in the second sight, of course, I am well aware that our modern science does not yet understand all the various thoughts and signals that the brain can absorb. And so I cannot say that it is entirely impossible that one person could pick up messages from another, in what could appear to be some sort of magical insight.

Say that Mrs. G might somehow intuit that a certain half-Scots Briton with a fondness for shepherd's pie would be staying to dinner. Father Michael is equally fond of same, and her admirable version of the dish would undoubtedly have been a strong possibility for the entrée on that reason alone. And I can say with great authority that Mrs. G was both surprised and pleased to see the duke walk me inside as she was bidding her good nights to Tommy and the priest.

At any rate, we shared a most convivial meal and discussion of various new books and other interesting matters. Consensus of the table: there are too many books of Lincoln's letters and not enough of people's recollections of the man, cities must work to find better ways for horseless carriages and traditional ones to coexist in the streets, and the Prince of Wales is really much too old to be misbehaving in such a fashion.

I need not tell you that no one went very far into the details of said misbehavior.

After we finished with Mrs. G's lovely meringue torte (which only added to my suspicions, because all that lemon curd for Preston's tarts leaves a lot of extra egg whites), we retired to the parlor for a bit. It felt quite like a happy family moment, sitting on the settee with Gil as Tommy and Father Michael played checkers, with the occasional outraged appeal to us. We were the very picture of appropriate courtship as we leafed through my album of postcards from our recent San Francisco stand, and Montezuma contentedly observed from the bookshelf, sharing his own happy memories: "Grapes! Sweet!"

"Extra! Extra!" came the cry from the street. "Verdict in the Van Vleet murder!"

"Extra! Extra!" echoed Montezuma. "Verdict!"

Tommy ran to the front door and quickly bought a paper from the newsboy, thankfully a *Beacon*, and we all gathered round.

"Not guilty," he read, though we could all see the banner. "She won't get the chair."

"Miss Hetty is likely downcast," Gil observed.

"Not even a little." I pointed to the paper. "She's got the byline on the extra. She wouldn't care if they'd proclaimed Mrs. Van Vleet Queen of the May."

"Absolutely." Tommy nodded.

"Still a tragedy, though," the priest reminded us. "A man's life taken in such a terrible way, and his wife's reputation ruined, whether or not she dies."

"All true, Father," Gil put in, "and there's still a killer at large. Hosmer Van Vleet surely did not stab himself fourteen times."

"Well, at least Morrison can't put Hetty back on hats anytime soon," I observed.

"Trust you to find the silver lining, Heller."

Chapter 13

In Which Benefit Night Becomes Far Too Interesting

Before the show next evening, Tommy and I had a difficult duty: talking to Ruben about that anonymous letter. Since nothing had come up in any of Toms's inquiries or mine, we weren't especially worried. But it might be something only Ruben and the letter writer knew, so we had to ask.

Ruben's dark eyes were worried and there was a small furrow between his brows when he knocked and walked into my dressing room.

"Is something wrong, Miss Ella?"

"We assume not, but we would be failing in our duty if we did not show this to you," I said, looking to Tommy.

"This was in our mailbox the other day." Tommy handed the letter to him, and we both watched as he read it, his face freezing and his caramel skin going grayish.

And then a shocking response: "Oh, no. I'll leave at once."

"What?" I gasped.

"Really?" Tommy gave Ruben a disbelieving glare. "Why don't you tell us about it first?"

"How much do you know about Birmingham?"

"Alabama, not England?" I asked.

A small rueful smile played about his lips. "Yes, Alabama."

"Very little, I'm sorry to say."

"They did not take their defeat well," Tommy said, sitting down on the dressing-table chair. "And I've heard reports of ugly incidents between the races."

"That's a way to put it." Ruben nodded. "Well, a boy named Royal Avery was born to freed slaves there a few years after the end of the war . . ."

I looked to Toms. He nodded, clearly understanding, as I did, exactly where this was going, and that we did not need to hear any more. That it was better in fact not to give voice to the rest. Ruben deserved to be judged on his talent, not the color of his skin or his parents, and we had no intention of allowing some anonymous enemy to change that.

"Well," I began, "I'm sure he had a difficult and fascinating life, but I don't know what he has to do with Ruben Avila, born in Havana."

"But I—"

Tommy very carefully looked him in the eye. "There've been any number of hurricanes in Cuba over the years. I'm sure you and your mother were lucky to escape with your lives, never mind any records."

"Oh." Ruben just stared at us. "So you—"

"We know exactly who you are," I said calmly. "A brilliant basso, an excellent performer, and a very good colleague. I have no idea what became of Royal Avery, but I'm quite sure there's no way anyone can prove Ruben Avila is anyone other than who he says he is."

"You think so?"

"I know so." Tommy nodded. "There are advantages to upheaval. Even in the unlikely event that someone should find records of Royal Avery's birth in Birmingham, or some such thing, there's no way to definitively prove a connection."

"And as far as we are concerned, we hired Ruben Avila and have no reason to suspect anything else. Full stop."

Ruben let out a long breath. "I don't know what to say."

"Absolutely nothing. Never speak of it again if you can avoid it." Tommy shook his head. "There's a lot of prejudice and unfairness in this world."

"And we won't add to it." I kept my tone cool, though my blood boiled for Ruben, as I'm sure did Tommy's.

We two nodded together. Someday, we surely hoped, the world would change enough that Royal Avery could have the singing career he deserved, but today all we could do was protect Ruben Avila. And that we would do.

"Thank you." Ruben's voice came out soft and shaky. "I—"

"Have a show to prepare for, as do we all," I said firmly. "This incident changes nothing for us, so don't let it change things for you."

He managed a genuine smile. "Right."

When the door closed, Tommy sat down on the settee. "So who would know—or suspect—that, and why would they threaten to reveal it?"

"I don't know. That feels a lot more like an attack on Ruben than on the company."

"True. Although surely anyone who knows us would know we wouldn't just throw him out . . ."

"Do they?" I stretched out on my side of the settee. "It's not just the prejudice, after all. We don't stand for lying, and someone might think we'd be angry about the deception."

"Deception for the best of reasons."

"For my money, it's not deception at all. It's survival."

"Right." Tommy nodded decidedly. "At any rate, that wasn't an extortion letter. That was intended to get us to dismiss him."

"True. So do we also have someone who's after Ruben?"

He sighed. "I don't know what we have. Nothing that makes sense for sure. How could that be connected to the murder?"

My tiny ormolu clock chimed the hour, and Tommy jumped up. "Blast it. I have to go fetch the Eaggers. You know tonight's the benefit."

I nodded. "In addition to everything else."

"At least we know we're doing some good."

"All we can do any day."

The usual after-show scene was a bit different that night. Marie slipped out immediately after curtain because small Polly was just getting over a cold. I didn't blame her; I was grateful she'd performed at all, considering. But of course she had, and like Anna and Louis, she had kicked in her share for the benefit, despite having never set eyes on Jamie Eagger or his family. That wasn't the point for her.

Jamie's mother and sisters, of course, came back to offer thanks, and Tommy and I were happy to greet them and catch up, even if their life in a somewhat nicer part of the old neighborhood was far different from our world these days.

Gil, newly promoted to friend of the company, seemed happy enough sharing a corner with Preston and merely observing the scene. All seemed amiable, if a bit crowded, until after Father Michael arrived to conduct the Eagger family back to their home, with Preston offering a little extra chaperonage for the grieving ladies on his way to the news office. But then a much less savory visitor came to offer his praises.

In neat black tie, his dark hair slicked back, Connor Coughlan could be any gentleman opera fancier, if you hadn't grown up in a part of town where you immediately recognized the menace conveyed in the walk and the cold shamrock-green eyes. Those eyes were the last thing any number of people who crossed him in Five Points had ever seen.

At the moment, though, he was in a friendly and expansive mood, smiling at Tommy and shaking hands, then giving Rosa a cheerful grin, which made her blush a little. And then he got to Gil.

"Well, I don't believe we've met," Connor said.

"Gilbert Saint Aubyn."

"British. Saint Aubyn. Where do I know that name?"

They sized each other up for a moment. Gil was a couple of inches taller, but Connor was wider, and clearly the more dangerous. I took a sip of my after-show mint tea and tried not to think about what might happen if this went badly. Didn't matter. I, and everyone else, might as well have been invisible.

"Duke of Leith, as it happens," Gil replied with a carefully modest shrug.

"Right. You related to the Saint Aubyn who stopped charging rents and gave food to his tenants during the Hunger?"

"My great-uncle."

I hadn't known about that, and he, of course, would never have told me, even though Father Michael was initially very leery of him, because most aristocrats had just let the Irish starve. The fact that his great-uncle had tried to help said a great deal about Gil's family . . . and him.

"You're all right, then." Connor held out his hand. "Connor Coughlan, old friend of the family. Nice to meet you."

"Likewise." Gil cut his eyes to me as they shook.

"So it's like that." Connor caught the glance. "See here, you're not sniffing around, thinking our Ellen is some bit of fluff for your pleasure—"

"Mr. Coughlan, I will thank you not to bring up such matters in front of a lady."

Connor blinked once, then answered with a lightly menacing tone. "Just making sure. There are a lot of toffs who can't tell the difference—"

"Between a soprano and a soubrette." Gil nodded, using the line I'd thrown at him at our first meeting. "I'm well aware that Miss Shane is a respectable lady and an artist."

"All right, then."

"And I would also remind you, with all due respect, that my friendship with Miss Shane is a matter for her and at most her cousin. I'm sure you're aware that Mr. Hurley has been known to have a word with anyone he finds unsuitable."

Connor's gaze turned truly icy. "If Tommy has a word with you, you'll need a doctor. If I do, you'll need a priest."

Gil returned ice for ice. "How kind of you to take an interest in my spiritual welfare."

For one long, terrifying second, their eyes held, the entire room tense and silent, as they assessed each other.

And then Connor laughed and patted Gil on the arm. "You're not bad for an English stick, Saint Audrey."

Gil opened his mouth to correct him, and I shot him a glance.

Connor turned to me and took both my hands. "Well done, Ellen. You and Madame Marie are in top form. You are making a recording for the phonograph?"

"Probably. It's a bit of a pain, but we'll likely at least do the death-scene arias."

His green eyes lingered on my face. "I still have the old cylinder of the 'Ave Maria' you recorded for me years ago."

I felt, rather than saw, Gil tensing a bit. While he knew, as almost no one else did, that I really don't enjoy singing "Ave Maria," because of my late mother and odd place between faiths, he couldn't possibly know the rest.

I'd sung it at Connor's mother's funeral because she was a friend of my aunt Ellen, and the cylinder had been a sympathy offering, a small thing I could do to ease a terrible pain I knew only too well. Even before that, Connor had placed me on some mythical pedestal, the girl who escaped into a different world. If he'd been a bit sweet on me back in the old neighborhood, these days his romantic interests ran more to chorus girls and other types of women I'm not supposed to know about.

"I'm glad." I smiled at Connor as he let go of my hands.

"Always good to see you, even if I always have a bit of a remembered headache from that fight on Orchard Street."

We laughed. Connor and Tommy had been scrapping over some imagined but desperately important slight when I'd jumped on Connor's back and yanked out a handful of his hair. I pretended now to take a careful look at his shiny black-Irish brown mane and smiled.

"Doesn't seem to have done permanent damage," I noted.

"Not at all. I have other engagements tonight, but I wanted to come back and thank you for the benefit."

"We were glad to help."

"Still the kindest heart I know."

"Thank you."

Connor made a formal bow, as graceful as any society gentleman, and turned to go. On his way out, he took one more hard look at Gil and nodded, as if making up his mind about something.

I hoped for Gil's sake that meant he'd passed muster.

Tommy and Gil tactfully took their leave as Connor walked out. I'm sure it was as much to make sure he left as to give me a chance to change into the simple grayish-lavender shadow-stripe merino dress I'd worn to the theater. Rosa was just helping me into my coat—the nice purple one, of course—when we heard the unmistakable sound of a gunshot.

I ran, with her on my heels, to the stage door.

Outside, on the landing, Tommy, Gil, and Connor were standing together, trying to look unruffled and mostly succeeding.

"What on earth?" I gasped.

Tommy nodded to the fresh bullet hole in the brick wall, easily visible in the streetlamps. "Someone fired at the theater."

"At the three of you," I said, looking across the lot of them.

"At one of us, anyhow, Ellen." Connor shrugged. "I can't say it's never happened before, but I'm terribly sorry it happened here."

"We're all safe," Tommy assured him in a calm tone deeply betrayed by his eyes.

"Whoever it was," Gil put in, looking at the divot from the bullet, "he's a dreadful shot. Missed us by a yard or more."

"And thank goodness for that." I spoke with a brisk calm I didn't feel. Connor brings a certain amount of unease with him, but he's never brought actual danger before. Thank God Marie was safely home.

"I'm truly sorry, Ellen." Connor stood before me, looking like the misbehaving street urchin he'd been, we'd all been, a couple of decades ago. "I would never want the dangers of my world to touch you."

Tommy and Gil both glared at him with the righteous fury of a lady's official protectors. It was all they could do, and they knew it.

"No harm done, thank heaven." I managed a neutral tone and patted Connor's hand.

He nodded. "It won't happen again."

Tommy and Gil nodded.

"Please take care, Connor." This time, my voice wobbled a tiny bit.

"I'll do my best." He bowed to me and cast a glance back to the others. "Leave this to me."

Tommy first and then Gil, following his lead, nodded again, a small but very definite gesture. As Connor walked away, I supposed I might have entertained a glimmer of shock that my two gentlemen were apparently pleased to allow what would almost certainly be a terrible punishment for whoever had fired that shot. But I already knew Tommy had a hard side, which I rarely saw, and I wasn't especially bothered to know that Gil might have one, too.

Chapter 14

Roses of the Wars

Matinee day is always a race to the finish, but one that pays off in some extra sleep or family time if all goes well.

After all the previous night's drama, I straggled in with less than twenty minutes before vocalization, to find an extravagant arrangement of yellow roses, at least two dozen, taking up most of the dressing table.

"What on earth?" I turned to Rosa, but Booth walked in just then.

"Madame Marie got one, too. Do you suppose it's related to last night's unpleasantness?" he asked.

I picked up the card, a plain white rectangle from Naylor's Florist. The key witness in Amelie Van Vleet's trial might indeed have constructed the bouquet, which really was lovely. The creamy yellow roses were large and filled the room with their fragrance. I usually find the scent of rose bouquets cloying, but these flowers had an appealing freshness.

The card was not nearly so pleasant. Unsigned, with two simple lines: *My deepest apologies. It will not happen again.*

Connor.

I knew, as any sensible person would, what that second sentence meant, and I couldn't repress a shudder.

"I see I'm not the only one to get a floral tribute," Marie said when she appeared in the doorway, a furrow at her usually smooth brow. "I understand there was a bit of excitement after I left last night."

"And not the good kind," Booth put in dryly.

"How true." Marie gave me a sharp look. "Do we assume this is all related to Connor Coughlan?"

"I'm reasonably certain."

"Well," Booth said, nodding at the flowers, "then this is the safest show in the history of opera."

The furrow in Marie's brow eased a bit. "How so?"

"He's right." I twisted the card between my fingers. "Knowing Connor, he not only eliminated the threat but also put out the word that we are under his protection."

"I'm not sure I like that." Quoth the lawyer's wife. "Will he want some consideration?"

"Not at all," I reassured her. "He would see protecting us as his duty in return for endangering us last night."

"Exactly." Booth bowed to us. "I'm sorry, ladies, but I need to check on the prop table, or *I'll* be in danger."

We smiled as he took off in his springy long-legged walk, waving at the propman.

"Seriously, Marie, if the scourge of Five Points is looking to our well-being—"

"We've never been safer. I know." She nodded and looked at the roses for a second, then turned back to me with a faint smile playing at the corner of her mouth. "Those flowers are quite a statement. I don't believe I've ever seen such a large bouquet. Are yellow roses some sort of calling card for him?"

I knew the answer to that and chuckled. "Not a bit. I know you haven't been courted in more than a decade, but it's the language of flowers."

"Oh, of course. Paul brought me enough Canterbury bells to build a cathedral." She smiled at the memory. "They mean constancy."

"Part of that campaign to win your trust."

"Precisely. So what is Mr. Coughlan telling us?"

"Forgive and forget."

She nodded. "Well, we'll forgive, but I'll warrant he won't forget."

"He never does."

Marie nodded, and the twinkle returned to her eyes. "I remember something else from the language of flowers."

"What?"

"Lilacs. The purple ones. Do you know what they mean?"

I glared at her. "They mean my favorite flower, and a color I wear often."

"Not a bit of it." She grinned. "First emotions of love. I wonder if your duke is trying to tell you something."

"He knows I like lilacs. Full stop."

"Full stop, indeed. Has he come up to the mark yet?"

"Of course not." I glared at her. "Far too early for that."

"You say. He came all the way over here to see you."

"Not to see me."

"Oh?" She sat down on the settee. "Tell."

"I don't rightly know why he's here. But I know it's more than me."

"Yes?"

"Some sort of business is all I know."

"And you . . . ?"

"Merely a pleasant aside."

She shook her head. "What are you going to say when he asks?"

"He's not going to ask."

"Oh, he is." Her eyes were suddenly sharp on mine. "Just don't say no, all right?"

"Marie."

"Ella, men keep asking after the first no only in books. In real life, if a man, especially someone like your duke, actually asks you to do him the honor, only to be rejected, he won't try again."

I heard something in her voice and returned her sharp glance.

She nodded and smiled ruefully. "Voice of experience."

"Really?"

"I actually had to ask Paul again. I'd told him no, told him I couldn't see a way for us to manage my career and a family life, and told him that wasn't going to change."

"And?"

"He stopped coming around." Her face turned sad and wistful as she remembered. "It took me a few weeks to realize what an idiot I was. There he was, a man who wanted me enough to allow me to have a career, and I'd handed him his hat. I was singing the Queen of the Night in a *Magic Flute* in Philadelphia, and I was just miserable. I sat in my room and cried when I wasn't in the theater."

"Terrible for the voice," I offered, hoping to get a smile.

"That too." She did smile. "Finally, I came home on a Sunday night and took a hansom right to his rooms. Absolutely inappropriate."

"And . . ."

"Only my first violation of propriety that night." The smile became a grin. "I marched up the stairs, knocked on his door, and asked if his offer was still good."

"And it was."

"And so was everything else."

My eyes widened a bit.

"No, no. He bundled me right into a cab and talked to my father the next morning." Another grin. "Whatever were you thinking?"

"Um, nothing."

"But yes, I didn't really need Grandma's whisky, though I was quite glad for the talk. You will be, too."

"I don't need—"

"One-hour call, ladies!" Booth knocked on the door. "Sorry to interrupt the hen party, but we do have a show to do."

We turned on him as one, and he ran off before we could throw things. Smart man.

Matinees tend to draw somewhat different audiences, especially parents who are hoping to give their children a bit of cultural polish. We also see some courting couples from strict families who do not approve of evening outings. I had been surprised and amused when Cousin Andrew the Detective asked if he might bring Miss McTeer and a chaperone to today's matinee but had happily made arrangements.

Given Father Michael's progressive and open-minded attitudes, I assumed that Miss McTeer's family was the old-fashioned one. After the curtain fell, I was quite looking forward to meeting her and seeing what sort of dragon chaperone her clan might have sent with her.

I was surprised on all counts.

Cousin Andrew squired his lady to my dressing room with a proud and joyful smile. He'd clearly made a significant effort as to appearance, his good gray suit perfectly pressed, his tie knot precisely placed, and his red hair fancily slicked back, betraying the time he'd spent. If that was not enough to make clear his feelings for Miss McTeer, the expression of absolute adoration with which he gazed at her would have done so.

Gazed up, I might add. Miss McTeer had a good three inches on him, but he didn't seem either aware of or interested in that fact. And no wonder. A classic black-Irish beauty with creamy skin, dark curls, and striking dark green eyes, she'd dressed up her best black dress with a garnet velvet spencer and matching glass drop earrings. She looked like a queen.

Queen of Cousin Andrew's world, at any rate.

Needless to say there was no mention of the previous night's incident or any other police matters. I'm sure he knew about the gunfire, and I'm equally sure he forgot every scrap the minute those lovely eyes landed on his.

Our lawman blushed as he presented his prize. "Miss Ella, Tom, I'd like you to meet Miss Katherine McTeer."

Katie McTeer smiled shyly and shook hands. "Lovely to meet you. A wonderful show."

"Thank you," Tommy and I said in unintentional unison, doing our best to maintain demeanor for Cousin Andrew.

"Katie here is a teacher at the primary school," the detective proclaimed. "She graduated top of her class at the Normal College."

Miss McTeer blushed, which only enhanced her loveliness. "I was fortunate to get a scholarship. Teaching is—"

"Not just any scholarship. The award for top girl at Saint Brigid's."

Tommy and I very carefully did not look at each other as Cousin Andrew warmed to his topic. No doubt he would start listing all her many virtues if we did not intervene.

"How wonderful," I said quickly. "I always wished I had been able to go to college. What did you study?"

Miss McTeer, no fool, took the lifeline. "Education, of course, and history. Which is why this show was such a treat."

"We do try to be as accurate as we can," Tommy agreed. "The character of Neville isn't entirely true to the real Neville, of course."

"But," she said, "it would be terribly confusing to have the three or more different men who were actually there."

"Exactly." I nodded and looked about a bit. "So did your chaperone enjoy the show?"

"Oh, our chaperone." Cousin Andrew's besotted expression gave way to a beleaguered sigh, and he reached behind him. "Miss Ella, Tom, meet Miss Mary Grace McTeer, Katie's sister."

Miss Mary Grace McTeer, a smaller and surlier version of her elegant sib, looked to be about twelve and seemed a little awed by me and Tommy and more than a bit annoyed with her sister's beau. Someone had seen fit to force her into a rather elaborate frilled bright pink frock that did nothing for her complexion and probably less for her humor, complete with rosy bows on her dark braids. I guessed this was a hand-me-down from a much daintier sister, confirmed when she hissed at the senior McTeer, "My name is Mack."

"Your name is Mary Grace, whatever your school chums may call you," Katie McTeer said to her little sister with a tiny trace of steel in her voice and gaze, likely all it took to control her primary-school cherubs. "Manners, dear."

Mack, as she preferred to be known, was no cherub, but she did look at least a bit sweeter when she smiled at me. "A wonderful show, Miss Ella. When can we come again?"

"Mary Grace!"

"You're welcome whenever you like, Mack," I said with a laugh. "We can always find a spot for a friend of the company."

Mack's face took on a happy glow. "Thank you, Miss Ella. Is sword fighting as much fun as it looks?"

"It's actually an art requiring great skill and discipline." I didn't want the poor dear running after the other neighborhood children with a stick.

"But she loves it," Tommy put in with a diplomatic smile. "Would you like me to show you around backstage?"

She clapped her hands. "Oh, yes. Please."

Tommy guided her out, bows and braids bouncing, and Cousin Andrew and Miss McTeer turned back to me.

"I'm sorry, Miss Shane. Of course she won't come again."

I shook my head. "She's truly welcome. You two are, as well. We really enjoy having friends and family about. And we have plenty of paying customers."

"Well, thank you kindly. You may live to regret that. Mary Grace is a caution," Katie continued. "She doesn't seem to believe in rules or demeanor."

"Neither did I at that age." I shrugged. "At any rate, I hope you are having a lovely afternoon out."

Cousin Andrew shot me a glance that meant it would be far lovelier without Mack, but nodded. "Indeed we are. I am going to take the ladies to the ice-cream parlor and deliver them safely home at a decent hour."

"An excellent choice," I agreed. "No doubt young Miss Mack has homework to do."

"And my da likes to know I'm home before he goes to sleep at seven," Katie said, betraying her family's humbler origins by her name for her father. "He has to be up at two to bake the bread."

"McTeer's Bakery?" I asked. "I knew it was a familiar name."

Katie smiled. "Yes. We all sometimes help in the shop. One Saturday afternoon, a friendly officer of the law wandered in."

The officer of the law blushed. "I haven't bought a crust anywhere else since."

"As indeed you should not."

"If I hope to see my next birthday."

As they bantered, I caught the little crackle between them and realized that they really were well matched.

"We often buy bread from McTeer's, as well. It is truly wonderful," I said. Mrs. G would forgive a small stretch of the truth in the service of true love.

"Thank you, Miss Ella," Katie said, still all asparkle from the little back-and-forth with her squire.

"Thank you, Miss Ella," Cousin Andrew echoed as he bowed. "We should go collect Mary Grace before she draws Tom into a duel."

"Probably true. Thank you for coming. Delightful to meet you, Miss McTeer."

"You as well. Thank you again."

"The pleasure is ours."

We all bowed once more, and Cousin Andrew followed Katie McTeer out the door.

"If he's not dead gone on her, I don't have eyes." Rosa laughed.

"I think if you get your dictionary and look up the word *smitten*," I said, joining her laughter "you will find a picture of our good detective."

Chapter 15

In Which We Enjoy a Quiet Morning at Home

"Miss! The duke is here!" called Sophia as Gil walked into the parlor.

"I gathered that." I shook my head as she returned to dusting, straightening, and now minimally covering the proprieties as chaperone.

I was relaxing on the chaise, with the newspaper, a book, and Montezuma keeping watch from the bookshelf, trying to recover my energy a bit after the stressful night of the benefit, followed so closely by the matinee. I'd awakened late and irritable, scowled at the autumn rain, donned a simple but pretty lavender-and-white floral delaine day dress, and put my hair up without much care or style.

Neither the dress nor a dab of my favorite rosewater hand cream had gone very far toward cheering me up, even though such girlish things often do. I will admit, though, that the sight of Gil, clearly delighted to see me, did much to improve my humor.

"*Alba gu Bràth!*" As did Montezuma's cheerful greeting of him, which earned birdie a bow before His Grace turned the table to me.

"I'm not interrupting your rest?"

"Not at all. I was just reading." I put the mark in my book, then allowed myself a long look at him. Even in his usual simple suit and overcoat, he was perfectly turned out, with the same careful attention to detail I recognized in Tommy and Preston, but without even the little hints of flash they allowed on occasion. No red tie or flower in the lapel for him.

Some might suggest his attire was a bit dull, but I appreciated the reserve. And the smile was quite showy enough.

"I was in the neighborhood after taking care of some business up near Fifth Avenue and wondered if you might be about."

"Ah." I knew the vague explanation had to do with whatever his other errand was, and decided to just let it rest. "Seizing the chance to see me, as it were."

"Just so." He sat down on the chair by the chaise. "Is this how you usually spend a performance day?"

"Mostly. I sometimes take a fencing lesson or go for a walk, but the comte is booked today, and the rain was a bit discouraging. What did you think of the show?"

"Well, until the unpleasantness after, quite impressive."

"Connor has enemies."

"I gathered that." Gil looked closely at me for a moment. "He will not be returning?"

"I doubt it. He sent extravagant floral apologies to Marie and me and vowed that it won't happen again."

Gil's eyes narrowed a bit. "You like extravagant floral apologies?"

"Not from Connor."

"I note that you call him by his first name."

I laughed. I couldn't help it. "He grew up in the same neighborhood as we did. It's difficult to revert to 'Mr.

Coughlan' after you've yanked out a handful of someone's hair."

"That wasn't a joke?" Gil's concern faded in amusement.

"Not a bit. I used to help Tommy when the other boys picked fights."

"You would."

"He didn't want me to, but I did." I shrugged a little sheepishly, noticing Sophia's shocked expression. "He was my protector, and God help anyone who tried to hurt him."

Gil smiled. "Even someone as dangerous as Coughlan?"

"He wasn't dangerous then. And really, still, he's harmless—to us. But I would not want to be the person who fired at him."

"I rather imagine that person is past their earthly woes by now."

"Better for them if they are." We nodded together, and I quickly changed subject. More than enough of this. "Marie told me that Albert's lawyer sent you the report?"

He colored and shook his head. "He did. I haven't had time . . ."

"It's all right," I said quickly, knowing I would get nothing I wanted by pushing him. "When you have time."

"Yes. Soon, I hope."

I nodded. Perhaps just a light and pleasant talk now. "About *The Princes* . . ."

"Magnificent. I'll enjoy seeing it again when I can."

"Whenever you like. I told you, you're now a friend of the company."

His serious mien gave way to a grin. "I rather like that."

"So do I." I basked in the warmth of his gaze for a moment, then decided to put my in-house critic to work. "And as a friend of the company, you must give me some thoughts on the show and the cast."

"Well, Henry Tudor is especially gifted . . ."

"Thank you, but I meant the others."

"Well, since I am calling on a lady, I should offer some compliments."

"Not required, but much appreciated."

He shrugged. "They had no lilacs at the florist, so pretty words will have to do."

"Lilacs are very hard to get this time of year. I still don't know how you managed to send me a bouquet for opening night."

"I have my ways. At any rate, the cast."

"Yes."

"Madame Marie is transcendent, naturally."

"If there is a better coloratura singing today, I do not know of her."

"She could probably spend her life in the best opera houses of the world if she wished."

"But then she wouldn't have her happy home," I reminded him. "It's not a fair trade to her."

"No doubt." He nodded. "At any rate, the rest of your cast is very good. The big ginger boy who plays Neville needs a bit of seasoning, but he's holding his own."

"Yes, Eamon. You're right. He is very green."

"But promising. And your Richard has a magnificent basso."

"Ruben is special," I agreed. "I hope he can develop to his full ability."

Gil studied me carefully. "Is there a threat to that?"

"Not exactly. But he's overcome a great deal to get here, and some people might not give him a chance."

"Some people don't like Cubans, do they?"

"Cubans," I agreed, watching his eyes. He knew.

"Well, I have always believed that a man—or a woman, for that matter—should be judged on their abilities and actions, not their pedigree."

If I didn't already like him a great deal . . .

"I'm certain you already know that, Shane."

"I do. But it's not a kind world for some people."

"True. This show should give him a good start, though."

I nodded. "Absolutely. And unless he's otherwise engaged, we'll take him to London, as well."

"That run will be good for the entire company."

"And its friends, as well, I think." Our eyes met as I said it, and for perhaps half a stanza, we just gazed at each other.

"So," Gil said briskly, breaking the moment with a cool tone to cover whatever he'd been thinking. "What are you reading?"

"A fascinating study of the Hawaiian Islands."

"Ah, a fantasy of the tropics on a gray fall day." He picked up the book. "Would you perhaps like me to read to you?"

"That would be lovely."

It was far more than lovely. I was utterly enchanted, as were Montezuma and Sophia, though likely for entirely different reasons.

No one had ever read to me before, at least not that I could remember. In novels like *Little Women*, reading to someone is an improving sort of activity that one might do for a sick relative or one's sisters while they darn stockings. *Improving* would not be the word I'd choose for this.

Intimate, more likely. Gil read elegantly, as I would have expected, and his voice was low and liquid as he described the sights of the tropical rain forest as if he were really reciting some particularly romantic piece of poetry. As he read on, his precise London diction slipped a fraction and a bit of the North crept in, making him sound more like the dangerous border lord he actually was. I reclined on my chaise, watching him and enjoying the fact that he was performing just for me, a complete reversal of my usual role in the world.

Whoever decreed that reading aloud was an acceptable activity for courting couples should really reconsider. Perhaps if the book is very dry and the reader not especially skilled. But an appealing man reading beautifully for an appreciative woman? One could quite easily see how this might lead to all sorts of trouble, even if one hadn't had Marie's glass of whisky and talk on the specifics of that trouble.

As he finished a chapter, I sighed a little. "Oh, well done. You are very good at this."

"I have a very good audience."

His eyes met mine over the volume, and I had a sudden and very nearly irresistible desire to just throw myself into his arms and kiss him, never mind propriety, principles or, for that matter, the Hawaiian rain forest.

"Good audience!" squawked Montezuma, and Sophia let out a little giggle just then, the two of them dashing some needed cold water on the moment.

"Er, well." He turned the page and fixed his gaze resolutely on the book. "Chapter Four, Volcanoes . . ."

Now, there's an apt metaphor.

"Heller! You awake yet?" Tommy called, barreling down the stairs.

"In the parlor!"

"Wait till you hear . . . Oh, hello, Barrister." Tommy looked from him to me to now blushing Sophia and back to me and smiled wisely. "Reading?"

"Just so."

"It's a good book." Tommy looked at me with a wicked twinkle in his eye. "You'll especially like the chapter on volcanoes."

"No doubt." Gil handed the book back, very careful

not to even brush my fingers, and stood with a polite bow. "I've probably kept you from your rest too long."

"Not at all."

"Coming to the show tonight?" Tommy asked him.

"Not tonight. Perhaps tomorrow, if I might."

"Of course." I very deliberately didn't ask more, choosing to offer a test of a different kind. "We light Sabbath candles in my dressing room at sunset before the show."

I waited to see his reaction.

A smile. "Are friends of the company welcome even if they are not of the tribe of Abraham?"

"Anyone of goodwill, Barrister." Tommy nodded approvingly. "You may have noticed we are not an especially doctrinaire group."

" 'Doctrinaire!' " Montezuma echoed. For some reason, the word *doctrinaire* is a favorite of his. Also *crustacean* and *fortissimo*.

"One of your best qualities." Gil turned to me, diplomatically ignoring the bird. "I am honored to be asked."

Another bridge safely crossed. "My pleasure."

We smiled foolishly at each other for a measure or two, before Tommy broke the silence.

"Well, before you go, let me share our good news."

"Good news?" I asked.

"I've added up the receipts from the benefit night—and we raised enough to pay off the mortgage on the Eaggers' house, with a bit left over."

"Wonderful, Toms!" I clapped my hands.

"Wonderful indeed." Gil, who had quietly taken Tommy aside to make his contribution before curtain time, gave him a vigorous handshake. "Well done."

"Everyone pitched in, of course, or it wouldn't have happened."

"But you organized it," I pointed out.

Tommy shrugged modestly. "It was what I could do."

"I assume Mr. Coughlan made a generous gift?" Gil asked.

"Oh, Connor," Tommy said with a twist to his mouth. "He did, not that any of us were happy to take his money."

"Why? The gunshot?" Gil's jaw tightened as he asked.

"That was just the final insult."

"Ah." A slow, cautious nod from Gil.

"Lord only knows what horrible things he does to get that money." Tommy shook his head. "I don't know all of what he's into, and I'm glad of it."

"As are we all," I added.

Gil took a long look at me. "He does seem to admire you."

Tommy caught the glance. "No, Barrister. Connor thinks she's some kind of angel on a pedestal."

"Really?"

I swallowed the giggle at Gil's faintly jealous expression.

"Connor's well supplied with companionship." Tommy's brows arched faintly as he looked at Gil, but he didn't elaborate. A message among men, of course. "He worships Heller from afar because he knows she'd never have him, even if he weren't the scourge of Five Points."

"I see."

"Barrister, you're the first man she's ever given the time of day."

"Tommy!"

"Heller!"

" 'Heller!' " Montezuma added, breaking the tie for Toms, as is his habit.

Gil laughed. "I don't wish to cause any unpleasantness between you two. Three?"

"Don't worry, you're not," Tommy said, shooting me a victorious smile. "I'll walk you out."

"Good day, Shane."

"*Alba gu Bràth!*"

Gil bowed to me again and let Tommy play host. I put down the book and took up the feature section of the *Beacon* instead, wondering uncomfortably what might happen if my men—and parrot—started conspiring against me.

Chapter 16

A Friendly Tea

Friday mercifully started with rest and quiet. I lingered long abed, enjoyed my coffee in my room, put on a simple skirt and plain pale violet shirtwaist, and took a brief but refreshing walk to the newsstand for the newest issue of a fashion book. It is true, I do enjoy reading about clothes, but I would never, ever expect dear Hetty to do the writing!

I returned to find Tommy in the midst of a most congenial discussion with our latest visitor. While I am not at all in the habit of entertaining multiple gentlemen, Cabot Bridgewater has fallen into the pattern of coming to tea with Tommy and me on occasion. We all share similar interests in literature, history, and improving our current society and enjoy lively conversations.

Obviously, he is merely a good friend to the two of us. I am, sadly, very well aware that he doesn't seem to cause the same sort of electrical disturbances in the atmosphere that happen when the duke is about, and he has never given me the slightest hint that he cherishes any deeper feelings for me. Cabot is simply excellent company to Tommy and me, and that is all.

I know that seems rather like protesting too much. But even if I had been minded to consider a courtship with Cabot, I had quite enough to contemplate with deciding what I intended to do when we took *The Princes* to London. Certainly now, with Gil back in town, I hoped I could keep the friendship as it stood.

Men, though, have been known to get rather silly about women having male friends, and I dearly hoped Gil would not do so. And equally that Cabot would not develop any strange ideas, though that seemed highly unlikely.

At any rate, if Mrs. G doesn't deem Cabot worthy of the teatime extravaganzas she launches for some guests, she surely finds him acceptable, as evidenced by the plates of cucumber sandwiches decorated with little rosettes of the same vegetable and small apple tarts finished with tiny pastry stars. She has quite a range of expression for showing her opinions of our visitors in the refreshments, with the lemon-curd tarts and fanciful garnishes whenever Preston or another favorite appears, and plain bread and butter sandwiches for those few she finds unworthy. She's usually right, so I am glad to see the embellishments when the senior Mr. Bridgewater calls.

She also provides well for his companion. What appeared at first to be a large tawny bear was stretched out in the foyer, a soup bone between its giant paws, happily asleep . . . and snoring. Noble, for that is the mastiff's name, generally accompanied Cabot to all but the fanciest occasions, quietly shadowing his master with a sweet adoration that belied his gigantic size. Noble is another example of Cabot's own kind nature; he took in the poor creature after some society acquaintance meant to destroy him. Apparently, the enormous animal was ordered at great cost from England, only to disappoint because he was not the expected ferocious guard dog.

Unwilling to disturb his dog dreams, I merely smiled at Noble and proceeded into the humans' tea.

"A lovely and generous table, as always, Miss Ella," Cabot observed as I poured.

Tommy shot me a grin, well aware of Mrs. G's habits. "I never turn down apple tarts."

I did my best not to glance longingly at them and contented myself with a cup of tea. As a little girl growing up on the Lower East Side, I'd never have imagined it, but since people in our current respectable circle can frequently eat five times a day, it's all too easy to become overfed, and a woman who plays slim boys for a living must be exceedingly careful.

I forswear most sweets before and during a run for that very reason and perhaps overindulge a bit for a week or so after. Not as disciplined as some singers I know, but it will do. In any case, apple tarts aren't my favorite, so it's *fairly* easy to pass them up.

"Mrs. G is quite impressive," I said.

"As is everyone in this establishment."

We smiled modestly, and the conversation moved into a discussion of our current reading material: a new biography of John Adams for Tommy, a study of court politics in the English Reformation for Cabot, and (because I had no intention of bringing up that book on Hawaii) the amusingly overwrought jeremiad against women's education that I had brought home from the lending library purely because it was so badly written and made me so mad.

"I'm quite certain you can find any number of other things to make you angry, Miss Ella," Cabot observed with a laugh.

"I've been telling her that for days." Tommy shook his head. "She keeps picking it up to read and lasts five minutes, muttering imprecations against the good Reverend Weems."

"We need to know what people like that think in order to defeat them," I said irritably.

"I don't disagree," Cabot said, taking another sandwich, "but you can surely take the main argument and then find something more enjoyable to read."

"I should." I nodded. "I have some lighter works from my last library visit."

"*Lighter* meaning that book on Hawaii and a new biography of poor Marie Antoinette." Tommy chuckled. "We really do need to get you to start reading sensational romances, at least during a run."

We three shook our heads together.

"Well, speaking of sensational," Cabot began, "I have been following Miss Hetty's excellent coverage of the Van Vleet murder in the *Beacon*."

"She's a terrific writer," Tommy agreed. "And it's a good chance for her to impress her editor."

"Who still wants to leave her to cover hats." I topped up everyone's cups with a scowl.

"Everyone isn't as progressive as we might hope, Miss Ella, even with our new century coming."

"True."

"In any case, I'm rather amazed by the whole thing, from murder to acquittal."

Tommy and I did our best not to snicker, and I took the reply. "Wives don't kill their husbands only in the poorer neighborhoods."

Cabot shook his head, and I noticed a trace of a flush at the top of his ears. "No, Miss Ella, I didn't mean to sound snobbish. My amazement is at the drama of his end. Hosmer was the dullest person I have ever known."

"I see."

"And the woman seemed grateful enough for her good fortune in marrying him, if very well aware of her own attractions."

I noted that he did not refer to her as a lady.

"Really." Tommy had, of course, followed the case every drop as closely as the rest of us. "I admit I assumed she married him out of love for his bank account and not his sensitive soul."

Cabot laughed. "I believe the sensitive soul must have had something to do with it, Tom. Hosmer wasn't really that well off."

We both looked at him in surprise.

He took a breath. The Bridgewaters, a genuine Knickerbocker clan who share a fortune of the Astor or Vanderbilt school, are far too well bred to speak of money in any detail. "Remember, he worked at the stock exchange."

We nodded. It was all he need say. Bridgewaters do not work to increase their fortune, and they leave the management of same to hirelings. If Hosmer, despite his own illustrious Knickerbocker name and Fifth Avenue manse, was dirtying his hands with stock trading, he was several notches down from Cabot.

Not, I hasten to add here, that he meant Hosmer was close to pushing a peddler's cart on Mulberry Street. Cabot's perspective is just a bit different. His family, whose original name was de Brede Wege, had already been quite well off when those scruffy Puritans arrived on the *Mayflower*, and the family stayed that way by buying large swaths of land. The other Anglicized version of the name is Broadway, and there's a reason one of the City's main thoroughfares carries it. Even the other storied clans are parvenus to the Bridgewaters, since they are so high up that everyone remotely respectable is basically the same distance away. Which likely explains Cabot's comfortable friendship with us.

"Risky business, stocks," Tommy said before taking a sip of his tea and cutting his eyes to me. "I prefer real property. Just not too much of it."

We, naturally, own the town house and Aunt Ellen's brownstone, as well as a couple of other buildings and the lots on which they stand. And while probably the only certain thing in life is change, still, real estate in New York City has a most satisfying tendency to gain in value if one holds on to it.

Just ask the de Brede Weges.

The current head of the clan joined our canny nods. "Quite so, Tom. In any case, it's all terribly unfortunate. Either we admitted a murderess into our circles, and she walked free . . ."

"Or an innocent woman was rightly cleared of a crime she didn't commit." I looked to Toms, thinking of another person who might be innocent.

Cabot shrugged and then put down his cup and turned to me with a faint smile. "I'm terribly sorry to bring up such dismal topics at our tea, Miss Ella."

"We talk of many things." I smiled back. "It's not distressing. I'm proud of Hetty."

"Women do not get nearly the opportunities they deserve, it's true."

We skated easily into a discussion of women's education and Cabot's plans to offer reading groups for young working women at his family's lending libraries. Soon, though, it was time for us to start preparing for the evening, and Cabot took his leave.

As is appropriate for friends, Tommy and I both saw him to the door, where we stood together at three corners, exchanging handshakes.

Just then, I felt a tap on my shoulder and turned to see Noble standing on his hind legs. Since this had happened before, I had a moment to steel myself before getting my nose soundly licked. Of course, we all dissolved into laughter and gave Noble a generous ration of attention before returning to our human farewells.

"Thank you for a lovely visit," Cabot said. "I'm glad you two managed to make time in the middle of the run."

"It was our pleasure." I held out my hand as I spoke, and Cabot held it for a moment, as he always did, rather than attempting a real or pretended kiss.

The gesture, which would have occasioned more than a small crackle of electricity with Gilbert Saint Aubyn, left me with nothing but the usual feeling of warmth and friendship. And unless I was sadly misreading Cabot, there was no lightning bolt for him, either.

Just as well, one thinks.

Undoubtedly, there are women who would be thrilled for any scrap of attention from him, since he is, after all, the head of the senior branch of the family and not merely unmarried, but never married. Meaning not only a lack of excess offspring to get in the way of one's eventual child, but also no lost angel taking up space in his heart. And, if that weren't enough, there was not the usual trail of chorus girls and other questionable companions one might expect in such circumstances.

All of which made him what the society mamas would call a catch.

Not that *I* would; I've never been interested in that game. I suppose one might make a perfectly happy and satisfying marriage out of a good friendship, mutual interests, and comfort with one another, eased along by pots and pots of money. But I can't imagine why.

Marie's Irish grandmother was probably too blunt, but there is something to the theory that much of the reason to marry is to have someone to keep you warm at night.

"I'll see you backstage again sometime soon, since you've extended the run."

"I'll look forward to it."

"And our next tea." He turned and shook hands with Tommy.

We three smiled and bowed, Cabot and Noble walked out the door, and the dog quickly pulled his master toward the park, apparently hoping for a good squirrel-chasing session.

"Always good to see a friend. And his dog." Tommy grinned. "When is the barrister coming again?"

"He's also a friend of the company," I reminded him.

"A rather special friend of the company. I wonder if *friend* is the word he'd use for you, Heller."

"There are friends and friends," I said briskly. I had no intention of discussing our "understanding" with Tommy until I knew what it meant myself. "I'm going to feed Montezuma before we go to the theater."

But as I offered seeds and carrots, I wondered how indeed Gil might describe me, and how I might like to be described.

Chapter 17

Candlelight and Dark Signs

Friday evening, Eamon knocked on my dressing-room door shortly before the two-hour call. Tommy was on the settee, reading a book, and I was idly leafing through the *Beacon*, enjoying our few moments of quiet.

"May I trouble you with a question, Miss Ella?" From the doorway, he glanced past Tommy, seeming a little awkward and uncertain, as he usually did offstage.

"Certainly. Come on in."

Tommy motioned him to the settee and lounged in the corner near the doorway. Just propriety. Whatever he claimed about scraps in the street, Eamon wasn't much of a threat to anyone in real life.

In tough neighborhoods, someone always wants to dice with the big man, and Eamon probably cultivated a certain amount of bluster there as self-protection. Here, still settling into his first major role, he was understandably scared and shy.

"So what do you need to know?"

"I've been invited to sing at one of Mrs. Corbyn's musicales in three weeks, and I'm not certain what I should offer."

"Well, of course you'll do Neville's aria," I assured him. "If you have a piece you're known for, you do that."

He nodded, watching me intently, focused like a student. "I can also sing King Richard's."

"I don't doubt that you can," I said gently, "but it's not the one you've been doing for appreciative audiences these past weeks."

His face tightened a little, and his eyes took on a slightly off cast. "I'm at least as good as Ruben."

Tommy met my eyes behind Eamon's head.

"That's neither here nor there, really. Those musicales are just awful, and believe me, you don't want to be trying out new material. In fact, I'd suggest your audition piece as your encore."

"Really?" He looked downcast.

"Yes, truly. It feels like a great honor to be invited the first time, and it is, I promise. But it's an entirely different environment and a different world. You will have many things to think about, and your music should be something you know so well it's part of your skin."

"That does make sense. Sunday suit and company manners."

"Oh, yes. And do remember to bow and kiss hands when they're offered. That crowd sets store on courtliness."

Eamon gave a sigh at least as wretched as anything Neville could offer. "My goose is cooked, then."

"Not a bit of it. I'm sure your mother taught you good manners. Just remember to add a little hand-kissing when it feels right, and you'll be splendid."

"I don't *actually* kiss their hands, do I? I've never seen visitors kiss yours."

"They'd probably like it," Tommy observed with a chuckle. "But no. Just bow over the hand when the lady holds it out."

The big ginger boy shook his head. "I see what you mean about making sure the music is something you know well."

"Exactly. And don't mention me to Mrs. Corbyn," I warned. "She does not have a good opinion of me at the moment."

"Oh?"

"She thinks Heller broke up her daughter's chance at a coronet." Tommy shook his head with a grin. "In fact, Miss Pamela had other plans."

"And good for her," I added.

"Very good for her," Toms agreed. "At any rate, Eamon, you'll be fine. Just keep your head and sing your heart out."

"Thank you." Eamon nodded to us both. He started to rise, then paused, his face sharpening with some new concern. "May I ask something else?"

"Of course." I motioned to him to stay seated.

"I know Ruben was supposed to go on as Richard a few times during the run before . . ."

"Right." Tommy's voice had a cautious edge.

"Would the same apply to me?"

The question was careful and neutral, but the expression in his eyes was anything but. Ambition is a good, healthy thing, but misplaced hope is dangerous to a singer. So, too, is trying for too much too soon.

Tommy looked to me, and I to him. From whom would it hurt less?

I finally spoke, slowly and gently. "I'm sorry, Eamon, but no. We really think you are doing a brilliant job as Neville, and don't want to push you into things you're not ready for."

"Oh." His gaze fell to his hands.

"She's too kind to tell you that it's for your own good," Tommy put in.

"What do you mean?"

"You're giving a strong and good performance, something you can really build on. But if you go out there as Richard when you're not ready and you turn in a terrible show, that's all anyone will remember. Don't go too far too fast."

Eamon and Tommy held each other's gaze for a full measure, and then Eamon nodded reluctantly. "I suppose so."

"We have nothing but great respect and hope for you," I said, "and of course you'll be coming to London if you wish."

"Oh." A smile. "That's all right, then."

"Yes." I returned the smile.

Booth knocked on the door just then. "Two-hour call, Miss Shane."

"Thank you."

As Booth headed down the row of dressing rooms, Eamon rose. "Thank you, Miss Ella."

"A pleasure. Would you like to join us for candle lighting shortly? You know you are always welcome."

"No, um . . . ," Eamon stammered, his face tightening in a scared and embarrassed grimace. "Just not for me."

I did not push, and he beat a hasty retreat, leaving Tommy and me exchanging significant glances.

"He's very young and awkward," I reminded him. "He may not have meant it that way."

"Or he did." Tommy's jaw tightened. "Do you really want that attitude with us in London?"

"We already asked him. And life has a way of enlightening people."

Tommy shook his head as he headed for the door and his own preshow work. "You're too optimistic, Heller. See you in a bit."

While Eamon wasn't interested, many other members of the company, and friends, were quite happy to come to candle lighting. I'd seen Mack McTeer wandering about the theater when I came in, as she'd done after school since the matinee, and I had meant to invite her, just to welcome her, but something had distracted me, and I'd never remembered to seek her out. She likely had to be home for dinner in any case.

The dressing room was full enough of people—and goodwill—as it was. Louis, Anna, and Marie were standing together, chatting about their children, as they often did, and clearly glad to share our little ceremony. Tommy gave Rosa an evening newspaper and teased her about her love for the yellow sheets, which they both knew was really a show of admiration for her reading and self-education.

We were almost ready to begin when the latest friend of the company appeared. Gil knocked on the door, then walked in with a shy smile and a bouquet of small sunflowers, not surprisingly from Naylor's.

"I understand flowers are always appropriate at such times. Our lady witness from the trial told me these mean gratitude, to thank you for inviting me."

"Lovely." I took the flowers with an unavoidable blush and waved him in, glad that I was still in the lavender floral jacquard afternoon dress I'd worn to the theater. It was newer than most of my usual choices for such moments and featured some very pretty ribbon-and-lace trim.

Though I'm sure God has no problem with my lighting candles in doublet and hose, I don't like to change until after the ceremony. Particularly when a gentleman whose opinion I value might be about.

Anna had set the candles in the holders, preparing to start the blessings. After Gil greeted her and moved on to Louis and Tommy, she shot me a grin. I handed her the matches with a wry headshake.

Marie did not scruple to send me a significant glance, either.

Gil and Tommy stood on either side of me as Anna began. Both bowed their heads, as good Christian boys do, while I shielded my eyes for a moment, as my mother had taught me. When I brought my hands down, I slipped one into Tommy's, glancing over at him.

His eyes were a little too bright, and his jaw was a bit tight. I knew he was still mourning Jamie Eagger's death, with the guilt and all else that meant. I hoped a few moments of spiritual comfort, and joy in our friends, might help. Tommy squeezed my fingers and nodded.

I felt a light touch on my other hand and glanced over to Gil, who laced his fingers with mine. He smiled faintly, and his eyes were very bright, too. Shabbat is a beautiful and moving ritual, even in the spare and simple way we do it.

We all stood there for a few moments in the light of the candles, silent, after Anna finished the last blessing. God in the room is really God in the people we love, I believe.

Finally, Louis let out a sigh. "Morrie is with his *bubbe* tonight, so we can't bless him, so I suppose we should go get ready for vocalization."

Anna nodded. "I miss him."

Louis put a gentle arm around his wife. "I do, too. You'll hold him tonight, when we get home."

She sighed as they moved for the door.

"A pleasure to see you this evening, Your Grace," Marie said, greeting Gil and me with a grin and an appreciative glance at our hands, still twined long after the end of the ceremony.

"A delight to see you, Madame Marie," he replied with only a faint note of guilt as I narrowed my eyes a tiny bit at her.

Just then Tommy, being Tommy, took note of Gil as he let go my hand, and grinned. "It is a lovely ritual, isn't it, Barrister?"

Gil nodded as he put his hands in his pockets, a minor violation of aristocratic protocol that meant he wasn't quite sure what to do with them. "Indeed. I've been to the Sabbath meal at my friend Joshua's home a few times. I'm not sure if we are really feeling God in the room or simply joy in each other, but it's surely a good thing."

"A very good thing," Marie observed as she swept on toward her dressing room.

I smiled at my men. "The effect is the same. Believe what you will."

The two exchanged glances and smiles.

"Heller doesn't trouble much with theology," Tommy said with a shrug.

"No need, really." Gil looked at the candles burning steadily on my vanity. "Best leave that to God. We mortals have quite enough to worry about."

"Don't we, though," I agreed, thinking of gangsters, dangerous letters, and Richard IIIs.

"One-hour call, Miss Shane!" Booth called, knocking on the door. To the best of my knowledge, Booth, renegade son of one of those tent-revival ministers, would never dream of attending church, but he often comes for candle lighting. He stuck his head inside and looked, downcast, at the candles. "I missed it."

"Sorry, Booth," Tommy said. "I came to get you, but you were talking to the propman."

"Reading him the riot, more like. One of Miss Shane's swords went missing."

"Missing?" Tommy, Gil, and I asked in suspicious unison.

Booth shook his head. "Damned if I know. Sorry, Miss Ella. It's just the small one you wear as King Edward. We have a duplicate, of course. And I've locked away your King Henry sword. I'll bring it to you when you change."

"Good enough," Tommy replied briskly.

"All right," Booth agreed as he and Tommy nodded together, the sign that much more would be said about this after the show.

"Miss?" Rosa popped up from behind the dressing screen, holding King Edward's doublet. "It's time to get ready."

"I know."

Tommy and Booth walked out, clearly counseling about this latest problem.

Gil, the Sabbath glow gone from him, too, paused before me with a troubled expression. "Is this a matter of concern?"

"I don't know that it's ever happened before. We simply do not have thefts."

His eyes narrowed. "With everything else that's been happening . . ."

"It raises more questions."

"Please be careful."

"Always."

He took my hand then and raised it to his lips. As my beau, with an "understanding," he had every right to place a careful, respectful, and harmless kiss on the back of my hand, and this he did. Careful and respectful it was, but with his eyes burning deep into mine, and the attraction crackling between us, it didn't feel harmless at all.

It was a good thing I had a show to do.

We stood there, hand in hand, for several measures, both likely wondering what might have happened if I hadn't.

"Miss?" Rosa chirped finally, and we broke apart, quickly returning to our appropriate demeanor.

"Have a very good night, Shane."

"Thank you. I hope you enjoy the performance."

"I actually have another engagement. I came only for the candle lighting."

"You did?"

"It seemed a rather appropriate time to see you." He suddenly looked a little shy again. Adorably so.

"A very sweet gesture."

"I will come for the show tomorrow night, if I may . . ."

"Friends of the company are always welcome."

"I am honored to be a friend, then."

"And I am honored to have you as one."

We bowed to each other, and he walked away without a backward glance.

I closed the door and let out a bit of a sigh.

Rosa pulled me behind the screen and started unbuttoning my dress. "Oh, miss, he's something else."

I bit back my smile with an attempt at a stern look. "That's rather unbecoming slang, Rosa . . ."

She just looked at me.

"And also undeniably true."

Chapter 18

Women on a Wheel

When we are cursed with a chilly autumn in the City, that rare sunny and warm day draws everyone out to enjoy what might be their last chance at pretty weather until spring. And so it was that Saturday, when the sun and the temperatures rose early and swiftly. I made a quick call to Hetty, and though her night had been no less late than mine, she was delighted to bring out her velocipede for one more run though Washington Square Park.

By ten, we had scrambled into our sports costumes, suits with ankle-length split skirts for safety and modesty, hers gray, mine navy blue, both topped with sweet little straw boaters, and started steaming down the paths. Everyone we saw was in the same joyful mood we were, soaking in the warmth and light for that last happy time before the snows descended.

Even poor Mrs. Early seemed to be a little less sad, offering a tiny smile when I gave her the coins as she sat in the sunniest spot on the bench. I tried not to think about how much cold she might suffer before spring came again.

Many other ladies and a few gentlemen were also out on their wheels, and for this one gorgeous day, there was a distinct decline in disapproving glances. Even though velocipedes are hardly the sign of an adventuress these days, cyclists do still draw the disgust and disdain of those who believe nice women should sit quietly in the house, waiting for something to happen. Or, more likely, for the next demand of their menfolk.

Today, though, even the older couple from MacDougal Street who make a point of glaring at Hetty and me most days managed to simply nod and walk on. An elderly lady I recognized from Sunday mornings at Holy Innocents gave us a friendly wave, and a knot of young men, college students from their dandyish clothes and carefree air, actually cheered us.

"Don't you have studying to do?" Hetty called back at them with a laugh.

"We like studying you!" replied the tallest one, a dark-haired fellow who wasn't half bad looking, if you prefer boys to men, which I do not.

Hetty, however, appreciates male attractiveness in all its forms and favored him with a flirtatious smile before moving on.

"Looking for a pet?" I teased.

"He'd probably be more fun than our old cat."

"Yes, but Lord Tennyson is house-trained."

"And you can at least count on him to keep the mice away."

We laughed together.

"It's so good to be out this morning. It's been pretty tough sledding in the news office since the trial. Winter fashions, holiday needlework, and yet more hats."

"No good follow-up stories?"

She sighed. "No one will say it on the record, but the sense I get from the prosecutor is that he's quite sure she did it, and equally sure that no jury will convict her."

"No justice for anyone."

"No. And she just flounces away."

As I watched Hetty's face tighten in irritation, I wondered again what was so awful about the woman. "Why does she bother you so much?"

"I wish I knew. You know we are very, very careful not to allow our biases to creep into our work."

"Of course. You're a professional. It's the code."

"Exactly. But we're also taught to listen to our instincts. And there's something off about that woman."

"What?"

"Ah, if I could tell you that, I could unravel this whole mess. But I can't. And so she's free, spending Hosmer's lovely money and probably up to some very unlovely business besides."

"Probably. But you won't have to think about her again."

"True."

We rounded a corner, to see Teddy Bridgewater and Mama B promenading slowly toward the fountain. People rarely recognized me on my wheel, since it is really an unexpected activity for a diva. But I was not to be so fortunate today.

"Oh! Miss Ella!" he cried, clapping his hands. "How delightful to see you and your friend."

We slowed enough to offer a brief greeting, all that propriety required, and to absorb a scorching glare from Mama B, who, as usual, refused to speak to me.

"I'm glad I don't have admirers," Hetty said as we pedaled on. "That one gives me the creeps."

"They're not all that bad."

"No?"

"Some are worse." It was probably the only time I had ever laughed at the thought of Grover Duquesne. We grinned together.

"The mother's a piece of work, too." Hetty shook her head. "Half the time, women do worse things to each other than men would ever come up with."

I nodded, thinking of all the society matrons who came backstage and delivered words of praise with condescension I was not supposed to appreciate and could not acknowledge. "As much as we think we'd do a better job running the world, I'm not at all sure."

"I'd like to take my chances for a while." Hetty watched the path reflectively for a few turns. "Really, men aren't so bad, if only they'd work with us instead of against us."

"Some do. Tommy does."

"Tommy, as you well know, is the treasure of the world. And there's only one of him. Even if he were the marrying kind, we couldn't all have him."

"No, but we can send good prospects to him for training." As she returned my smile, I decided not to press that any further, since neither of us needed to chew over romantic complications in the midst of such a lovely outing.

"Perhaps. In the meantime, I need to stop thinking about how unfair it is that Amelie Van Vleet is walking away free and start looking for a new exposé."

"Absolutely. But first, we still have some time and sunshine." I turned onto another path, enjoying the breeze and the warmth, the sweeter for knowing it might be months before I felt them again.

At the next turn in the path, we were speculating about whether we might get one more pretty day before the cold returned when she looked at the watch pinned to her bodice.

"I can't believe we've been more than an hour. Soon back to the newspaper."

"Soon back to the dressing room."

"But at least we got to enjoy the sun." She had a downcast look, which suggested she was sad about far more than the coming cold.

I turned my wheel toward the gate to the street. "Come on. I'm sure Mrs. G can fortify you with some kind of baked good before you head off to the office."

"And back to hats."

"Hopefully, just for now."

"Your lips to God's ears."

Whether it was the sunny day or just a flurry of activity as we rounded the corner before our final week, Saturday afternoon found many of us at the theater early, for any number of reasons. I had made a quick and very successful stop at the bookshop nearby, having found a marvelous copy of *Volcanoes of the World* in the window. It would make an entirely appropriate, if somewhat cheeky, gift for Gil. One can always give one's swain an improving book, after all.

Ruben was coming out of the music shop a couple of doors down, and we walked the last few blocks together, chatting about the books we planned to read when we had time and concentration after the run. As it happened, we shared an interest in the courts of the English Renaissance and traded reading recommendations.

As we stepped backstage, I had one of those odd moments where you feel someone's eyes on you and turned to see Edwin Drumm, the hand who'd been glaring at Ruben during his first practice as King Richard. I met his scowl with a cheerful smile and a hello, usually the best way to lighten such moments, and he mumbled a greeting and went back to moving a set piece.

Strange. Maybe a tinge menacing. Not that I had time to give it much thought at that exact moment.

Marie was in the costume shop, having her dresses taken in a touch more, with the slimming effect of several weeks of performing. I would have been concerned, except that she explained it to me as the last little bit of remaining weight from her confinement with Joseph and promised she was quite delighted.

As he did many Saturdays, Paul had taken the two older ones to the library, leaving Joseph in Marie's charge, and ultimately mine. Not a difficult chore at all. Master Joseph Winslow, very nearly one year old, was a pudgy ball of happiness. Admittedly, he got into quite literally everything, but since I caught him before he'd had his late-afternoon nap, it was safe enough to take him into my dressing room, let him play with my charm bracelet for a few moments, and rock him to sleep.

It is not unusual for me to play fairy godmother or amiable auntie to the wee Winslows. Marie has observed that unlike most women who have chosen not to marry, I not only acknowledge her children but also enjoy them. That has been true since big brother Jimmy was born; he, Polly, and Joseph are all sweet, happy babes, far different from the cranky, snotty creatures my younger cousins were when I had to play nursemaid as a girl.

In the past few years, I suppose it's become rather more than that. I've gradually come to the conclusion that I might not mind having a child of my own. If I didn't have to give up everything else in my life in return, that is.

My thoughts were running in that direction as I watched Joseph drift off, less imp and more angel as he settled into his baby dreams. I was more than a little tired myself from all the late nights of the run and from the fresh air and sunshine of my velocipede ride. While I might usually have read the *Beacon* or an improving book of some sort, I was just as glad to hold the little fellow and half doze myself for a few minutes.

For this one brief moment, only between wee Joseph and me, I wondered what it might be like to hold one of my own. And allowed myself to come to the conclusion that it would be a very nice thing indeed to feel the unexpectedly heavy weight of a fuzzy small head on my shoulder and the warm grip of a starfish hand around my finger.

But such pleasures come at a terribly high price, if they come at all. My throat tightened a little, and my eyes prickled with the beginning of tears.

"Shane?"

Gil, knocking on the half-closed door. Why now, of all times? Embarrassed, I blinked hard and turned, to see him gazing down at me and tiny Joseph with an expression I'd never seen before. Transfixed or shocked perhaps.

"Oh, hello." I tried for a cool tone, but it came out sleepy and husky.

"I didn't know you were in the habit of babysitting in the theater."

I sat up very carefully, and the baby just stirred in his sleep and snuggled closer into me. "Marie's having a fitting. I'm seeing to Joseph for a while."

"He seems to like you."

"He's a sweet little thing."

Gil sat down beside me on the other end of the settee, a proper distance still between us, the door wide open so we were not inappropriately alone. "An appealing vision."

I smiled at him.

"I read a rather interesting article on Mr. Darwin and heredity not long ago," he began.

"Really?"

"I don't believe all the swill about white master races and so on, you know, but some scientists have rather intriguing theories about how features are passed on."

"Do they?"

"The way I understand it, two blue-eyed people are quite likely to have a blue-eyed child. But I wonder what happens when one person's eyes are closer to green?"

He held my gaze, and I knew this had nothing at all to do with science. I tried to keep my voice neutral. "An interesting question."

"Perhaps worthy of investigation in due time, under appropriate circumstances."

"Quite possibly."

For a long moment, we studied each other, both well aware that this conversation was part of the surrender negotiations. Appomattox Court House indeed, Toms.

But why does anyone have to surrender? Perhaps we could settle on a draw.

I wondered if Gil was thinking the same thing as he reached over and carefully touched a curl that had escaped my knot, asking: "And what do you suppose that means for dark hair or light?"

"I've heard it depends on whether there are other light-haired people in a family."

"My mother and sister have red hair."

"As did my father."

"A ginger would not be unwelcome."

I had a sudden, and not at all unpleasant, picture of him holding a wee redheaded bundle. We might still be sitting there on the settee like that, me cradling Joseph on my shoulder, Gil leaning down to watch him, all comfortable and safe and happy together, except that like many small people, Joseph was not in on the game.

His bright brown eyes opened suddenly, and he saw me, immediately realized I was not his mama, and started howling. I knew enough about young children to know that it had nothing to do with me and everything to do with wanting Marie.

I rubbed his little back and tried to calm him. Gil put a soothing hand on his head, and Joseph took a breath— then let loose an even louder wail. That was enough for Gil, who backed away and stood there, looking like he desperately wanted to do something but had no idea what it might be.

"Fetch Marie," I said, bouncing Joseph a bit.

Gil turned for the open door, and just then, thankfully, Marie swept in. I stood and handed her son over and within about a half second, he was back to cooing, making a special point of looking at Gil and me and smiling to be sure there were no hard feelings.

Marie grinned at Gil on her way out. "You're welcome to sit with Joey anytime, as well, Your Grace. You might be glad for the practice."

I blushed. Gil even colored a touch. He had, after all, sired "an heir and a spare," though he'd almost certainly had little to do with their care. The boys, now on either side of twenty, would likely have gone straight from the nursery to boarding school, all probably overseen by his wife until she died ten years ago, because that was the way it was done in his world.

Joseph might well have been his first experience with an upset infant, since nannies generally present aristocratic parents clean and perfect little cherubs at playtime. He hadn't done badly, considering.

He might actually be good with children. The children I hadn't thought I wanted or needed for most of my adult life.

Once again, we stood there, just watching each other. It was almost time for vocalization, and we both knew it. Gil finally reached over, took my hand, and kissed it, one of the few socially acceptable gestures available to him.

He held my hand for a long moment. "I shall not forget our little scientific discussion."

"Neither shall I."

The rest of the night unfolded according to the usual plan. Ruben was getting better every time. Marie remained transcendent, and I was certainly close to my best. Even Eamon was losing some of his awkwardness. We were not yet falling prey to late-run tiredness, so I was well pleased.

It was only after the show that the evening became noticeably less pleasant.

We could not blame the newspaper contingent for this. Hetty was, of course, doing her duty with hats and society while nosing around for more substantive stories; Yardley was covering a boxing match, quite possibly with a small covert wager on the undercard; and Preston . . . Well, we would only know if there were leftover lemon-curd tarts when we arrived home.

A long run guarantees more visits from stage-door Lotharios, of course, and so it came to pass. While the Captain of Industry appeared to be seeking greener pastures at the moment, Cabot's friendship guaranteed the presence of the other members of the clan.

Cabot, a good friend and no fool, immediately took the temperature of the room, greeted Tommy, and exchanged quite amiable introductions with Gil. If there was any tension there, I didn't see it, because the three quickly moved into an easy chat about the unseasonably cold autumn and the various inconveniences of transatlantic travel.

As for the other Bridgewater, it was over quickly. Not only was there no reference to this morning's passing glance, but there was almost no conversation at all, Teddy being twice as intimidated by the combination of Tommy and Gil, and Mama B taking far too much interest in the duke. And not because she was making offensive assumptions, either.

"That woman looked at me as if I were the Christmas joint of beef," Gil said with a shudder as she shepherded her son away.

Tommy chuckled. "Would you like me to have a word?"

"Er, no, but good heavens, what are American women coming to?"

"Perhaps she's never been so close to a British aristocrat," I offered meekly.

"It wasn't my pedigree she was studying, Shane." Gil shook his head and looked a little sheepish as he realized what he'd said. "At any rate, you may wish to limit your association with that branch of the Bridgewater clan."

"You don't fancy a wealthy widow?" Tommy teased.

"Agh." Gil turned to glare at him and laughed when he saw Tommy's face. "Really, Tom, you should give her the same treatment as that vile Mr. Duquesne."

"I'll do my best, Barrister."

They laughed together, and I realized how comfortable they were with each other. Always good to see my men getting along. Though the reference to the Captain of Industry told me someone had been taking a close interest in my backstage visitors.

My men, indeed.

The next knock announced far more surprising visitors. Rowan Alteiss and his freshly acquitted client. I did vaguely remember Alteiss as an opera fancier; perhaps he'd come backstage at some point.

As impressive as he was in court, Alteiss was rather less remarkable in person. In the same line as his suit in court, his black tie was of good fabric and likely expensive, if too loose on his skinny frame. But his gray eyes were kind and friendly, and his smile was warm and honest as he bowed over my hand.

"A pleasure to meet you, Miss Shane. Did I see you in court during the closing arguments?"

"You did. Congratulations on your victory."

He bowed modestly. "Thank you kindly. Do you know my client?"

"I haven't had the pleasure."

Alteiss motioned Amelie Van Vleet forward, and I determinedly banished Hetty's opinion from my mind, doing my best to give the woman before me the benefit of the doubt. She was barely appropriate in a black dress of dull silk. The neckline seemed a trifle much for a recent widow, as did the diamond pendant in her décolletage, but that was none of my business.

Up close, she was older than I'd thought. Definitely a few years past me, and I suspected harder years from the tightness of her carefully rouged mouth and the faint lines beside her deep blue eyes. But her nut-brown hair was shiny, her skin pale and soft, and her figure generous, so I could easily understand the appeal.

Amelie Van Vleet smiled at me. "So nice to finally meet you, Miss Shane. My late husband and I saw your Romeo in San Francisco on our honeymoon, a few years ago."

"Ah." I bowed modestly as I caught the first odd note: her peculiar accent. Well, her name was Amelie. Perhaps she was French. "Yes, the Paris of the West."

"A marvelous city. And a marvelous performance." She nodded to me. "It was a delight, but this new work is amazing."

"Louis is brilliant, and we are lucky to perform his work." As I gave the anodyne reply, I tried to place her voice. It was definitely an attempt at a French accent, but like one of no French person I'd ever heard. Very strange.

Hetty did not have my grounding in the French language, but she had certainly been around a number of native speakers over the years, so she might have caught the odd inflection without necessarily knowing what it was. For a skeptical journalist, it might be enough to place a permanent question mark. Perhaps I had at least solved that little mystery.

"Miss Shane is, as usual, far too modest. It takes a magnificent talent to truly realize a great work." As the lawyer spoke, I noticed Gil tensing as he observed the scene, his gaze focused intently not on Alteiss, but on his client. Odd.

"Thank you very kindly." Genuine compliments like this are always a gift, never to be taken for granted. "We will be taking the production to London soon."

"Perhaps Mrs. Van Vleet will see it again," Alteiss said. "She has been considering a trip to look after her husband's business there."

"Well," I offered neutrally, wondering if the prosecutor would really let her out of his sight, "we should love to see you again."

"Of course. I do love London," Amelie Van Vleet said with a distinct lack of conviction.

"And don't we all." Alteiss smiled politely.

Something very peculiar was swirling in the air, but I did not have a chance to sort it out, because Gil stepped forward at that moment. "Mrs. Van Vleet. How delightful to see you."

That expression, the blood drained from her face? I actually saw it happen at that very moment.

"Gilbert Saint Aubyn, Duke of Leith," I intervened, smoothly moving into the formal introductions, "may I present Mrs. Hosmer Van Vleet."

She held out her hand like an automaton, her eyes flat. "Your Grace."

"A pleasure," he said, bowing over her hand and taking another very long and careful look at her. The kind that might well suggest some sort of interest if it weren't happening inches from the woman with whom he had an "understanding." The master swordswoman with whom he had an "understanding."

"Indeed." She choked out the word, which, even more strangely, came with an inflection that was much more London than Paris, and bowed quickly before turning to her lawyer.

Once again, Alteiss spoke for her. "We'll take no more of your time, Miss Shane. I merely wanted to congratulate you on your success."

"Thank you so much." I bowed.

"A . . . a pleasure." Amelie Van Vleet's voice wobbled as she took her lawyer's arm, and I could have sworn I saw her hand tremble just a tiny bit.

"Thank you for coming," I said, carefully watching the two of them walk out of the dressing room, noting that Gil was doing the same.

Once the door was closed, I turned to him, and carefully keeping my voice and expression casual, I asked, "Do you know her?"

"We are not acquainted."

The careful lawyerly answer was more than a little suspicious. I watched him and waited for a moment.

"Obviously, I know her reputation. We may have briefly crossed paths in London." He held my gaze as he said it, and I understood that this was part of whatever he couldn't tell me. But why did he have to look so closely at her?

I decided a light touch was best. "Ah, well, at least she didn't look at you like the main course."

"She looked at you like the hangman," Tommy said quietly.

Chapter 19

In Which We Learn More of a Poor Boy of Summer

That night, after the show, Tommy went out with some of the boys from the gym for one last drink in memory of Jamie Eagger. It sounds like an excuse to carouse, but it's not at all. It actually marks the end of the formal mourning, and the morning after, the fellows wake up with their headaches and go on with life, knowing they've properly paid tribute to their friend.

I hoped he'd feel better in the morning, not only for all the obvious and good reasons, but also because we were heading into the last week of the run, always a tense and exhausting time. Of course, I, too, had much on my mind.

Gil handed Rosa and me into our hansom and wished us a good night, but he seemed distracted. And I was quite sure that the distraction had begun when Amelie Van Vleet appeared in the dressing room.

Surely not.

Whatever else I might, or might not, know about Gilbert Saint Aubyn and the world at large, I could say with a high degree of certainty that any man who might find Amelie Van Vleet appealing would not take the trouble to cultivate an "understanding" with me at the same time. If only because I had the distinct impression that she would be a far easier conquest.

Not kind at all, no matter Hetty's speculations and the woman's unfortunate legal history. I had no right to make assumptions about her virtue or lack thereof. Nor did I have any right to assume that Gil would show interest only in me.

Yes, the "understanding." But more importantly, I reminded myself of Aunt Ellen's excellent maxim, deployed when one of the older cousins came home sobbing because her beau had cast eyes on some other girl: "They'll look until the lid's nailed down, *acushla*. It doesn't mean anything. Men are men. Learn it now."

Learn it now, indeed.

I should note here that while Uncle Fred of beloved memory always had a sparkly Irish rake smile for a comely female of any age, he also never so much as thought of straying, and until his last breath he professed his adoration for Aunt Ellen and amazement at his incredible good luck in winning her. So in that case, the look was indeed just a look.

And Amelie Van Vleet certainly offered much at which to look.

Rosa noticed my quiet but left me to my thoughts for the ride home. As usual when we share, I had the hansom drop her at her home first. When I finally slipped into the town house, still feeling maddeningly blue and lonely, I wandered down to the kitchen for a soothing cup of mint tea, only to discover I wasn't alone at all.

"Miss Ella!" Mrs. G was at the stove, fussing over something, and Preston was sitting at the table. Both appeared more than a little guilty. And absolutely adorable.

Just the happy surprise I needed.

"Hello." I carefully controlled my smile. "So kind of you to drop by to start the baking for tomorrow . . ."

She happily played along. "Just so. Mr. Dare was seeing me back from a most improving talk at the museum, and I remembered that I hadn't set the sponge for the bread."

Remembered also, I was sure, that you can't possibly have a civilized conversation with a gentleman caller in your flat with two nibby children in their late teens lurking about. I glossed right over that, noting that while Preston wasn't blushing, his ears were turning pink. "What sort of talk?"

"Oh, it was fascinating. A gentleman who'd been exploring in the Antarctic talked about what he'd seen. You and Mr. Tommy must read his book. You'll love the pictures of polar bears."

An improving talk at the museum was one of the few appropriate ways for a courting couple of any age to spend an evening together away from the prying eyes of family. More, the very public nature of attending a lecture together was an announcement in itself, which I knew I'd best not acknowledge.

"Polar bears sound very interesting, indeed." I smiled. "I've just come down to make another cup of mint tea so I can sleep and—"

"Little Rosa is a dear thing, but she probably doesn't know how to make a proper cup of mint tea. I always add a pinch of lavender flowers for the calming effect." She took down a cup and set it down beside the other two on the counter. "I'll make it for you."

"Thank you."

"Of course. I'm already making a nice little pot of tea for Pres . . . Mr. Dare."

"Yes. Very kind of you to squire Mrs. G here and home."

He tried to glare at me and failed miserably. "Always happy to protect a pretty lady."

Mrs. G blushed.

"But I stopped by because I wanted to tell you what I've learned about poor Florian Lutz," Preston continued.

I sat down at the table. Preston and I both knew that he could easily have passed on this information at tea next day, since it was Sunday, but it made a convenient story. Far be it from me to ruin that.

"That poor young man Albert Reuter is accused of killing?" asked Mrs. G.

"Yes. He played for the Cleveland Spiders, so I asked the boys and did a little digging in the morgue."

Mrs. G winced.

"Newspaper morgue," I clarified quickly for him. "It's where they keep all the clippings and stories."

She nodded, and we both waited. Preston is an excellent storyteller and loves an appreciative audience.

"Well, as you know, nobody makes a living playing baseball," he began, "so he was actually training with his father, the cabinetmaker Ernst Lutz."

"Ernst Lutz? Lutz Pianos?" I asked. I *knew* I had heard the name Lutz before.

"The very one."

The kettle whistled, and Mrs. G bustled for a moment while I thought about that. Like many furniture makers, Ernst Lutz produces the occasional piano between sideboards and whatnots. Unlike many others, his pianos are ones we'd want to play. While I have an extremely good, and insanely expensive, instrument in the studio upstairs, the Lutz upright in the drawing room is better than serviceable, at a reasonable price.

"So Florian had a connection to music," I said after everyone had tea and a plate of lemon tarts had appeared by magic, "before he ever met Albert's sister."

"That's how he met Albert's sister. Seems the Reuters were buying a piano so he could practice, and she went along because she played, as well."

"And Cupid's arrow struck."

"So to speak."

"Poor children." Mrs. G shook her head. "I hope they were happy while they were together."

Preston smiled, not so much at the wish, but at the sweetness of she who offered it. "No reason to think they weren't."

I sipped my tea and left them to their smiles for a moment, before carefully pulling the conversation back. "At any rate, Albert claims he hadn't seen Florian since his sister's death—until he saw him dying on his dressing-room floor."

"I don't know about that, but the timing is at least possible." Preston took a tart. "Florian stayed with the Spiders after the killing, and he was good enough that someone with the team found him an off-season job there."

"So why was he back here?"

"Broke an ankle early this past season. Came home because he had nowhere else to go."

"Sad." I said it, but Mrs. G and I nodded together.

"Losing his wife was tragic," Preston agreed. "But having to remake your life is simply a setback. He would have had to find something other than baseball eventually, after all. I'm told he was working on new pianos with his father and becoming very good at the craft. He would have been all right."

"If he had lived." Mrs. G sighed.

We were all silent for a moment, drinking our tea. I could not let Preston and Mrs. G's happy evening end on this dire note, so I finally, firmly, changed subject.

"Tell me more about the polar bears."

"Oh, they're truly amazing." She smiled. "Ten feet tall and pure white. Ferocious too. They eat men, you know."

I grinned. "I will get that book at the library for certain."

"She should tell you about the penguins," Preston put in.

"Such adorable birds. Three or four feet tall, if you can imagine. Black and white—and they waddle."

Preston leaned back in his chair, happily watching Mrs. G.

They're really well matched, I thought.

After a few more stanzas of travel stories, I picked up my tea. "I'm quite exhausted. Thank you for coming over to start the baking, Mrs. G. I'm sure Mr. Dare will be happy to see you home."

He gave me a tiny scowl but nodded. "Have a good night."

"You too."

I did not observe that they were almost certainly having a far better night than me. It would absolutely not have been fair.

Chapter 20

In Which We Duel the Duke and a Few Assorted Demons

The next day, Gil appeared about halfway through my fencing lesson, claiming he needed a bit of practice to stay sharp. Something in the way he said it suggested there was more to it than that, but I was not displeased to trade Monsieur du Bois for a more appealing opponent.

"*Alba gu Bràth*!" Montezuma called, then got a friendly "Love the birdie" in response.

The comte handed his foil to Gil with a sniff and a glare and leaned against the piano to observe and scowl. Montezuma decided this was a good time to lighten the mood with a drinking song, fortunately one of the less offensive ones in his repertoire.

Gil and I were both smiling as we stepped into position.

"En garde." I tapped my foil on his. "I'm glad you decided to visit me instead of seeking out Mrs. Van Vleet."

He laughed outright, damn him. "I'm sorry?"

"Well, you certainly seemed fascinated by the lady in the dressing room last night."

"Shane, are you jealous?" He easily fended off my attack.

"No more jealous than you are about Mr. Bridgewater's

visits." Since it was really all I had, and not much at that, I just threw it at him, I admit in hopes of getting a response of some kind.

"Which Mr. Bridgewater?" Parry.

"The senior, of course." I launched a new attack, hoping to make him work a little harder.

"*Cabot* Bridgewater?" He blocked the strike easily and held his ground with a confident smile. "You cannot be unaware that he's a confirmed bachelor."

"He is unmarried, yes."

Gil shook his head and launched an attack of his own, clearly thinking about what to say next. "Shane, he's not unmarried the way Mr. Dare is unmarried."

Block. Thrust. "What?"

"He's unmarried like your cousin is unmarried."

I almost dropped my foil, but his discomfort at saying it balanced out my error and left us pretty well even.

"Well . . ." I launched a new attack. "In any case, I would never look at Mr. Bridgewater with such interest in your presence."

"It wasn't that kind of interest."

"What kind was it?" Thrust.

Parry. "This is part of what I can't tell you."

"I see."

"Surely you can trust me for a while. I promise to explain all as soon as I can."

For several very long seconds, there was only the sound of steel on steel. I didn't like this one little bit. But since he had framed it as a matter of trust, I had no choice. "Very well."

"You won't be sorry, Shane."

I backed him toward a corner. "I'm sorry already."

"I do owe you an apology in one area."

"What's that?" I launched a new attack.

"I still haven't looked at the autopsy report in the dressing-room stabbing." He faltered a bit, and I pushed him back. "I really will get to it."

"Please do." I allowed a little coldness to creep into my voice as I blocked a strike.

"On another topic, would you happen to know why Connor Coughlan felt the need to see me?"

"What?" I lost my advantage as I thought through all the possibilities, none good.

"He just happened by as I was walking in the park a few days ago."

"Connor doesn't just happen by."

"I gathered that."

"Tommy and I will discourage him from contacting you again."

"There's no cause for concern."

"No?"

Gil chuckled. "I am not supposed to tell you this, because it was a conversation among men."

I remembered Connor's assessing glance in the dressing room. I had a strong inkling of what was coming next. "Just tell me he didn't order you to marry me."

He almost missed the block. "Close enough. He allowed as how you'd look lovely in a tiara."

"Of course he did."

"I gather you did not put him up to this."

My turn to almost miss. "Indeed not."

"I didn't really think so. But apparently, your Mr. Coughlan has decided that I am an appropriate match for you, and he is doing what he can to speed the course of true love."

I shook my head as I started a new attack. "Of course he has. Connor thinks I should be properly settled, and there's not much more proper or settled than being a duke's wife."

"Well, I assured him that my intentions are honorable,

but that I also respect your right to sing, and we have a bit to work out."

"To which he said?"

Gil laughed and colored a little. "In much less delicate terms, he said I should marry you and have a wee one or two, and you won't miss the stage a bit."

"Typical male answer. Give a woman a baby, and she won't want anything else."

"I didn't agree with him, Shane."

"I didn't think you did." I smiled and pressed my attack. "You're one of the good ones."

"Thank you kindly." His eyes were close on my face. "It's not that you don't want children . . ."

"I've come to the conclusion that I do." It says a great deal about me that the admission was easier with a sword in my hand.

He almost missed the block, then managed a carefully casual reply. "Wee Joseph has had his effect."

"But I'm like Marie. I'm a woman *and* an artist. Not one or the other."

"I'm not certain Mr. Coughlan understands that concept."

"Just tell me you didn't try to explain it to him."

"Not at all. I assured him that I was doing my level best to win you, and we left it at that."

"Excellent answer for your safety," I said, backing him into a corner. "Whatever the truth."

"Perhaps we take this discussion up again after the run?" he offered, trying one more attack.

"An excellent idea." I fended it off easily. "I'm not giving you a draw. I win."

"Not just the duel, Shane."

We bowed. He took my hand and kissed it, then held it for a long moment after.

"You know, don't you, that I have no interest in Mrs.

Van Vleet's company?" he said, eyes steady on my face, fingers twining with mine.

"You know Mr. Bridgewater is a good friend and no more."

We might have stayed thus for days if the comte hadn't broken in with a growl. "Monsieur le Duc, do we have to have that discussion again?"

Gil sighed. "Monsieur le Comte, someday, it is going to give me great pleasure to tell you to mind your own business."

"And it will give me great pleasure to congratulate you on your happy news when that day comes."

Despite all the serious currents swirling in the air, I couldn't suppress a smile at the two of them, real aristocrat and fake, glaring furiously at each other.

"Fine figure of a man!" Montezuma contributed, clearly throwing his support to the British Empire.

I glared at the bird and bowed to the alleged Frenchman. "Thank you for an excellent lesson, Monsieur le Comte."

"I'll teach you a lesson!" Montezuma produced a perfect imitation of a sports writer, likely Yardley, who'd shooed him away from his whisky.

I had no doubt it was only a matter of time before Montezuma shared some of the other things the sports writers had taught him, including words I am not supposed to know. I motioned to the gentlemen. "Shall we leave Montezuma to his contemplation?"

As we walked down the stairs, Gil straightened his waistcoat, and the last button came off as he did. "Drat."

I held out my hand. "Give it to me. I'm still capable of a little mending."

I bowed the comte out and motioned Gil into the parlor.

Sophia was already there, dusting the whatnot, so there was no concern about chaperonage. Gil handed me the waistcoat and put his jacket on without it, a nod to the proprieties that would have made me smile at any other time. I pulled the mending box from its drawer, set it on the table, and picked out the materials, with the sick little twist in the pit of my stomach I have every time I take up a needle.

Mostly, I leave mending to Rosa, but once in a great while, I'll sew on a button for Tommy or myself, usually only if it drops off in my hand. I can't do needlework without remembering those last days with my mother, each one finding her thinner, paler, and sicker, coughing harder and longer, her eyes becoming wider and more anguished. It was so cold, and I was so scared. And the only thing I could do to help was pick up the piecework.

I should not have offered to sew on the button for Gil. I knew that by the time I had threaded the needle. I didn't look at him as I sat down on the settee and quickly set to work. It would take only a few seconds, and then it would be done—

Of course I stabbed my finger on the third stitch.

I winced and muttered something unladylike as my eyes filled and the shivering started.

"Shane? What's wrong?" Gil's voice was sharp with genuine concern.

I shook my head and put my stuck finger to my mouth for a second, turning away from him.

"I'm sorry. I should not have let you do this." He sat down beside me, tossing the waistcoat away, and took my free hand. "You told me once that you did piecework as a child."

I was stunned that he remembered an offhand mention intended to explain my facility with a seam ripper months ago. I turned back to him and nodded.

"Do you want to tell me more?" His voice was gentle, and his hand warm on mine.

"Not much to tell." I took a breath and tried to stop my

shivering. "The last winter. She was dying a little every day, and all I could do to help was sew."

"Your mother?"

"Yes."

"The two of you were alone?"

I nodded and looked down at my lap. I was afraid I'd see pity or worse in his eyes. In his world, things like this happened only in the works of Mr. Dickens.

"How old were you?"

"Eight." As I forced out the syllable, a couple of tears spilled over. There was actually a good bit more to the story, but I knew I could not tell it now. He might not even believe me.

There's a reason the illness that killed her is called consumption. It devours a person from within, one racking cough at a time, until nothing is left. The last winter, Mama was fading every day, and we both knew. But neither of us would admit it.

She didn't want me to be frightened. I didn't want to add to her suffering.

At the end, even on the rare days when we could afford a fire in our little stove, she could not really get warm. She never complained, and neither did I, even when we had only one meal of bread a day, because I didn't want to hurt her by asking for more. When we huddled together in the blankets that passed for a bed at night, all I felt were loose clothes and bones—but it didn't matter, because it was still my mother's embrace, and even as an eight-year-old, I understood that I would not feel it much longer.

The last week or so, I lied and told her the public school was closed for some American winter holiday, because I wanted to be home with her. As best I know, it's the only real lie I've ever told. She almost certainly knew the truth, and the simple fact that she allowed me to stay home from school should have been a sign of very serious trouble.

But I did not recognize it. I was just grateful that she let me stay by her side. All I could do to protect her was sit with her and take up the piecework when she let me. I believed, with my child's mind, that if I just watched over her, I could keep her safe.

In the early darkness of winter, when there was no longer light to work, she would tell me stories. Of the beautiful redheaded Irishman she met at Immigration. Of the day they met once again on a Lower East Side street. And of the day they ran off to marry, knowing full well that it would cost them their families, their friends, and their faith. All worth it, she would say, because they were bashert—meant to be together.

Then she would spin her dreams for me. Usually vague, rosy things. How I could do anything, become anything: a teacher, a social worker—even a ballet dancer—if I worked hard enough. Mama didn't know much about ballet, only that dancers were beautiful and adored.

What she wanted for me.

That last night, as we drifted off to sleep, she kissed the top of my head and told me she loved me. I do not remember saying the words back to her, but I tell myself I did.

The next morning, my teacher, concerned that I had missed more than a week of class, stopped by our room. Miss Wolff found me curled up beside Mama, hoping she would awaken when the sun came out. She would never wake up again.

I wasn't frightened at first, because she looked really happy for the first time I could remember.

My teacher scooped me up and took me to the school wrapped in a blanket. I carried a bundle containing my mother's candlesticks and the few scraps of clothing we hadn't been wearing. I spent that day in the teachers' office, drinking hot sweet tea, my first taste of sugar since a *stray bit of Christmas candy months before, eating bread with the shocking treat of butter, and waiting to see if I would be sent to the orphanage.*

I knew it was probably where I belonged, because I didn't have anyone anymore.

The nice ladies who fed me, fussed over me, and told me my mother had gone to heaven also told me it was all right to cry if I wanted to, that I did not have to be brave for them. I knew they were wrong. I had to be brave for myself now, because nobody else would be.

I didn't know I was safe until late that afternoon, when Aunt Ellen swept into the office, saying that Frank's girl wasn't going to any orphanage. Until that moment I hadn't known that she existed, never mind that I'd been named for her or that my mother had sent her a last, desperate letter.

She took me home, and she and Uncle Fred made a place for me in their already large and struggling family. I spent the rest of that winter sleeping in the warmest spot by her stove, because, as she told the cousins, "the poor little creature hasn't been warm for months." I made sure nobody saw me cry for my mother after the funeral, because it didn't seem grateful.

I could not trust Gil with this yet, if ever.

"A cold, frightened little girl stitching for her life," Gil said quietly, his faint Northern accent suddenly more pronounced. He leaned closer and wiped away one of the tears, and as I gazed back at him, I saw something like admiration. And affection. "I'm sorry, sweetheart."

I took a breath and tried to regain my composure. "Everyone has losses and difficulties."

I couldn't quite steady my voice or stop the shivering, and he put his arms around me then, an innocent, protective gesture, like something Tommy would do. I leaned on his shoulder for a moment, glad for the comfort and reas-

surance, even if it was almost certainly a violation of propriety. His arms were warm and strong, and I could just
faintly hear his heartbeat.

"It's all right. You're safe now." He stroked my hair,
whispering something that sounded Scottish Gaelic.

Safe indeed. I'd never felt so protected and cared for in
my life. *Cherished*, I think, is the word.

After a stanza or two, I managed to stop shivering and
control my breathing. I carefully moved away, though I
could cheerfully have stayed in his embrace. "I'm sorry."

"No cause for apology." He smiled a little. "But I never
want to see you take up a needle again."

"You won't." I picked up the waistcoat, tied off the
thread, and handed it to him. "It'll hold until you can get
it to a valet."

Gil nodded and stood, quickly donned the garment, and
briskly buttoned it, not looking back at me until his jacket
was on and he was once again appropriately dressed.
"Thank you. I'm sorry it was so difficult."

"You couldn't know."

"I should have suspected." He studied me for a few long
seconds. "But of course you would not discuss your early
life unless forced to do so."

"No."

"Too painful, and I'd guess you don't want people feeling sorry for you."

"Perceptive as always, Barrister."

"Anyone with sense would just admire you, Shane." He
gazed down at me with what looked like awe. "You truly
are the bravest person I know."

I noted that he said "person," not "woman," and just
accepted it. "It's not brave to do the only thing you can."

"The ability to see only one way forward is courageous
in itself."

"I'm told that sometimes life closes all the doors except

the right one." As I said it, I remembered Preston once telling me not to close the door on the right man.

"That's a way to put it."

As I stood and carefully rearranged myself into the appropriate demeanor, I remembered that whispered Scottish Gaelic and wondered. "What did you call me?"

"What?"

"You said something in Gaelic. I think it was an endearment."

He looked a bit abashed. "It was. *Mo chridhe.* Essentially 'sweetheart,' just a little more so."

I smiled. "Rather nice."

"Well, perhaps I'll use it on a happier occasion one of these days."

The gleam in his eyes left no doubt as to what sort of happier occasion he had in mind, and I realized at that moment that I'd been in his arms and held his hands, and that even now I was at close proximity to him, and there'd been none of the weird electricity that usually crackled between us. Just comfort and safety, nothing else.

"Perhaps," I agreed.

He took my hand. "Is this the one you injured?"

"Yes."

And suddenly, while the comfort and safety were still there, the electricity came roaring back. I caught my breath as he turned my hand over and ran his fingers gently over mine.

"Well," he said carefully, a trace of a naughty smile playing about his mouth. "Perhaps I should kiss it and make it better."

"Perhaps you should."

He was pulling my hand to his lips when the front door slammed.

We broke apart, both guiltily clasping our hands behind our backs, as Tommy blew into the parlor, closely trailed by Father Michael, as they continued some minor argument at full volume. Sophia, who had apparently observed the entire scene, quickly returned to her dusting, with a telltale blush of her own. Poor dear, what *will* she expect when she's old enough for a courtship?

Tommy stopped when he saw us, and his eyes immediately took in the mending box and focused coldly on Gil. "She doesn't sew."

"She never will again, if I have any say," Gil replied, calmly meeting the glare.

"I offered to sew on a button," I explained quickly. "I shouldn't have."

"Really, Heller." Tommy shook his head at me and then looked to Gil. "You know?"

"I know enough."

"All right." Tommy took a long glance at me, then returned his attention to Gil. "I keep telling her to spare herself."

Father Michael shook his head at the two of them. "When have you ever known Miss Ella to spare herself?"

"Too true." Gil nodded to the boys and turned to me. "Walk me to the door?"

"Certainly." I offered a reassuring smile, hoping all of this was behind us, at least right now.

In the foyer, Gil picked up a flat wrapped parcel of suspiciously familiar size and shape from the small occasional table. "I saw this at the bookseller's near the theater and thought of you."

I burst out laughing. "Wait one moment."

He gave me a puzzled and almost hurt look but did as he was bid while I went back to the parlor and picked up an identical parcel from the shelf where I'd left it. I held it up as I walked back into the foyer, and said: "I thought of *you* at the bookshop."

The puzzled expression gave way to a grin as we

exchanged the books. "Surely you're not reading my mind now."

"I do not believe in the second sight," I said firmly. "I *do* believe that science has not yet explained all the workings of the mind."

"And perhaps people sometimes share a connection and similar thoughts."

"Perhaps." I busied myself opening the parcel rather than meeting his intense gaze.

"Volcanoes of the World." We spoke in unison and gave in to a laugh likewise.

"Oh, you two are a pair!" Father Michael stood in the doorway, of course laughing, too. "Look, Tom. They bought each other the same book!"

"Mother's going to love this," Tommy teased. "Who's the one with the second sight now?"

"Just admirable taste in literature," Gil put in, trying for ducal demeanor even though he was blushing as badly as I was. "Simply an improving book."

"Improving," Tommy said with a wicked smile. "So that's what we're calling it."

Chapter 21

Calisthenics, Mental and Otherwise

Back on the women's beat for the moment, Hetty found herself forced to investigate the new vogue for ladies' calisthenics and dragged me into attending on Monday. Better, she'd managed to dragoon our friend Dr. Edith Silver into trying the class, as well, in hopes of getting her professional insight on the alleged health benefits of same.

We were also planning to investigate the health benefits of Mrs. G's meringues afterward, since she was trying out a new recipe ahead of the end-of-run reception on Thursday. And using up egg whites again. I was quite certain now that there was some connection to Preston's favored lemon-curd tarts, though I, of course, said nothing.

MRS. HELVETICA'S HEALTH STUDIO FOR LADIES read the sign on the door of the brick building near Waverly Place, and we dutifully trooped upstairs to find out what Mrs. Helene Helvetica, expert in women's health and vitality, might have to teach us. Her pamphlet, which we had scanned earlier, promised a class to awaken our inner energies and help us "flourish in our femininity." It also claimed she'd served by appointment at several European courts (unnamed) and provided private instruction to many ladies of important position.

I had sung at a European court or two over the years and had never heard of Mrs. Helene Helvetica, but I saw no need to point that out, at least for now. Especially since I was really curious about how I was going to awaken my inner energies.

Whatever inner energies I had seemed to respond well to a good cup of coffee, but who knew?

"So what, exactly, are the inner energies, Dr. Silver?" Hetty asked as we ventured up the narrow stairwell.

Duly accredited doctors of medicine do not snicker, so we will assume Dr. Silver was merely sniffling a bit from the damp. "Sadly, they weren't covered in anatomy and physiology. I'm guessing they reside somewhere on one of those old phrenology skulls."

"Well," I said as we reached the door, "I can hardly wait to find out about flourishing in my femininity."

Hetty shot us both a mild glare. "Behave now. We'll have a lovely snipe session over coffee later."

The doctor and I nodded together. We were there to support Hetty, after all.

"Lead on, Macduff," I said.

A plump and blasé matron awaited us at a rococo pink enamel desk in an office reminiscent of a boudoir in a Watteau painting. I wasn't sure what the point was of the Louis XVI allusion, other than over-the-top femininity, but I did dearly hope that at some point they would let me eat cake.

We maintained our facades of appropriate curiosity and interest as Madame Cleary—pronounced Cle-ray here, but probably Clear-ee in any other part of the City—handed us what she called our *vêtements*, and led us to the *chambre de préparation*.

"If you laugh, I'll rip your hair out with my bare hands," Hetty hissed at me as I did my best not to react to the pretend *français*.

Dr. Silver gave us a glance she'd probably perfected on her fourteen-year-old daughter and that excellent young lady's unruly friends. "Let us maintain an open mind, ladies."

We nodded meekly, and I bit back a smart comment about *ouverting* my mind. I concentrated rather on the fact that the *vêtements* were clearly properly scrubbed between awakenings of the inner energies, so I didn't need to worry about any residue of the previous incumbent's flourishing femininity. *Heureusement.*

Several other ladies were preparing in the *chambre*, to gauge by the feet sticking out under the pink floral curtains in the warren of cubicles, and we repaired to our own spaces to change into whatever Mrs. Helene Helvetica considered appropriate attire for awakening the inner energies. I did not expect anything as comfortable as my fencing breeches and old shirts.

Comfort, I supposed, was not really an issue as long as one managed not to look at oneself or, worse, see the expressions on the faces of one's friends. The little suits with split skirts Hetty and I wear for our velocipede rides are generally called sports costumes, of course, but these really *were* costumes: full navy-blue cotton bloomers topped by navy-and-white middy blouses, the ensemble crowned by the final insult, giant white mobcaps finished with comically expansive navy-blue bows.

Quelle horreur!

"Well, so much for professional respect," Dr. Silver said, straightening her mobcap. It appeared that her open mind had not survived the closing of the bow on the cap.

"We're here now," I observed, looking gloomily down at my blouse and bloomers as I realized they were made for a much shorter and wider female. Anyone hoping for a glimpse of my dainty ankle would actually get most of my calf. So much for modesty.

"It's all women here, Ella. Nobody will be looking at your legs." Hetty, poor thing, had gotten even a worse fit than me and was drowning in a costume that pooled at her ankles. "I'm not sure I still have them."

Dr. Silver, whose costume was almost a perfect fit, if every bit as silly as ours, permitted herself a small smile. "Thank goodness you didn't bring a photographer, Hetty."

"How true. I may come back later for a picture of a class."

"Without us." I said it, but Dr. Silver joined and magnified my basilisk glare.

"Entirely without you. Let's just see what Mrs. Helvetica has to teach us." Hetty nodded toward the door marked LE STUDIO.

"Ladies! Ladies!" Mme. Cleary appeared at that exact moment, clapping her hands. "Time for class."

"Back of the room." Dr. Silver grabbed Hetty and me and firmly steered us to a hopefully obscure corner of the studio, which was just the same sort of large, light room as my own rehearsal space, without Montezuma and with a rack of large pink hoops and a bar of equally pink scarves.

Mrs. Helene Helvetica was ensconced at the front of the room, in a similar costume to ours, only properly fitted and pink, where ours were navy. She was not slim and, from her posture, might even have been wearing stays, which made me wonder exactly what manner of athletic activity we were going to accomplish here. A few fat blond curls escaped her mobcap, softening her face and covering any frown lines that might have marred her alabaster brow. Her eyes were blue and friendly, at least until they lighted on our little group.

It probably wasn't recognition, but it was definite calculation, as she studied us with far more care than we deserved.

"Did you arrange this with the studio?" Dr. Silver asked.

"Yes."

"She doesn't look like she wants the attention," I observed.

"Oh, she does. Madame Cle-ray practically drooled over the idea." Hetty shook her head. "I told her we would participate like ordinary students, and I'd interview Mrs. Helvetica a day later."

"Ah. She's sizing us up, then." I understood the look now. A good duelist likes to know what she's up against.

"Well, bright, shiny faces, girls," Hetty said. "We don't want to give anything away."

"Just so," Dr. Silver agreed.

"Into formation, ladies," Mrs. Helvetica called in a carefully cultured voice. She nodded to us. "Our new students may follow along from the back. We don't want anyone to feel conspicuous."

I wasn't sure whether to be relieved or annoyed. Either way, the three of us settled into our spaces the same way as the others.

Mrs. Helvetica nodded to Mme. Cleary at the piano. "Let us begin."

A thunderous major chord, the standard musical exclamation point.

"Breathe, ladies! Let us awaken our inner energies!"

And so commenced an hour of breathing, arm swinging, and the occasional deep knee bend. It was neither especially strenuous nor especially challenging, though I suppose if you were used to sitting in a room and doing embroidery, it would have been a relief to move about a bit. For active women like us, it was rather dull.

Except for Mrs. Helvetica's patter, which was truly extraordinary. She urged us to nourish our energies, flourish in our femininity, and become one with our higher selves.

It was amazing, though probably not in the way our esteemed instructor intended.

Soon enough, thankfully, we took our higher selves back to Washington Square to nourish them with the promised meringues, which Mrs. G had seen fit to sandwich together with orange marmalade, as well as good coffee.

"So, Doctor, what did you think?" Hetty asked after we'd stopped giggling and helped ourselves to refreshments.

"It's quite silly," she admitted after taking a small, thoughtful sip, "but not especially harmful. I suppose it might encourage women to seek out physical culture, which is definitely a good thing, so overall, I'm not concerned."

"Really?" Hetty's eyes widened in surprise.

"Really. We're all quite active, of course, but something like this, silly as it is, might be the encouragement women need to get moving and start tending to themselves. Not a bad thing."

"Makes sense to me." I had taken only one meringue, since I still had a while to button that sleek velvet doublet. "Every woman isn't going to be comfortable just hopping on a velocipede and taking off."

"Exactly. And anything that encourages women to understand and care for their bodies is a good thing. So, even though Mrs. Helvetica makes us want to giggle, she's not doing any harm."

Hetty scowled. "I was hoping for a good exposé . . ."

"Not here, sorry." The doctor contemplated for a moment. "But surely there's more with the Van Vleet matter. Somewhere out there is the person who stabbed her husband fourteen times."

"Not you, too," Hetty grumbled.

The doctor smiled. "Not at all. I know women can and do kill all the time, and unlike quite literally every man I know, I have no trouble accepting that she'd do it in such a bloody way."

"But?" I asked before sipping my coffee.

"But there was no reason for her to kill him like that. If she had wanted him dead, she'd have quietly poisoned him. There are still plenty of poisons that are hard to trace, despite all our modern science."

Hetty took another meringue, probably as consolation. "That does make sense."

"I rather liked the Frenchman, I admit," I put in, to electrified glances. "As a suspect!"

They laughed.

"I did, too," Dr. Silver agreed. "And most definitely only as a suspect. Certainly, we agree, the aggrieved lover might decide to end matters in blood. But . . ."

We waited.

"Again, it makes more sense to do something like poison, which might be taken as an illness or accident. Ferocious attacks like that happen in the heat of the moment or in the street."

"Perhaps Hosmer told Lescaut to stay away, and violence ensued." Hetty nibbled on her meringue.

"Perhaps." Dr. Silver took another meringue, too. "But the extreme violence reminded me more of a street fight. I've patched up any number of neighborhood miscreants who've ended up on the bad end of such things."

I nodded.

Hetty put down her cookie. "Hmmm. Hosmer was in financial straits a few months before his demise. And then he suddenly wasn't."

We looked at each other. As New Yorkers aware of the shadier parts of town, we knew what that likely meant.

"There are any number of ways to get money. It does not have to be something evil or dangerous." Dr. Silver's eyes narrowed as she carefully placed her cup on her saucer.

"True," I agreed. "And it's possible that someone of his status had something of value to sell or pawn."

Hetty returned both of our gazes coolly. "But we all know it was far more likely to be some kind of shady loan."

"Which opens up a world of ugly possibilities." I picked up my coffee cup again, to distract myself from grabbing another meringue.

"It surely does." Dr. Silver shook her head.

Hetty, however, smiled brightly and popped the last of her meringue in her mouth. "I can work with this."

Both the doctor and I started to remonstrate.

"I'm not going chasing gangsters, silly. A lot of the sports writers like to bet. And if you have a bookmaker . . ."

I nodded. "You have to have a moneylender."

"And it's probably not my aunt Myriam." Dr. Silver chuckled.

"Exactly." Hetty nodded.

I reached for a meringue and stopped myself, to smiles from the others. "Well, as exciting a motivation as illicit love may be, money will kill you every time."

The doctor nodded to Hetty. "And if anyone knows about scrounging for money, it's the boys in the news office."

"So true." Hetty smiled and held out her coffee cup. "Here's to a new lead."

I refilled all our cups.

"And to mental calisthenics, instead of Mrs. Helvetica's," Dr. Silver said as we toasted.

Chapter 22

A Morning Walk

Tuesday morning found me walking out with Gil, in my best purple coat lavishly trimmed with nutria fur and the new broad-brimmed violet velvet hat topped with a satin bow, plumes, and a sparkly pin, not to mention wasting half an hour fussing with an elaborate hairstyle from one of the fashion books, only to decide on my usual soft knot. Walking out, like attending an improving lecture or the opera, can be something of a public announcement of courtship, a fact that had clearly not escaped either of us, since Gil appeared at the appointed hour, looking as if he'd spent a bit of extra time on his appearance, as well. The dead giveaway was the dark blue tie that set off his eyes; I'd never seen him wear anything but various shades of gray.

For the barrister, it was practically dandyish.

I was not, of course, unaware that whatever Gil was doing might require him to maintain the appearance of a courtship as an explanation for his presence. But when he turned from amiably grousing with Tommy about the once more chilly autumn weather to greet me, the expression in his eyes left no doubt that the appearance was not the heart of the game at this exact moment.

I hadn't seen him since my unfortunate upset after our fencing match on Sunday, and to my considerable relief, he made no mention of it. But I did notice a bit of added protectiveness and gentleness in his manner toward me. It was as if he valued me the more for knowing those awful truths about my childhood. Probably the last reaction I would have expected, and one that absolutely warmed my heart.

Someday, if we continued our acquaintance, I might tell him all of it.

"Washington Square Park?" he asked as we walked down the stairs.

I took his offered arm, glad for the excuse to be close to him. "I know no better place. Unless you would like to go shopping for fripperies on the Ladies' Mile."

"Fripperies are hardly my area of interest."

I grinned. "Neither mine."

"And what is your area of interest, Shane?"

His eyes held mine, and I was suddenly, sharply, aware of the warm muscle of his arm under the wool cavalry-twill sleeve, the faint scent of some sort of herbal shaving cream, and the closeness of that ice-blue gaze. *Oh, dear.*

"At the moment"—I took a breath to propel myself in a more appropriate direction—"probably Marie Antoinette's deleterious effect on political matters in the last months of her husband's reign."

Gil laughed, breaking the spell. "Well played. I would not have thought you a student of the French Revolution."

"Well, I'm not especially interested in it, except as it affects the fate of Marie Antoinette. One of the other books I am currently reading."

"I don't even have that much interest, I'm afraid. I

know I should care very much about how people who started out merely wanting to create a working government ended by slaughtering thousands, but I can never make myself wade through the blood and terror to understand."

"True. I've reached the king's trial, and it's very hard sledding."

"No one is making you finish it," he pointed out.

"But I hate to just put down a book."

"Such a diligent scholar." He chuckled a little. "No one will quiz you on it, after all. So skip to the dramatic scene of the guillotining and then find a more congenial volume."

"It might be the thing at that," I agreed as we turned the corner toward the park.

"And by the way, sweetheart, I've asked Mr. Reuter's lawyer to send me the correct autopsy report."

"What?" I stared at him.

"I picked it up last night, ready to do my part, only to discover that I was looking at records from the demise of one Florence Lantz. Apparently, a mistake at the medical examiner. His defender—who really ought to have caught the error—is getting the right papers."

"I'm sorry."

"Not your fault." He gave a wry little chuckle. "Mrs. Lantz, by the way, died of entirely natural causes, if anyone was concerned."

We exchanged a small smile.

"A penny for a poor widow?" Mrs. Early was on her usual bench, and I had the usual coins.

"Please wait here." I slipped quickly away from Gil and gave the widow her mite, exchanging blessings, as always.

"That your gentleman?" she asked as I turned to go.

"Yes." Close enough.

"I had someone who looked at me like that once. Good luck, sweetie."

"Thank you."

Gil had indeed waited compliantly, and when I returned, he offered his arm once more. "Another of your many kindnesses, Shane."

"It's a cruel world for some people. I can't fix everything, but I can make things better for people within my reach."

His eyes lingered on my face. "That you do."

"Life has been good to me. I should share it where I can."

After a breath or two, his serious expression faded, and he said in a teasing tone, "Our swashbuckling heroine has a heart of gold."

"Kindly don't tell anyone." I returned his smile. "Come, you promised me a walk in the park."

"Indeed I did."

We walked happily on, well matched in pace and stride, and moving quickly enough to be quite comfortable despite the chill. I reflected that I might enjoy doing this more often, though I surely didn't relish the idea of moving to London for the privilege.

Also, that I would be an absolute fool to ruin a lovely promenade with such serious thoughts.

"Why, Miss Shane, is that you?"

Grover Duquesne was on a bench just inside the park, reminding me of one of those large, nasty spiders that sit in their burrows, waiting to devour unsuspecting insects as they pass. I might have preferred the spider.

I nodded to him as his eyes swept over me in the usual repulsive fashion. Gil's arm tensed under my fingers, and he cleared his throat.

"Ah, and your duke. How delightful." Duquesne pretended a jovial expression for the next comment, which in fact was anything but a jest. "I was beginning to think you'd been quite seduced and abandoned."

For one terrifying full measure, I had the distinct impression that Gil might just give the Captain of Industry the broken jaw he so richly deserved for a remark like that, however carefully delivered to sound like a joke.

"Mr. . . . Duquesne is it? I am assuming we once again have some sort of misunderstanding." Gil's eyes narrowed, and the temperature dropped several more degrees as he smiled, not soothingly. During our previous misadventure, Gil had backed him off in similar fashion, allowing him a pretense to climb down. Now, though, my swain was leaving less room for doubt. "No decent man would jest about such matters with a lady."

Duquesne swallowed hard, looking more unnerved by Gil's calm menace than he'd ever been by the prospect of a "word" from Tommy or Preston, and finally managed to speak, attempting joviality. "You know, different English on different sides of the pond. How nice to see you again."

"Indeed." Gil managed a barely genuine social smile. "Miss Shane has kindly agreed to walk out with me, since I am in town on business."

"Ah. Didn't I see you in the gallery at the Van Vleet trial?"

They held a tense gaze carefully for a measure or so, each clearly trying to determine the other's game, and Gil was apparently curious enough to allow the conversation to continue. "Yes. Quite the sensation."

"Quite a thing, indeed. I suppose just as well that she wasn't convicted. Terrible thing to electrocute a woman."

"Terrible."

Gil's eyes flicked toward me and back to the Captain of Industry, who swallowed again, with a blotchy flush creeping up under his whiskers. I wondered why he had any expectation that Duquesne would know where the line of appropriate conversation lay.

"Er, quite. You know, it was bound to end badly. Poor Hosmer never saw her coming."

"Oh? How so?" Gil asked.

I could have jumped into the discussion, but this was clearly something among men, and really, why would I want to dignify the Captain of Industry's existence? Better to listen and observe.

"Yes. He went to some summer resort in Maine two years ago and came back engaged. He was widowed, and she just snapped him up."

"Perhaps she was a match for him."

"She was something, all right." Duquesne gave a filthy chuckle, and his porcine eyes glanced from Gil to me and back. "Men sometimes make mésalliances in the middle years, you know."

"Do they, now?" His voice was cool, but the cords in Gil's arm were like steel cable under my fingers.

"A man sometimes thinks he has to marry a woman when really—"

"I warned you before, Mr. Duquesne. That is really quite enough."

Duquesne's flush bloomed into full, repulsive effect. "I meant no—"

"I am sure you did not." The words came in an arctic tone, with London diction sharp enough to cut glass. "But as you are clearly utterly unable to maintain polite conversation, we are going to walk on. And while it is not my decision, I am going to strongly suggest to Miss Shane that she forbid you from the house."

And with that, we indeed walked on, leaving the Captain of Industry gaping, and now looking rather more like a distressed bullfrog than a spider.

As the properly defended lady, it was, of course, my

place only to follow along, but I was rather stunned by the whole thing. Terribly polite and terribly dangerous. And Gil taking up for me with such intensity.

Perhaps rather more than one might expect with merely an "understanding."

"I'm very sorry, Shane," Gil said perhaps a hundred yards later. "But I'm quite sure you know the outlines of what he was saying about you, if not the exact details."

"I do."

"And if I had listened for just one more instant, I might well have done something quite violent."

"Really?"

"It is, unfortunately, one of the drawbacks of being courted by a man who's half Scots, sweetheart." He looked down at me, eyes still burning, and I noticed the faint Northern accent creeping back into his speech. "When that vile man insulted you, I wanted to behave like a wild Highlander and defend my woman."

I blushed to the roots of my hair.

Gil took a breath and shook his head, and his angry expression faded. "I am, of course, well aware that besides being a respectable lady and an artist, you are also an admirable swordsman and more than capable of fighting your own battles."

I was still back at "defend my woman," which had struck me speechless.

"I hope you were not offended, Shane."

I cleared my throat and hoped I wasn't blushing too badly as I spoke. "Not in the least. Actually, though I may be banned from the next suffrage march for it, I rather liked being defended."

"I won't tell the Women's Rights Committee."

We exchanged grins.

His expression turned a bit more serious as he patted

my hand on his arm. "I don't mean to be overprotective of you, but it has been a long time since I courted a woman . . ."

"Has it?" I wondered if he might tell me about his late wife. All I knew was the line in *Debrett's* listing her as more than ten years dead, and his brief comment months ago that influenza had killed her.

"You are curious." A faint smile.

"Of course I am. I would never bring up painful topics, but if you want to tell me, I'll gladly listen."

"Kind and diplomatic, as always, Shane." The smile turned wistful as we turned down another path, one lined with the dying vegetation that is all that remains this time of year. "I was a twenty-four-year-old barrister in training, still well removed from the title, when we married. May— her name was Millicent, but I never called her that—was the widow of a friend of mine."

"A widow."

"I admit to envying Edward a little when he married her. And, of course, when he died in a ridiculous train mishap half a year later, to feeling terribly guilty."

"Not guilty enough to not court her."

Gil's face took on the "bad little boy" expression I love. "Well, no. At least not after she informed me that it was past time I started."

"She did?"

"Indeed she did." He shook his head and chuckled. "We were all of the same social circle, young lawyers and their wives. Remember, people married much earlier then."

"Some people." This was not the moment to point out that Irish women who hoped to have a relatively secure life had always married rather late, in order to have time to save up some money.

"True. Once one had the wherewithal, though, there

was no reason to wait. And certainly not when a lovely acquaintance rather pointedly informed one that she was six months past the end of mourning."

"Ah."

"She was not at all like you, Shane. Small and dark haired, gray eyes, which she gave our younger son."

Suddenly, I was not at all sure I had been right to follow my curiosity.

Gil turned to me. "But in the only ways that mattered, she was very like you. Intelligent and well read, not to mention fiery and determined to have what she wanted as she wanted it."

"Not a bad thing."

"Not at all. And ferocious in her defense of those she loved." The Northern burr became stronger as his voice went softer, and his face clouded. "She had the Russian flu, and she ordered me to keep our children out of the sickroom, even at the last."

My father, while dying of typhoid, had given the same order to my mother. It had probably saved my infant life. As his May had saved their children at the same unimaginable cost.

We stopped walking for a moment, and he looked down at me, a muscle flicking in his jaw and the skin around his amazing eyes tightening a trace. "When she was sick, she told me to marry again."

I nodded.

"It was unthinkable." He took a breath. "For many years, absolutely unthinkable."

I didn't speak or even breathe. I had to let him say what he needed to say.

"It no longer is."

I met his gaze and held it for a stanza or more. When I finally spoke, it came out a little rusty with my own emotion. "Marriage was unthinkable for me for most of my career."

"But?"

"No longer."

For what seemed like a very, very long time, and likely was, we just stared at each other. It was too much too soon to go any further, and yet, we both knew the most important question between us had been answered.

Finally, we both took a breath at the same time, and we allowed the moment to break on a laugh.

"In any case," Gil said, nodding to the path ahead as we started walking again, "that repulsive man—"

"Why don't we just agree that the Captain of Industry brings out the worst in us all?" I offered.

"That he does." He nodded. "Even if he might have useful insight."

The Van Vleet matter? I wondered. "Not useful enough to justify this trouble."

"I entirely agree. Now, shall we circle the fountain?"

"A lovely idea. I may drop in a penny for a wish."

"What might you wish for, Shane?"

"Ah, that would be telling . . ."

Chapter 23

In Which Our Detective Finds a Clue

That night, after a rather routine performance, with none of the favored friends of the company making an appearance, Rosa was helping me into my coat and Tommy was on the settee with a book when Cousin Andrew appeared in the dressing room with a rather serious face.

"So," I asked after greetings were exchanged, "how did the Miss McTeers enjoy the show?"

The thought of Katie softened his aspect for a moment. Dead gone indeed, to use Marie's expression. "They loved it. I'm told the little one has been sniffing around the stage door?"

"She's come over after school a few times, I'd guess." I nodded. "We don't mind, and it's harmless enough."

"Mother McTeer probably wouldn't like it much if she knew, but she's not likely to notice as long as homework is done and everyone is at the dinner table."

"Sounds like my mother." Tommy laughed. "Your chaperone is perfectly safe with us, and, of course, someone always bundles her out the door well before dark."

"Oh, yes." The detective gave a vaguely uncomfortable nod. "She's always home of an evening."

Tommy gave him a wise smile at that. "She really is your chaperone."

"And a very dedicated one. Mother McTeer has seven, and a husband who's asleep at the dinner hour because of the bakery, so she has no time to supervise a courtship herself."

"I imagine an observant twelve-year-old will do nicely." I chuckled a bit.

"Observant little tattletale." He sighed again. So did we, because sighs are contagious among the Irish.

Then his amiable face turned serious. "At any rate, I thought you should know that a body was found in the East River early today."

"A body?" Tommy asked, eyes narrowing, whether at the unpleasant topic in my presence or the actual information, I wasn't sure.

"Poor fellow was from one of the Five Points gangs, and he'd been beaten to death. Not quickly."

Tommy's eyes sharpened on Cousin Andrew, likely over that nasty little detail of the unfortunate's demise.

"Five Points," I said. We all knew.

"An underling to one of Connor Coughlan's rivals, I'm told." Cousin Andrew watched us both. "I'm also told that Mr. Coughlan ran into a spot of danger during the benefit for Jamie Eagger and assured you that it wouldn't happen again."

"All true." Tommy nodded. "I doubt the incident was the first such thing to happen to Connor. But he was very troubled that it happened here."

"As he should be."

"So he did what every Irishman does," I cut in, giving my two undeniably Irish gents a wry face. "He turned overprotective and assured us that he's looking to our safety."

Cousin Andrew and Tommy both ignored the dig, a very bad sign.

"He put out the word that the show is under his protection, you think?" Cousin Andrew asked.

"Very likely," I said.

"Some of my superiors are worried about the possibility of a new gang war. Might I be able to offer them a little reassurance?"

Tommy shrugged. "You know all that we do. Someone came after Connor here, and he apparently took care of the danger."

I did my best not to think about how.

Cousin Andrew gave Tommy a hard look. "You two don't actually know Coughlan—"

"Tommy decked Connor when he was sixteen, that's all." I didn't want our detective looking for connections that did not exist.

"With some help from Heller," Tommy added quickly. "He is proud of her accomplishments . . ."

"And yours!" I added with some heat.

Tommy glared at me for a second. "He admires her from afar and probably does take a certain amount of pride in having fought me back then. We might see him once a year."

The detective nodded. "I didn't really think you had any business with him, but I had to ask."

"Of course." Tommy shrugged. "You're looking into things."

We're both far too familiar with the ways of law enforcement to be troubled by such questions; Tommy's late uncle Jim was a desk sergeant, and we have a few more distant relations on the beat. Not to mention the fact that we are hardly the only Irish people to have connections on both sides of the law. Unless I misremembered, a few years before, Cousin Andrew and Father Michael had buried another cousin who'd been up to no good in Five Points.

Cousin Andrew gave him a grateful nod. "Well, Cough-lan was here . . ."

"Just for the Jamie Eagger benefit," I explained.

"Jamie Eagger. Terrible thing." The detective shook his head. "His mother is a cousin of Katie's father."

"A terrible shame." Tommy's face tightened again at the mention of Jamie Eagger, and I noticed that the shadows under his eyes hadn't quite gone away. When the run was over, we should take a little time for rest, I thought. At least a week of sleeping in, without any responsibilities.

Toms carries too much, I thought, not for the first time.

"And all of that after the Florian Lutz killing," the detective said.

"Do you think—" I began.

"I don't think anything, Miss Ella. But there's nothing coppers hate more than coincidences and cases that seem too easy. And I know you and your world well enough not to let those headline grabbers at the Broadway Squad write it off." His scowl left no doubt of his disdain for Manhattan's most famous, and most chronicled, detectives.

Tommy and I nodded, exchanging glances. We'd somehow fallen into some kind of internal police battle, in addition to everything else.

"At any rate, Andrew, we all need to get some rest," Tommy said, moving to give the detective a graceful escape. "I'd invite you back to the house for a cup of cocoa, but . . ."

"No, no. I understand." Andrew looked at his watch. "It really is quite late."

"I'm going to go get our cab. Do you mind walking Ella to the door once she and Rosa collect their things?"

"Not at all." He actually seemed quite pleased by the prospect.

Tommy walked out, and Cousin Andrew turned to me and stared for a long second with an awkward little smile that made me wonder what might come next. "You're a woman."

"I believe so."

"And you love your work."

"Also true."

He took a breath, thought about it a bit, and then just jumped in, words tumbling out in a rush, his face tight with distress. "Katie won't marry me, because she doesn't want to stop teaching. Says she needs more than a home and children. Should I just give up? I love her, Miss Ella."

I carefully kept my face neutral, thinking that we were about to find out how modern Cousin Andrew was. "First off, don't give up."

His miserable expression brightened a bit. "No?"

"Not if you really love her."

"I do."

"Enough to accept a wife who works?"

He considered for a moment. "As long as the wife is first and the work second."

Really, not bad, I thought. Probably as good an answer as one can expect from a New York Irishman in the last months of 1899. "Well, then, you find a way."

"You think? How? The city schools don't allow married women teachers."

"They aren't the only schools, after all. I imagine a settlement house or some other private concern would be grateful for some of her time."

"Oh." He smiled, relieved.

"What matters is you're willing to meet her partway."

"It's Katie, Miss Ella. I'd move heaven and earth for her."

"You don't have to do that." I shook my head. Men always want to be our heroes, when all we really want is a helper. "You just have to let her be herself."

He looked a bit puzzled.

"You are the man who loves Katie McTeer, but that's not *all* you are, right? You're a detective and a son and a friend . . ."

"Right." The light dawned. "She needs her work."

"Exactly. Not as much of it, maybe, when you have wee ones, but she needs to be Katie, as well as Detective Riley's wife."

"Good insight, Miss Ella."

"Only if you use it."

"I surely will."

"Don't expect her to believe you right away. A lot of men, even good ones, don't understand this."

"Does your duke?" Not for nothing is Andrew Riley a detective.

"I think so . . . but I'm in no hurry, either."

The little copper grinned. "Well, I hope the two of you will dance at our wedding one of these days."

"First, you convince her of your earnest."

"Right. And perhaps get Mack to leave us alone for a bit."

"You don't mind calling her Mack?"

"She's Katie's chaperone. I'll call her the Princess of Wales if she'll let me walk Katie to the door alone."

I joined him in a sigh. It seemed other courting couples appreciate a bit of privacy in the foyer, as well. I wondered if Mack lurked in the parlor doorway at the McTeer house the way Tommy and others did at Washington Square. If Katie's upbringing was even remotely similar to mine, and

I had no reason to suspect otherwise, the precautions were silly and pointless, but Irish families guard their girls' virtue as much for appearance as for practicality.

"You would think an officer of the law could be trusted for a respectful good night."

"No, Miss Ella, there you would be very wrong. It's just as well Mack is always about."

Chapter 24

In Which the Matinee Takes a Dangerous Turn

On our last matinee Wednesday, the audience got a much more sensational final duel than they'd bargained for.

As Louis imagined that ultimate confrontation, it is eerie and wonderful. Richard has already sung his last aria, "I Prevail or Die," and while he and Henry Tudor battle for the kingdom and, not incidentally, for their lives, the only music is a soft and spooky a cappella Latin chant. As the fight goes on, the chant very slowly resolves into the prayers for the dead and finally, as Richard lies vanquished at Henry's feet, into silence.

In that silence, I take the diadem from Richard's head, then pause to offer a prayer, perhaps for his soul, perhaps for the strength to rule the nation that is now mine. I stay for a measure or two in absolute quiet, on one knee beside his body, holding that crown. Then I stand, and as I settle the crown—and its weight—on my own head, the triumphant music of my final aria, "Mine the Kingdom," begins.

Amazing theater when done well.

Both Ruben and I have to stay entirely concentrated to

make the duel work, and it's actually more difficult than the final aria. In the aria, after all, I have to worry only about myself.

That afternoon, all started as usual, the male chorus falling into their chant as Ruben and I circled each other, following the very precise fight blocking we'd done several dozen times in rehearsal and performance now. Ruben makes the first strike; Richard wants this to end in victory or death. I meet the strike and battle back, Henry's life and honor equally in the balance.

We clashed, matching parry and thrust for several stanzas, as the chant grew louder. At the climax of the fight and the music, Ruben moved to make a killing stroke over my head.

Every other time we did this, I blocked his blade with mine, then made a quick thrust toward him, sending my sword harmlessly past his torso and onto the stage side to give the impression that I'd run him through. This time, though, his sword broke when it hit mine on the downward strike. Two large pieces of metal and some shards flew between us, and we stepped apart for a second, still working to stay in character.

Ruben stared at me in horror. I gazed back in equal shock for an instant, then quickly recovered myself, gave him a grim final nod, and took my kill thrust according to plan, finishing the battle as if the mishap had simply been the way it was intended to end.

He crumpled to the stage floor as always, but his breathing was ragged, and as I took the diadem, I caught a glimpse of his eyes, stunned and frightened.

As I'm sure mine were, too.

I know I sang the finale, and I know it was good, but I don't remember doing so. What I do remember is giving him a hand up after the curtain dropped, as I always did, and seeing a smear of blood on his cheekbone. "Ruben . . . are you all right?"

"What?" He shook his head. "I was concerned for you."

"What in the living blazes just happened here?" Tommy stomped onto the stage and grabbed the two large pieces of broken sword from the floor. "Where's the propman? Booth!"

On his call, Booth and the propman both ran up with confused and worried faces.

"Look at this! Somebody could have been really badly hurt," Tommy snapped. He handed the pieces to Booth, his eyes already on Ruben and me. "Do I need to call Dr. Silver?"

"No, no, not for me." Ruben dabbed at the small scratch on his cheek. "We have bandages and such in the dressing rooms."

"What about you, Heller?" Tommy took a hard look at my face, and it was really only then that I understood how terribly close we had come to disaster.

"What happened, kid?"

Oh, precious joy. An angry and upset Preston walking in from the wings. Just the addition we need to the scene.

"I'm fine." I put my hand to my head, which was when I, and everyone else, saw it. A slash in the shirtsleeve on my forearm, and blood staining the white fabric.

Cue a chorus of concern, which culminated in me being dragged off to my dressing room, where the company and friends stood watch or offered mostly useless medical advice. I ignored them, rolling up my sleeve, taking the medicine box Booth had produced and Tommy had grabbed from him, and setting to work on patching up what was really quite a minor injury. Bloody, yes, and fairly deep, but a simple straight cut, which would heal quickly enough if kept clean and bandaged.

"More iodine, kid. You don't want that getting in-fected," Preston urged as he unrolled a bandage. "Looks like the bleeding is slowing down, anyway." Something very dark in his voice reminded me of his comment that he'd been at Gettysburg.

I did my best not to wince as I painted on another coat of the tincture. Once my arm was nicely wrapped, with some entirely too proficient help from Preston, I moved on to tending to Ruben. It gave me something constructive to do.

Booth, who'd been responsible for informing the audi-ence that there'd be no curtain call or backstage visits this afternoon, returned as I set to work on Ruben. The stage manager's bony, handsome face was grim as he knocked on the open door. "Is everyone all right?"

"No thanks to the propman," Tommy snapped. "Send him—"

"Not so fast, Mr. Tom," Booth said, handing him back the two large pieces of Ruben's sword. "This was no acci-dent. Someone filed that blade so it would break."

Tommy took a careful look, then threw the metal down. As the clatter echoed in the small room, he stalked out, shouting, "Eamon Morrissey! I want you here. Right now!"

As I dabbed more iodine on Ruben's cheekbone, his face tightened, and not from the pain of the antiseptic. He spoke through gritted teeth: "Eamon."

"What?"

"It makes sense. I've had a few odd little things happen lately. The heel filed down on one of my boots—which could've caused a nasty fall—something odd smelling in my tea before the show . . ."

"Damn it," I said. Ruben's eyes widened. "I'm aware of the words. I don't usually use them. Why didn't you tell us?"

"I didn't want to bother you . . ."

And perhaps, horrifically, he thought it was just something he had to face in life. What a terrible world this is at times. "We'll take care of this, Ruben. I can't fix everything, but I can make *damn* sure people treat my singers well in my own blasted theater."

Ruben just blinked at me.

If he thought I was a picture of righteous fury, I could only imagine what he thought when Tommy dragged Eamon into the dressing room and shoved him against the wall.

Eamon, though an inch or so taller and sturdier, didn't fight back. He was blue-white with fear, just staring at Tommy. Everyone knows he's a former champ, of course, but even in the ring, he was known for his calm. On the vanishingly rare occasions that Toms gives in to rage (as opposed to yelling for show, as Irishmen always do to keep their women in line), it is absolutely terrifying.

Tommy held him against the wall and snarled right in his face. "Someone could've lost an eye! What the hell were you thinking?"

"As God's my witness, I wouldn't do that." Eamon looked like he might cry. "I admit it. I did put a little ipecac in Ruben's tea . . . and sand down his boot heel. I just wanted one chance. I didn't mean for anyone to get badly hurt."

"You could have blinded or even killed them if that sword had broken the wrong way."

"I'm telling you!" It came out almost as a wail. "I didn't tamper with the sword."

"If you didn't, who did?"

"Me."

We all turned to see one of the hands, a small, sinewy,

narrow-eyed older man who was new for the run, scowling in the doorway. I vaguely remembered his name was Edwin Drumm, the man who'd been glowering at Ruben during his first walk-through—and at the two of us when we walked in together last week. "I don't hold with that *Cuban* being on the stage with good white people."

"What?" Tommy let go of Eamon and turned on Drumm, leaving the young singer to slide down the wall and try to catch his breath.

"You heard me. I don't want the Irish boy to lose his chance. I did the sword. I'm sorry Miss Ella got hurt, but she shouldn't be playing with the likes of Ruben, anyway."

"Get out!" Tommy roared as he pointed to the door.

"Glad to. And I'll be glad to tell anyone who'll listen what you people are really putting onstage."

Tommy took two huge strides to him and grabbed him by the collar. The point at which Mr. Edwin Drumm found his feet dangling in the air is likely when he realized his error. "The hell you will."

"I'll . . . ," Drumm choked out.

"If I hear any such thing, I will know where it came from. And I will happily go down to the police station and swear out an assault charge for the sword." Tommy smiled terrifyingly. "I will also be happy to let certain friends of the company know that you deliberately endangered Miss Ella."

"All right." Drumm knew which friends he meant. "Let me go."

Tommy did. "Now that we understand each other."

Even though he was still fighting to regain his balance, Drumm gave Tommy one more glare and Ruben a long gaze of undiluted hatred. "I'm leaving."

"Damn right you are," Preston snapped. "I didn't watch my friends die at Gettysburg so some prejudiced fool like you could hurt good people."

That struck everyone speechless for what seemed like hours but was probably only a few seconds.

"I'll take this trash the hell out," Booth said finally, grabbing Drumm by the scruff of the neck. "Sorry, Miss Ella."

I swallowed a tiny smile at the courtesy.

"Now, about you." Tommy turned back to a still pale and terrified Eamon. "I should send you away without a character."

"I know. And I'm sorrier than I can say to Ruben and Miss Ella and—"

"Shut up," Tommy said coolly. "I don't need apologies. I need a bass-baritone who knows the role for the next three days. Don't take that as a reprieve. And if you so much as look crosswise at Ruben . . ."

"I understand. I really am sorry." Eamon looked to me. "Miss Ella, I—"

"I think we've talked enough," I said with the same arctic note as Tommy. "You can leave."

He took one long glance around the room, perhaps hoping for some kind of sympathy or encouragement, but he got none, as he deserved. Then he turned and walked away.

"All right," I said once he was gone. "Can someone get a spare sword for Mr. Avila?"

Everyone except Ruben turned on me with various angry remonstrations. He just nodded gravely, because he knew.

I held up my hands. "No. We have to rehearse the duel again right now. If we don't, the mishap will always be in our minds, and we could make much more dangerous mistakes later."

No one was happy about it, least of all Ruben and me, but everyone understood the importance of jumping right back in before the fear had time to settle. So duel we did, smoothly and uneventfully.

Marie, the two young sopranos who played her ladies-in-waiting, and the entire chorus joined the others watching from the wings. Everyone was as silent and concentrated as we were. They knew how important this was.

When Ruben went for his killing stroke, I saw his face tighten a little, and I knew he saw mine do the same. But all that happened was the usual block, and I made my final thrust wide on the stage side, as always. I saw the relief on his face as he crumpled to the stage.

Before he even landed, I was bending down, with my hand out. "Magnificent."

He took my hand, as he did when I helped him up every night, and sprang to his feet, and we stood there for a second, still breathing a little hard from the duel and the relief that it was over. We shared a smile and a nod. We were going to be just fine.

That's when the applause started. Marie, her ladies, and the rest of the company gave us a loud, raucous ovation. I lifted Ruben's hand up and led him in a bow.

After, Marie made a special point of hugging Ruben, and Preston shook his hand. By now, everyone knew or suspected enough to make those significant gestures. Preston nodded to us all and walked out, looking grimmer than I'd ever seen him.

Then Marie turned to me. "What next?"

"Please no," I sighed. "The one question we must never, ever ask."

With that, the longest matinee day in opera history finally came to a close, and we broke to go home for our various medicinal beverages. At least that's what Tommy and I did.

* * *

It was full dark, and Tommy and I were relaxing in the parlor, I with brandy, he with whisky, when we had time to catch our breath and talk. Mrs. G had offered to make us a nice healthful dinner, but neither of us had much appetite after all this Sturm und Drang, so we had sent her on her way for some relaxation of her own. I doubted she'd see Preston that night.

"Some hell of a day." Tommy took another sip of his whisky and stared into the fire. "Do we think ugly little Mr. Drumm and his prejudice were the center of the trouble?"

"I suppose we have to take him, and Eamon, at their word. At least for now."

"I guess. I'd like to take them out in the street and teach them a good lesson about treating people with respect."

"I'd like to help you."

We shared a nod.

"Three days, and then I can send that rotten boy back to the bog he came from." Tommy shook his head.

"In the meantime, I think he's scared enough to behave."

"I suppose. I'm just glad everyone is all right."

The doorbell rang.

Tommy looked at me. I looked at him, and we both glanced at the clock. It felt like midnight, but it was only seven.

"Sophia's gone home," I said.

"I'll see who's troubling us. Stay and rest."

"It was a scratch." I didn't need him treating me like a delicate flower.

" 'Marry, 'tis enough.' " As he growled Mercutio's famous line, I shook my head. There is nothing like a protective Irishman.

Unless it's a protective half Scotsman.

"Well, Barrister. A pleasant surprise."

"Quite." Gil barely managed a friendly handshake with Tommy before striding into the parlor. "I heard there was a mishap."

"How?" I asked wearily.

He held up a newspaper, the *Illustrated News*, which was not his normal reading matter. Unless perhaps he'd taken an interest in the gossip column. "Apparently, your admirers at the Lorgnette were enjoying the matinee."

I took a look.

> *Swashbuckling diva Ella Shane gives further evidence of the bravery that only adds to her beauty. A mishap with swords in the final duel of today's matinee of* The Princes in the Tower *left our heroine and her adversary with real wounds, but despite blood dripping onto the stage floor, she finished the triumphant final aria as magnificently as always. Miss Shane is said to be recovering well at home, and the run continues. Brava, diva!*

I shook my head and sighed. "Not nearly so serious. Yes, Ruben and I were both hurt, but it was nothing a little iodine and a bandage didn't fix."

"I see." His face relaxed and took on a shy, sheepish cast.

Behind Gil, Tommy was smiling a little, for the first time since the show.

"Apparently, one of our stagehands doesn't approve of Cubans and decided to make his feelings known," I said, shaking my head.

Gil's eyes narrowed.

"He is no longer one of our hands," Tommy assured him. "And has been appropriately cautioned about sharing his thoughts on Mr. Avila."

"Good."

"Would you care for a cup of tea?" I asked. "Mrs. G has gone for the day, but I'm perfectly capable of making one."

"No, no. You need your rest. I, er, should make it an early night, as well."

"You're welcome to stay awhile, Barrister." Tommy's eyes gleamed.

"Really, I just wanted to see that you are . . ." Gil shook his head, with an embarrassed chuckle. "I was concerned about you, Shane."

"I'm quite fine." I pushed up the sleeve of my wrapper and held out my bandaged arm. "See? Very, very minor."

He took my other hand and kissed it. "Not minor when we're speaking of you. Or of such a dangerous incident."

"We're treating it with the appropriate gravity." Tommy said. He and Gil shared one of those glances among men that annoy me so much.

That was quite enough for me after a trying day.

"Perhaps the two of you will enjoy a nice manly conversation." I picked up my book and rose from the chaise. "It was very kind of you to drop by, but I do in fact need my rest."

Gil, blast him, grinned at me, divining the exact nature of my irritation. "I should take my leave. Good night, Shane."

"Good night."

He glanced at Tommy and returned his gaze to me. "Don't be too hard on us, Shane. New century or no, men cannot help being protective."

I sighed and patted his arm in exact imitation of the good patriarch reassuring the little woman, which both of my protectors recognized. "Of course you can't."

They smiled, and I bowed, then started up the stairs. After I was out of sight but not earshot, I heard Gil's voice, more bewildered than bothered.

"She really does fight one at every turn."

"Now you're learning, Barrister."

Chapter 25

In Which We Entertain an Unexpected Guest

Amazingly, after a good night's sleep, we were able to put the worst of the upheaval behind us and move on. Part of that was the simple fact that it was the day of our end-of-run reception, a very exciting thing, indeed.

While chorus girls no doubt spend their entire runs celebrating the success of same, we know that serious, disciplined artists do not have the luxury of such misbehavior. But as a successful production draws to its close, we have always enjoyed entertaining the friends of the company and a few choice acquaintances at a small reception in the final week. It clears all the social obligations incurred during the show with one simple late-night buffet and gives the ensemble a chance to relax a bit before the last few performances.

And so, after the Thursday show, our cast adjourned to Washington Square. I slipped upstairs to put on my evening gear, leaving Mrs. G to final preparations and the gentlemen of the ensemble to amuse themselves. Unlike my counterparts, I don't just have to change from diva to hostess; I also have to change from man to woman, forcing me to start from scratch with hair and clothes.

The quick change gave Rosa yet another chance to show her talents; I am glad for Anna that she is moving on as Louis's lyricist and as a costumer, but I would have dreaded going without a good dresser. More, the fact that training a new dresser also got me a lady's maid was an unexpected bonus. A bonus for Rosa, too, since, of course, a lady's maid commands a higher salary and gets a variety of perks, not least the chance to sneak in some extra reading time.

She was most definitely meeting her new responsibility, stepping up in speed and skill, and I smiled at her as she carefully buttoned the deep back of my lavender velvet evening gown. Despite the color, it wasn't really my usual style; instead of my preferred ribbon or lace trim, it had simple but dramatic silver embroidery at the low neck, short sleeves, and skirt. Rather stark and sophisticated.

I kept a light lavender silk wrap around my arms to hide the bandage.

Rosa swirled my hair into a soft knot, twirled a few loose curls, helped me fasten my charm bracelet and the little amethyst heart pendant Tommy had given me on my last birthday, and pronounced me perfect.

"I'll do till perfect comes along, at any rate," I agreed, adding a tiny dab of rose-petal salve to my lips. There were still faint smudges of stage liner around my eyes, accentuating them in a way that one couldn't achieve with the limited cosmetics available to respectable ladies, and on the whole, I thought I did come out rather fetching. "Thanks, Rosa. Are you all set for the night?"

Rosa was staying over in one of the spare rooms; it wasn't fair to leave her to get home on her own so late, and she was probably glad for a night away from her boisterous family.

"Oh, yes. Mrs. G is making me a plate, and I've got a new novel from the library."

A quiet night alone in her own soft bed with some dainty treats and a good book. It was likely her idea of heaven. Quite close to my own, for that matter.

At least until the past few months. These days, my heaven might be a bit less bookish. Perhaps less solitary, too.

"Excellent. Enjoy your night."

"You, too, miss. I imagine the gentlemen will like what they see."

I shrugged modestly.

"Especially the duke." She gave me a cheeky little smile as I headed out the door.

"Off with you, now."

As I headed down the stairs, I caught some threads of animated talk. A woman was describing a recent trip to France in a tone intended to inspire envy in her listeners. Several men were comparing the relative merits of baseball and boxing. A mixed group seemed to be discussing education, and possibly women's need for it. The usual conversational gunpowder at our house.

Our guests were circulating between the dining room, the drawing room, and parlor, the pocket doors having been thrown open and furniture moved to accommodate them. The foyer appeared empty, since everyone else had arrived while Rosa was buttoning me into this elaborate frock. Nothing wrong with a grand entrance in one's own home.

"Shane."

Gil was standing at the foot of the stairs, watching me. I hadn't noticed him until he stepped out of the shadows and spoke.

"I always forget what a beautiful woman you are."

The soft, liquid tone of his voice told me it was meant as

a compliment, but it didn't come out quite that way. I shook my head and laughed, and so did he.

"Why do I always seem to do this with you?" He took my hand as I reached the last step, and the current between us turned the simple gentlemanly gesture into much more.

"I've no idea. But you are quite adorable when you do."

He gave me a rueful smile. "I was attempting to tell you that you look amazing tonight."

"Thank you."

"I might suggest somewhat more elaborate jewels with evening wear, but . . ."

"I've no need or desire for jewels."

"You shine quite enough on your own."

We stood there for a measure or so, eyes locked, my hand still in his, the electricity practically visible between us. I'm surprised something in the foyer didn't burst into flames.

"Why, there you are, Miss Shane. And Your Grace."

Instantly, guiltily, we broke apart. The insinuating little voice with its odd accent was unique, but I was still surprised to see Amelie Van Vleet standing there in a dull black silk gown, the appropriate fabric again rather neutralized by the very low cut, the embellishment of jet beads to emphasize the exposed flesh, and the diamond necklace. Merry widow, indeed.

Her surprisingly sharp dark blue eyes flicked from me to Gil, and I could practically hear the counter in her head adding up what she'd just seen. This time, though, she did not seem afraid of Gil. Perhaps I'd imagined it or there had been something else at play. She had been only a few days out of the dock, after all.

"Mrs. Van Vleet." I bowed. "How kind of you to come."

"Mr. Bridgewater was a friend of my husband. He invited me along. I hope you don't mind."

"Of course not." I glanced into the drawing room, where Cabot and Tommy were in the midst of an animated conversation, and very subtly caught Mr. Bridgewater's eye.

"And Your Grace. I *do* believe we met in England." She moved toward him with a careful, practiced smile that didn't reach her eyes. A lifetime on the stage told me she was performing, but I couldn't tell the objective of the show.

"We may well have done." He took her outstretched hand and bowed over it with what I recognized as absolute, freezing formality. "I'm terribly sorry I do not recall."

She managed to run her fingers across his as he released her, and gave him another vulpine smile. "Ah, well. I'll have to work harder to make sure you remember me this time."

"The work should be mine, Mrs. Van Vleet."

There was just the faintest thread of something else in his voice. If I hadn't known that he was constitutionally incapable of being anything other than respectful to women, I would have taken it as menace.

Mrs. Van Vleet took, or pretended to take, it as flirtation, which was the one thing I was reasonably sure it could not be. She batted her literally sooty lashes and beamed at him. "Hopefully, it will not be work."

I felt Gil tense beside me and stepped in to smooth it over. But not without giving in to my wicked curiosity about that peculiar accent.

"*Alors,*" I sighed, taking her arm for a little woman-to-woman aside, "*on sait que les hommes ne se souviennent de rien.*"

Amelie Van Vleet gave me an absolutely blank look for a damning quarter second. And then, quickly: "*Mais oui.*"

Men, I thought, *aren't the only ones who can't seem to remember anything.* I let go her arm and smiled, smoothly pretending I hadn't caught the expression. "Well, I must tend to my guests, and I'm quite sure that Preston and Tommy would like to see you, Your Grace."

"Ah. I wanted to speak with Mr. Dare about his latest article."

"Mr. Bridgewater is likely wondering what became of me," Mrs. Van Vleet agreed, her odd, and definitely not French, voice steady again, but her eyes, very sharp, were on me.

As we walked into the drawing room, Gil's hand brushed mine. A casual observer would have taken it for an accident, but when I looked back at him, he nodded to me. I smiled a little and proceeded into the party.

It was going to be a fascinating night.

Chapter 26

A Genteel Reception at the Diva's

"Heller! About time you got in here." Tommy shook his head. "I was just about to tell you to throw on your wrapper and come down."

"Well, I don't know what that is, but I know it's no wrapper," Yardley said with a laugh. "Nice, though."

"It is," Hetty cut in, rolling her eyes at her own expertise, "panne velvet with silver embroidery worked in a bold floral motif at the neckline, sleeves, and hem. Very fashionable."

"And hopefully, you won't need that knowledge for a long while," I said, taking her arm and heading for the punch bowl.

"Your lips to God's ears. What is that woman doing here?"

"Apparently, Mr. Bridgewater brought her."

Hetty's mouth pursed as she topped off her glass. "Surely not suitable in a respectable home."

"I certainly would not have invited her." I sighed as I ladled my own generous portion. I would tell her about my odd little French conversation with Mrs. Van Vleet at a more appropriate time. "But since a friend brought her, I'll treat her like any other guest. That's my duty as hostess."

"You're too good, Ella."

"A scene would be far more damaging," I added darkly before taking a sip of the punch, which was mostly various fruit juices with a dash of a few tasty and spirituous cordials. It is almost impossible to get sloppy on good punch, but it serves to take the edge off entertaining or being entertained.

"But far more satisfying."

We had almost worked our way over to Marie, who was ensconced in a chair with a glass of punch and was nibbling from a plate that Paul was holding as he sat on the arm. They are such a sweet couple together—she tiny and blond, and he tall, dark, and serious—and always solicitous and adoring of each other. Marie had chosen a China-blue satin gown with abundant lace trim, so it turned out well that I'd skipped the frothier frocks tonight.

Marie looked up from her punch. "Ella, Hetty. Lovely party. It's so nice to get out among friends."

"I didn't offer invites to the stage-door Lotharios," I admitted. "We've a few society names from the boards and all, but I didn't think we needed the Captain of Industry and his ilk."

"Good thing," Paul growled. "I saw the way that Duquesne man looks at women."

"You're a lawyer, Paul, not a pugilist," Marie reminded him with a teasing grin.

"And if he gets within a hundred feet of you, I'll find a way to sue him."

We ladies chuckled lightly. None of us mind the male impulse to protect us (as long as they don't take it too far), but sometimes we are amused by the way they express it.

"Miss Ella."

I turned to see Cabot Bridgewater, a glass in his hand and a furrow at his brow. Noble, of course, was home and probably happily asleep by some fire at the Bridgewater manse.

"Mr. Bridgewater. Delightful to see you." I nodded to the others, who no doubt knew that I had to have a bit of a word with my dear guest.

I held out my hand, and he took it for a moment, as usual. "Miss Ella, my apologies for bringing—"

"It's quite all right. She's a friend of yours, and that is all I need to know."

"That may be so, but I should tell you she was exceedingly interested in seeing you and your circle."

"Really?"

"She also asked me if the duke might be here."

I could feel my jaw tightening. "Did she now?"

"I felt it better to bring her and let her see the ensemble rather than have her approach at some untoward time."

"Ah. Keep her where we can see her."

Cabot smiled. "Exactly. Very wise, as always."

"And really, it isn't fair to ostracize someone who has not been convicted of any crime. Whatever people may think."

"Well, true." He clearly had his own opinions on the matter, and no intention of sharing them with me. "Thank you for your understanding. Don't be surprised if I express my appreciation with an extravagant floral tribute."

I laughed. "Just not lilies of the valley or red roses."

He knew about that, but not the lilacs. "Of course not."

We smiled together, balance restored, both of us knowing, if not acknowledging, that somehow this incident had moved us closer as friends and further from any pretense of a potential courtship.

Cabot drifted off, his eyes carefully, but unobtrusively, on his companion, while I circulated a bit, happily accepting introductions to families of the ensemble, then managing a bit of anodyne chat with the knot of society matrons who'd parked themselves near Mrs. G's elaborately decorated tray of jam tarts.

One of the matrons motioned Louis and Anna over, ostensibly to praise their work, but really to show off her own lessons in musicianship and ultimately beat the others to the mark by asking them to write a "little entertainment" for her next bal masqué. Such a lucrative commission, though perhaps not an artistic triumph, would give them plenty of money to buy time to work on things they really enjoyed.

They gave me a subtle glance, which I returned, and the ladies never noticed as I made a graceful good-bye. Someday, we little canaries might sing, or write, only for our pleasure, but this was not that day.

My rounds next took me to Ruben and his mother. She was beautiful, clad simply but elegantly in a high-necked, garnet-colored taffeta dress, with skin like honey and the same deep brown eyes as his.

"Miss Ella, my mother, Susanna Avila." Ruben presented me with a shy, but proud, smile.

The little I knew about Ruben's situation was enough for me to understand that it was a great mark of trust for him to bring his mother to our gathering. He needn't have worried. If anything, his mother looked more believably Cuban than he, and after the incident with Edwin Drumm, the company was firmly united in our acceptance of him, which clearly extended to her.

"An honor." I greeted her warmly, shaking hands and putting a hand on her arm. "Your son is amazing."

"He's a good boy." Susanna Avila smiled. "Good singer, too."

"We agree on both counts."

Mrs. Avila and I made conversation for a few more minutes, and I found myself drawn to her and not really shocked by her voice. I'd met a few people from Cuba and the waning Spanish Empire over the years, and she didn't sound in the least like them. While she'd clearly and carefully lost any accent she once had, a faint echo in the rhythm of her speech reminded me of a young soprano from Georgia who'd understudied on our first tour, before quitting to marry the boy back home.

Whatever part of Havana—or Birmingham—was Mrs. Avila's original home, she was a lovely, charming woman who'd done a magnificent job with her son, and I was delighted to know her. And their secrets were safe with us.

As the party wound down, I finally managed a return to the punch bowl and, hopefully, my own plate of treats, not that there were many left.

"Hey, kid. Tom and I saved some for you."

Preston handed me a plate that did indeed have a selection of my favorites.

"Aren't you sweet."

"We know you." He refilled his own glass. "I know why you serve this stuff, but I don't think there's one real drink in that entire bowl."

"There's not, and that's why we serve it."

"Probably wise. Imagine that bunch after a few belts." He nodded at the matrons, who had presumably had their fill of critiquing the party and me, and had moved on to looking at each other with all the affection a mongoose shows a cobra.

"I'd almost change the recipe just to see it."

We chuckled together.

"Don't you dare. Gret . . . Mrs. Grazich outdid herself, and we don't need drunken socialites in the punch bowl."

"Mrs. G did indeed produce miracles," I agreed, ignoring the slip. "I couldn't do this without her."

"Hmmm." Preston sipped his punch. "What if, say, she found something else to do with her time?"

"Something else?" I strongly suspected what he meant. "Well, she's a free woman, after all. I'll just have to find another cook. But unless she takes religious vows, perhaps I can beg or bribe her to make an occasional batch of cookies and cater a special party once in a while."

"I think it might be something a bit more secular."

"Good thing. Being a nun doesn't sound like any fun."

Preston smiled a little. "She'd probably be willing to pitch in for you sometimes if you really needed her."

"And if her other employer didn't object?"

"Wouldn't be your usual employer, kid."

"So she'll have room to negotiate."

"I'd guess."

"Well, if she has a good opportunity, she should take it."

"Yes?"

"And if," I said, carefully keeping my eyes on my plate, "someone were thinking of offering her an opportunity, they should perhaps get on with it."

"Would she take it, do you think?"

"If it's the opportunity I think it is, she won't let him finish the sentence."

Out of the corner of my eye, I saw Preston smiling.

"Heller! You have to settle this!" Tommy called from across the room, where he was clearly having some minor argument with Yardley and Cabot. "You're the only one who actually remembers all of Henry VIII's wives . . ."

"My public calls. You always tell me not to let fear stop me."

"I do, don't I?"

The matrons took their leave quite early, soon followed by the Winslows and the rest of the artists. In a particularly interesting twist, Cabot offered to squire Hetty home, as well as Mrs. Van Vleet, which my reporter friend accepted with an acquisitive gleam in her eyes.

The party was quickly running down to Tommy and the sports writers, which would be my cue to take to my bed for what beauty sleep I could manage. I put down my glass and began one last circle of the house to be sure I hadn't missed anyone, to find Gil in the drawing room, studying our bookshelves.

"You and your cousin are quite widely read."

"One or the other of us will read anything." I shrugged. "Would you like to borrow something, since you can't have brought a good supply along?"

"Thank you. I would, actually." He pulled out an edition of John and Abigail Adams's letters. "They were a fascinating couple."

"Well matched. And he greatly respected her judgment."

"As any man with a clever wife should."

"I'd like to think so." I smiled at that.

"But also very much in love, I've read. He missed her terribly when he had to go abroad."

"Being apart is an awful strain on a marriage."

"Duty is all well and good, but a man should try to stay with his wife if he can."

"Should he?" I had the feeling we were no longer talking about the Adamses.

"Well, if one is fortunate enough to find true love, it makes no sense to then sit on opposite sides of an ocean."

"Even with true love, it's not always so simple."

He looked up from the book then, his eyes on mine in the light of the nearby oil lamp, bottomless and intense. "Perhaps it should be."

"Perhaps."

For a long moment, we stood there, just gazing at each

other. *Want, love, need* . . . Whatever word I could've chosen, it would have been inadequate. No denying the attraction, but it went far further and deeper than that, a real connection of mind and soul.

"Heller! Want to play checkers with the boys?"

For the second time tonight, we stepped apart guiltily, this time, though, we weren't even touching.

As he walked into the room, Tommy chuckled and smiled at Gil. "You're welcome to stay for the tournament."

"I'm sorry," I said briskly, "but you'll be playing without me. I'm so tired, I hardly know what I'm doing." I bowed to both. "Good night."

"Good night, Shane." Gil bowed. "Sleep well."

"Get some rest, Heller."

As I headed upstairs, I heard Tommy and Gil talking, but I couldn't make anything out and, really, had no need to know.

Chapter 27

Not Holmes, but Marry, 'Tis Enough

His Grace appeared in the parlor just before noon the next day, with a sheaf of papers and a troubled expression that didn't lift, despite his approving glance at my pansy-print day dress.

"Am I interrupting your preshow rest?"

"Not at all." I had just risen after a night of rather unsettling dreams. And no, not happily unsettling. "This close to the end, we float through in a fog of memorization and exhaustion, anyway."

"You never seem to be slipping away."

I grinned at him. "Then I'm doing it right."

He did not return the smile. "And I haven't done right by you, and your unfortunate baritone."

"What?"

"I only just looked at this autopsy report. You will want to send it to your friend the detective after I explain what I found."

"I will?" I returned his sharp glance with my own.

"I am reasonably convinced they've arrested an innocent man."

"Oh, dear."

He nodded to the coffee table. "Here. I'll lay it out for you."

"All right."

We sat down on the settee together, any romantic undercurrents between us obviously buried by our mutual concern for Albert.

"These things aren't normally matters for ladies, of course, but as you've studied such reports before . . ."

I couldn't hide my indulgent smile.

"You are the woman I am courting, Shane. Allow me to observe at least the outlines of the forms."

"Of course."

"Right, then." He put the report on the table and pointed to a sentence. "It's exactly as you suspected. The issue is indeed the wounds."

I read aloud what he indicated. "Deep stabbing laceration of the carotid artery in a downward trajectory."

"How tall is Albert?"

"His exact measurements are in Anna's costume book, of course, but he's a bit taller than me and noticeably shorter than you. Say, just under six feet."

"Before we go to the appropriate authorities, we'll want the precise number. But that's close enough. Florian was six feet two."

"So there is no way that Albert, five feet ten or so, could stab *down* at his neck in a standing surprise attack."

"None."

We nodded together and just looked down at the report for a moment, absorbing the enormity of it.

"Shane, I'm sorry I didn't believe you—"

"You agreed to take a look for my sake, believe or not. That's quite enough."

"I should have done it immediately. That envelope sat on my bureau for days, even after they sent the right report."

"You're working on other matters, as well." *Which I am not going to ask about.* "Let's just worry about clearing Albert now."

"All right. So what do we do? I hate the thought of that poor young man in the Tombs."

"It's about as you said. I'll send word to Cousin Andrew, and you'll lay out the evidence for him. He'll probably be the one to go to the DA." And to rub the Broadway Squad's face in it.

"How long do you think it will take to free him?"

"I don't know."

"Perhaps closing night at least."

I just stared at Gil then, impressed and amazed that he understood what would matter most to a singer.

"I am a friend of the company, after all," he added.

"That you are." I smiled at him but shook my head at the thought of poor Albert. "I doubt he'll be in any shape to finish the run."

"Likely not, after all that time in gaol. Another loss for him."

I turned my mind to the practicalities. There *was* a fairly simple solution. "We don't really need two Richards in London, but many companies do travel with doubles for lead roles."

They might alternate as Richard and Neville, actually, since Eamon certainly wasn't welcome on this tour.

"And you and Tom can likely put in a good word here between now and then."

"We certainly will." I nodded. "It won't make up for losing this opportunity, but he's quite good, and we'll help him find more."

Gil finally smiled. "Your new project?"

"I imagine so." I thought about it. "First, we get him out. Then we get him back to form and start working on recovering his career. And finish the run, of course."

"And then you prepare for London."

A different note in his voice made me look up at him. Our eyes locked, and despite everything else, for a second we just sat there, drawn together. London would mean a real, formal courtship . . . and then what?

"Yes," I said slowly. "London. Assuming we all live that long."

I'd intended it as just a touch of wry gallows humor, but Gil's gaze sharpened on me with real concern. "If not Albert, who, Shane?"

"Someone who means the company ill, I suspect." I remembered Tommy's earlier speculations, when it had been nothing but an outside, fantastic possibility. Not a fantasy now.

"What do you mean?"

"Well, if Albert didn't kill Florian, then someone else is out there. Which makes me wonder about some of our other incidents, like the gunfire after the benefit."

"I assumed it was aimed at Mr. Coughlan."

"As did we all. Not to mention the sword theft—"

The front door slammed. "Heller!"

Gil and I reflexively moved to opposite corners of the settee as Tommy walked in, assessing the situation with a smile.

"Paying respects after the reception?" he asked.

"Not quite. I've just finished explaining to Shane that Albert Reuter is almost certainly innocent."

"He is?"

"Not tall enough to deal the fatal blow," Gil said.

The three of us looked at each other, all ticking through the list of tall men who would be found backstage. It would almost have to be someone who did not attract notice from the company—a hand or even a member of the cast, horrible thought though that was.

"Was the night of the benefit Mr. Coughlan's first appearance?" Gil asked.

"And his only one." Tommy shook his head. "He stays away from respectable precincts unless he has a good reason."

Gil reflected. "He's also somewhat shorter than either of us, if I recall."

"He is." Tommy nodded.

I ignored the note of satisfaction in Gil's voice at literally topping Connor. "Booth is taller than both of you, but . . ."

"I surely hope not." Tommy's face tightened. "He's been our New York stage manager for years, and I can't imagine . . ."

"Anything is possible, but he's a good man, with no reason to wish us ill." I thought about it. "At least a couple of the stagehands are tall enough. And many of them are new for the run."

"Yes, including the wretched Edwin Drumm."

"He was too short and would never have done anything that might benefit Ruben," I pointed out.

Tommy gave me a very concerned glance. "An accomplice we didn't catch?"

Gil offered another candidate. "What about that large redheaded young man who plays Neville?"

"Eamon." I winced as I said his name. "But he confessed all."

"No." Tommy shook his head. "He confessed all we'd caught him at."

Sickening thought, but not impossible. "He knew Albert."

"And he certainly gained by his disgrace." Tommy scowled. "Not to mention his little campaign of sabotage against Ruben."

"He'd killed once and didn't want to have to do it again?" I asked. If that bloody scene had been Eamon's first murder . . .

"Maybe." Tommy swallowed hard and cleared his throat as he remembered the gore. "Or feared he would get caught."

Gil had been carefully observing all of this and finally added his own thoughts. "A great deal of dangerous work to move up in the company. Is it really worth so much?"

"A starring role is worth your life if you're a singer." Tommy nodded to me.

"No question. And certainly worth someone else's."

"What you are saying is that you would kill or die for your career?" Gil had an expression of shock and quite possibly disgust, one that I'd never seen before.

Tommy very subtly glanced to me.

"No, no. *I* wouldn't." I met Gil's gaze steadily. "The people I love are worth my life. A role isn't."

"But?"

We were suddenly right at the heart of the matter. Is the music worth everything else in my life, and if not, how much am I willing to give for the rest? And what is he willing to give for me?

"But . . ." I took a breath as I collected my thoughts. "A leading role, a chance, *feels* like your life. If you're a bit unbalanced to begin with, who knows?"

"And singers do sometimes become unbalanced over the need to succeed," Tommy agreed. "Unfortunately, I've seen it a few times. People who simply don't have the talent to make a profession of it but want it so much that they can't admit that."

"So such a person might be dangerous?" Gil asked, with a relieved expression that belied the words. Relieved, I didn't doubt, to pull back to the safer matter of murder.

"Could well be dangerous," Tommy agreed. "It may have been in front of us all along."

"Eamon." I had to admit, at least to myself, that we might have another villain among us. Villain. "Richard III."

"What?" Tommy and Gil asked in unplanned unison.

"Richard III. Eamon would be the third Richard if he managed to get rid of Ruben."

The men just shook their heads, giving me almost exactly the same wry face.

And then Tommy grinned. "Mother was right."

"What?" Gil and I both spoke, though I quickly realized what Toms meant.

"She said the second sight told her Albert was innocent." He laughed. "And this time, she was right."

"We'll never live this down." I shook my head. "Too bad she didn't see the real killer, too."

"Too much to hope for," Gil said, carefully keeping a neutral tone. "We have plenty of suspicions."

"But we can't prove anything," Tommy agreed. "We've got enough to clear Albert, but nothing more than a theory pointing to Eamon or perhaps a stray stagehand. And still two shows to go."

Gil nodded to him and turned an icy glare on me. "And you are not to go out and look for evidence."

"I'm staying in and resting before the show."

"And that's all you're doing, Heller." Tommy joined Gil in the glare. "Or you'll answer to us both."

I sighed and put my hands together for a mock bow of submission. "Yes, O great masters."

Like my beau's Queen and Empress, they were not amused. (Not that she ever actually said that!)

"Come along, Barrister." Tommy pointed Gil to the door as both loftily ignored my sarcasm. "We need to talk to Cousin Andrew the Detective."

"Is he really the Father's cousin?" Gil asked as he stood. "Or yours?"

"Father Michael's, for sure. Ours, probably not, but with Irish families, you never really know."

Gil chuckled. "Rather like the British aristocracy. We know we're all related, but only a few genealogists—and obsessed great-aunts—know precisely how."

They smiled together as they headed for the door, but then they turned back to me.

"Yes?" I said.

"Have a very restful afternoon, Shane."

"Or else."

While I did not obey the letter of the orders from my protectors—and at least one of them surely did not expect me to!—I did obey the spirit. I had no intention of launching a confrontation with Eamon or any other foolish thing they might have thought I'd do.

I also wasn't ready to give up on the idea of a stage-hand. Booth hired the hands, and it was fair to say that we did not look exhaustively into the bona fides of casual scenery movers. There had never been a need to do so.

We probably should have had Booth take a good look at the rest of the hands after the incident with Drumm, but quite honestly, I hadn't had time to string together two thoughts that didn't involve the show, the end-of-run reception, or keeping my injured arm clean. All right, a few thoughts of Gil, too. I am well aware that this is not even a decent explanation, never mind an excuse.

With everything in the air, though, I had to do something. Even if I had no plan to take rash action, I had less than no intention of sitting on my chaise, waiting for the next thing to happen. There's nothing wrong with research, after all. And the best source of information was the morgue. The *Beacon* morgue, that is.

I put on my boring dark blue coat and my second-best purple hat, because there was no need to be *that* inconspicuous, grabbed a small basket of molasses cookies from a suspiciously blooming Mrs. G and a program that listed the stagehands, since I didn't remember all their last names, and set out for the news office.

"Back to hats once more," Hetty groused as I handed over the basket.

"No."

"Oh, yes. Morrison says as soon as I find a new investigative story or another woman murders her husband, he'll happily let me at it, but until then, somebody's got to handle the girly stuff, and that somebody is me."

"Well, there's something up at the theater, and you might well find yourself a lead."

Her eyes gleamed. "Really?"

"Too early to be sure, but there's a good chance you can get an exclusive interview with a man who was wrongly accused."

"What do you need?"

"I don't know yet. Right now, I just want to see whatever you have on Florian Lutz and the parish where he, Albert, and Eamon lived." I held up the program. "Perhaps also to see if any of these stagehands have a history of trouble."

"To the morgue, then."

We didn't get very far with the unfortunate Mr. Lutz. There was one brief article on the murder of his wife in Cleveland, a feature on Lutz Pianos, and nothing more until he was the victim himself several weeks ago.

Last year's feature on Lutz Pianos proved surprisingly helpful, though. The reporter described the building of a piano and the skillful work of Papa Lutz and his helpers, including one Eamon Morrissey. He would have known Florian's story well then, and quite likely the man himself, making it very easy for him to lure the poor fellow to Albert's dressing room. That surely put him at or near the top of the suspect list.

Even so, there were signs of rather serious trouble in the wings. Two of the stagehands had been involved in minor scrapes over the past couple of years. One had been arrested after a particularly nasty bar brawl in the Theater District, an incident in which Edwin Drumm was also taken in. The other had been accused in a burglary and later cleared when another man was arrested. The address of the break-in was a street away from the Lutz workshop. So the alleged burglar, too, might know everyone involved well enough. All unsettling, but proving nothing, especially since I could not say with certainty how tall either of them were.

Except that the wrongly accused burglar, Rodney Jones, had the same last name as a man who died in a scrap that had ended in a stabbing in Five Points a year ago. Of course, many people, including several named Jones, die in stabbings in Five Points in any given year and not all of them have anything to do with us. Or Connor.

"Five Points again," I said.

"Your old gangster friend who got shot at on his way out of the theater?"

"Not a friend."

"Safer that way."

"No question. But it does make one wonder."

"Surely does." Hetty chewed reflectively on the end of her pencil. "Especially since the sports writers agree that if you're borrowing money, the money's coming from Five Points, and it best be paid back on time. With interest and plenty of it."

"Do they now?"

"They do. They also warned me to ask no further, since

gangsters won't harm a good woman, but they're not sure a reporter would qualify."

"Men." I sighed. "A working woman isn't a good woman?"

"Just the same foolishness you get on occasion."

"Ah, yes, the legions who can't tell a singer from a soubrette."

We shook our heads.

Hetty toyed with her pencil. "At any rate, I've also managed to learn from the stock sale records that Hosmer had made a bit of a killing in recent weeks."

"So he paid it back."

"Well, you'd surely think so. No one would be fool enough to try to cheat the gangsters."

"No one's that stupid," I agreed. "I still prefer the Frenchman as the killer, whatever Dr. Silver thinks."

"Me too. I've come to the conclusion that it's all nothing but a nasty fight over a woman, just in a Fifth Avenue mansion instead of a grubby tavern."

"And what a woman," I said. "You're right to doubt her."

"How so?" Hetty's eyes gleamed.

"She affects a French accent to match the name, right? But it didn't sound quite right to me, and I spoke to her in French last night."

"And?"

"Didn't understand a word. Gave me a rusty little '*mais oui*' in response."

Hetty grinned. "I knew there was something wrong with her."

"There is definitely something going on there. What, if anything, it has to do with the rest, who knows?"

"I'll nose around a bit."

"A whopper of a story either way." I borrowed the phrase from the sports writers.

"So true. Enough for a really good follow-up article."

"And by then, there will probably be another case."

She looked sharply at me.

"It's New York. We all know."

"We do."

"And I know," I said, with a look to the clock, "that I have to start thinking about getting up to the theater."

"Two more nights." She smiled at me.

"I'll miss the show, but the London run is coming."

"Ah, London." She chewed her pencil again. "And what are you going to do when you get there?"

"I wish I knew."

"He does seem like a good man."

"He is. But even the best men . . ."

"Are still men."

I took a breath. "In any case, expect to hear from Toms or me this evening, once we know how everything turns out. Hopefully, we can get you away from the hats for a bit."

"A resolution for which I shall devoutly hope."

Chapter 28

The Capture of the Sword Thief

After my trip to the morgue, I headed down to the theater. I was a bit early, but I'd been in no mood to dally about the house.

Before I arrived in my dressing room, the stagehand Rodney Jones, of all people, walked up to me. Definitely tall enough, dark haired, and fairly young, and I thought new for this run.

"Miss Ella? A moment?"

"Of course."

"The rest of the crew just wants you and Mr. Ruben and Mr. Tommy to know that we don't hold with Edwin Drumm's nonsense."

"Oh. Thank you so much." It warmed my heart that he—and they—had actually taken the time to talk among themselves and to us. "You told Mr. Ruben?"

"Absolutely. A lot of us—and our das—remember missing out on jobs because we're Irish or Italian or Jewish, and we don't want him thinking we're like that."

"Thank you." I patted Rodney Jones's arm, smiling at his way of referring to his father, which marked him as the same kind of Irish as Tommy and me.

He nodded. "I'm ashamed that anyone on our crew would do that. And I thought Morrissey was better than that."

"You know him?"

"Not well. He and I grew up in the same parish as Albert and that poor man who got killed."

I marked the way he described it. "You don't think Albert . . ."

Rodney Jones sighed. "I really don't know. We all got along back then. Guess I just don't like the idea of someone my baby sister made First Communion with being a killer."

"Understandable." I gave him a reassuring nod and said the only thing I could until I was sure Albert was free and safe. "He's a good man, Albert. It will come out all right."

"Sure hope so. Thing is, I—and the rest of the men— really didn't like the idea of that Drumm fellow making us look bad."

He was very deliberately bringing the conversation back to his main point. What I could not say for sure was whether it was with good intent or to distract me from looking too closely at his connections to Albert, Florian, and Eamon.

For the moment, I took it at face value. "You're a very good crew. I know you won't come to London with us, but I hope you'll be available next time we have a run here."

"And I surely hope you're not involved in any of the mess in this run," I didn't say.

"Thank you, Miss Ella. Mr. Booth has already written me a very nice recommendation for the new revue moving in across the street."

"Excellent. Thank you again."

"Glad to. Some things just aren't right. It's New York, Miss Ella. We're better than that."

We shared a proud smile, as New Yorkers of every

stripe sometimes will. "Absolutely, we are better than that."

Since it was the next to last night of the run, once back in my dressing room, I spent a little time collecting some of my extra things so they could be easily scooped up and taken back to Washington Square. And then a treat, a chance to sit down on the settee with a fashion book for a few minutes of relaxation.

I was puzzling over a diagram of a new design for garters—who knew such things required diagrams?—when Booth walked into the dressing room, holding young Mack McTeer by the scruff of the neck. Actually, the collar of her school uniform, but the point is made. My missing sword was in his other hand.

"Look who I found trying to return this to the prop table."

I just shook my head. "Oh, Mack."

"Miss Ella—"

"I'm sure it's all a misunderstanding, Booth. I'll deal with this." I stood and took the sword.

"We should turn her over to her future brother-in-law." The stage manager scowled down at Mack, who at least had the grace to look suitably terrified. "But if you prefer to mete out appropriate punishment, I won't argue."

"Thank you. I'm sorry for the trouble."

He nodded and bowed himself out. "Good luck with that one."

I motioned to the settee. "Sit."

Mack complied, watching me with big scared eyes. Good. I needed all the help I could get. On the fairly rare occasions I dealt with children these days, they were small and adorable, not half-grown and obstreperous.

"So?" I asked.

"I wanted to see what it was like. I wasn't going to keep it."

"All right." I believed her, and I was starting to feel at least a little sorry for her. "You are obviously not normally in the habit of stealing things."

"No."

"So why did you take my sword? Do you want to be a singer or an actress?"

"I don't think so." Her voice was small and tight, and she wasn't looking at me.

"Well, then?"

"I'm tired of being a good little girl."

"Ah. What does that mean?" I sat down on the arm of the settee. "You want to be bad?"

"No." Mack shook her head and looked up at me, her mouth working and her eyes fluttering as if she was about to cry. "I don't want to be what everyone tells me to be."

"Now, that makes some sense." I smiled, but she didn't smile back. "So what *do* you want to be?"

"I don't know. I just know I don't want to be somebody's wife or mother or servant or something."

My sympathy for her grew. "I understand."

"You do?"

"I wasn't an especially good little girl, either."

"Really?" Her eyes widened, and she gave me a small smile.

"And I definitely didn't dream of growing up to be at someone else's mercy, be it a husband or children or whatever." I patted her arm. "But I also understood that I have to obey the rules to get what I want."

She dropped her eyes and drooped a little.

"I'm sorry, Mack, but everyone has to learn what the rules are and where the lines are in this world."

"But the rules are stupid!"

"Some of them are. Some of them are actually very important, because they show us how to treat other people right."

"They are?"

"The trick is knowing the difference."

"Maybe." She shrugged. I wasn't at all sure what I was supposed to do with this girl, but she clearly needed a bit of extra care. I suspected neither overwhelmed Mother McTeer nor her older sister, who would soon have a great deal more on her plate, we hoped, had the time for it.

Neither did I, really, but the show *was* ending, and perhaps a feisty young lady would at least provide some useful training if I did indeed have a child of my own one day. The thought suddenly occurred that any offspring of Gil's and mine would be at least as incorrigible as Mack.

Probably more so. I did not need an article on heredity to guess that.

Not a line of thought I needed to pursue with all the other matters hanging fire at this exact second. I decided we'd best move on.

"So here is how we are going to proceed." I put my hand on her arm again, and she turned to me. "First, you will make this right with a very pretty apology to Mr. Booth and the prop master. Just tell them how sorry you are for their trouble, and that such a thing will never happen again."

She nodded and snuffled a little.

"And then you're mine."

Mack's eyes widened. "What? What does that mean?"

"Well, I'm not entirely sure, but you clearly need someone to take you in hand a bit."

"Maybe. Ma's busy taking care of the little ones, and all I hear is, 'Mary Grace, go do something constructive.'"

"Constructive we can do." I was starting to get an idea. "We'll start with a reading course. What are you interested in?"

"Everything?"

"Good answer." I stood and walked over to my trunk,

where I'd packed away the books I'd been reading during the run. "Well, next week, once I've rested up from the show, we'll go to the lending library and start working our way through the stacks. For now, perhaps something here will be a start."

She came over to me but hesitated at the trunk. "Can I?"

"Certainly. See what you like."

She spent a few minutes carefully picking up books and turning them over in her hands, reading the first pages, opening to the color plates, and gently closing them before picking up the next one. When I was her age, books were the treasure of the world. Still are, at some level.

"Is this one all right?" Mack held up one of Tommy's books that he'd left with me at some point: *The Steam Engine and Other Inventions.*

"Of course." I smiled reassuringly again. "Enjoy."

"Thank you, Miss Ella."

"Just bring it back without any odd marks, or Toms will kill me."

"Right."

Booth knocked on the door. "Two-hour call, Miss Ella."

I looked at Mack. "Time for your first lesson."

To her credit, she straightened up and nodded to me. "What do I do?"

"When he walks in, look him right in the eye and apologize." I gave her a reassuring nod. "When you make a mistake, you admit it and do what you can to fix it. It's not just the right thing to do. It also usually ends a lot better than you think it will."

I opened the door. "Booth, Miss Mack here has something to say."

She choked out an apology, and he took it with the gravity it deserved, with only a small glance over her head at me. They ended by shaking hands.

"Now, Miss Mack, since we've mended fences, perhaps you'd like to help me make the calls?"

She beamed. "I'd love to. And then I'd best go home."

"Thank you, Booth," I said, exchanging smiles with the stage manager.

"Candle lighting as usual?" he asked.

"Of course."

An hour later, Tommy blew in just before Anna lit the candles, and he quickly whispered that Albert was on his way home. Gil was nowhere to be found. But I wasn't troubled by his absence; this was still a special and joyous moment, our last Shabbat together as a cast before London.

"God in the room, Heller," Toms said after Anna finished the blessings. "And joy."

We smiled together, and I realized his eyes were the happiest I'd seen in weeks. He was starting to heal a little. Perhaps helping Albert had helped him.

"Joy is a good thing," I said.

"I'll take it."

Chapter 29

In Which We Ruminate by the Stove

After a surprisingly uneventful show that night, neither Tommy nor I felt like going right to bed. We slipped down to the kitchen to forage.

"Oh, dear! Miss Ella! Mr. Tommy! I was just setting some cinnamon rolls for brunch . . ."

Mrs. G's pink cheeks and her usually implacable opposition to brunch would have been quite enough to give the lie to that without Preston's presence at the kitchen table, with a cup of coffee and a plate of what certainly looked like the favored lemon tarts.

"Hello, kids." He gave us a hard look that dared us to comment.

Toms and I are cheeky, but not idiotic.

"Well, how kind of you to stay and walk Mrs. G home," I said gracefully, sitting down at the table.

He gave me a little smile and took the lifeline. "Even in this comfortable neighborhood, a lady really shouldn't be without escort."

"Exactly right, Pres." Tommy took the corner chair and stretched out toward the cookstove. "Is there maybe a drop more coffee?"

Mrs. G gave us a relieved smile. "Wouldn't warm milk be better for you two, considering you still have one show to go?"

"It's been quite a day and night." I sighed. "I'm not sure we'll be sleeping."

Mrs. G shook her head. "I'll make you some nice cocoa."

"We don't want to be a bother," Tommy said quickly.

"No bother at all."

"And I've been busy with that welterweight bout to-night. What's been happening in the world of arts?" asked Preston.

Tommy took a lemon tart. "Quite a lot. Starting with the release of Albert Reuter."

"Release?"

"I never thought that poor boy did it," Mrs. G tutted a bit as she poured milk into a pan for cocoa. She'd met Albert exactly once, when the company came over after final dress, but that was apparently enough to settle matters for her. "Such a sweet boy. Loves his mother."

Preston shook his head. "So, too, did John Wilkes Booth."

"Nonsense, Pres . . . Mr. Dare. I knew he was a good boy."

Preston smiled. We carefully didn't and were wise enough not to bring up the fact that Aunt Ellen shared Mrs. G's belief in Albert's innocence, whether by the second sight or the clear fact that a boy who loved his mother must be all right.

Tommy just shot me a glance and moved on. "At any rate, the barrister figured out that Albert wasn't tall enough to strike the fatal blow. We talked to Cousin Andrew today, and Albert should be home with his mother by now."

"Singing tomorrow?" Preston asked.

"I doubt it." Tommy shook his head. "I spent a few minutes with him while he was waiting to be freed, and he had a nasty cough. It'll take time to recover."

"Pity." Preston shook his head.

"We'll take him to London, of course," I said, "and perhaps he and Ruben will alternate."

"I've already sent word to Henry to start looking for good roles for him as soon as he's able to sing again." Tommy took another tart. "And he's talking to Hetty tonight, so people will get his side of the story."

Preston smiled. "And she'll get above the fold."

"Well, yes," I agreed. "But it's really about doing what we can to help him get back his reputation."

Tommy nodded. "We can't let Albert pay for someone else's crime."

"Who else's?" Preston asked, looking sharply at us both.

"There are at least two stagehands who are the right height," I said rather reluctantly. "And even though one seems to be a very good fellow, both have had brushes with the law. After Edwin Drumm—"

"He was mean and reckless, not homicidal." Tommy shot me a glare. "Eamon is a better possibility."

"That big redheaded wretch? The one you should have sent packing two days ago? You're still sharing a stage with him?" Preston wheeled on Tommy. "And you're allowing it? There's a scene where he smothers her, for God's sake."

"We have no proof, Pres. And I'm with her all the time . . ."

"And she's still in the hands of someone you know is rotten and might be a murderer!"

"Really, Pres . . . Mr. Dare." Mrs. G tried to calm him.

"What does the barrister think of this?"

Not only had Gil not appeared at the theater, but I had been too busy thinking about other tall men to spend much thought on that or his opinion on my activities. Just as well.

"We haven't discussed it." Tommy glared at Preston. "And you're not going to."

"Gentlemen, I am perfectly capable of defending myself."

Both of them turned on me with scorching glances. I knew what that meant. If I argued, they would yell at me and then do exactly what they wanted to do to protect me. Or I could just skip the yelling.

"Oh, just do what you want," I said with an irritated sigh.

"Men do, anyway, dear." Mrs. G shared a knowing and exasperated glance with me.

"All right, Tom, so why don't you round up some of your sturdy boxer friends for some extra security tomorrow night?" Preston suggested.

"Eamon might notice," Tommy pointed out.

"I hope he does. If the barrister is right, he'll be cornered, and maybe he'll just confess and be done with it."

"And when has any murder case ever ended that way?" I couldn't resist asking the sarcastic question.

"Well," Preston said with a wry little smile, "it's pretty close to the way the murder of Florian Lutz's wife ended."

"Really?" Tommy asked.

"Here now. The cocoa's ready." Mrs. G handed out mugs. "And Mr. Dare can tell us the story."

The cocoa was, as always, magnificent. So, too, the storytelling, even if the material didn't rise to the same level.

"Just a few sentences, really," Preston began after taking another lemon tart. "It was the hottest day of the summer in Cleveland. No breeze, no air, a horrible time to be living in a tiny little room above a cookshop. Which is exactly what Florian and his wife were doing, because it was the only place they could find."

He paused and flicked an apologetic glance at the ladies. "He might really have done better to stay at a players' boardinghouse. But rumor had it his wife was concerned that he might partake of the pleasures of the road."

Mrs. G and I nodded solemnly, understanding that Preston would offer no further details to spare our womanly sensibilities.

"At any rate, the poor thing, apparently a tiny, delicate blond girl, was keeping house in that hot little room while Florian played ball."

"No children," I said, not asked.

"Mercifully, no."

"Really a blessing not to bring a baby into that." Mrs. G shook her head sadly.

"Indeed." Preston put down his half-eaten tart and took a sip of coffee. "So, on this very hot afternoon, Florian came home from yet another loss and found his wife stabbed to death in their apartment."

"Terrible." I looked down at my cocoa. "What an awful shock."

"Horrible," agreed Tommy.

We all knew Preston was thinking of his wife and child, dead in a cholera outbreak thirty years gone. He took a breath and another drop of coffee and continued. "The police, of course, talked to Florian first, as the husband, and then started through the building to look for witnesses."

He strung out a pause carefully. "And downstairs, they heard yelling in the kitchen of the cookshop. That's where they found the couple who owned the place. He was sobbing. She was holding a bloody knife."

"Oh, dear," Mrs. G sighed.

"And she saw the cops at the door and confessed at once."

"Did she hang?" Tommy asked.

"It's Ohio, so you'd think she might, right?"

We all nodded. Cleveland was not known as a center of enlightened, progressive thought.

"But no. She ended up in the mental hospital—probably wishing she'd hung. Apparently, the husband had been watching Berthe, and Berthe, being a flighty young thing, had smiled back and been friendly."

"Nothing wrong with that," I said, thinking of all the times I'd smiled at men toward whom I had no intentions at all.

"Not a bit." Preston no doubt knew what I was thinking. "But the wife saw it the wrong way, and that hot, hot day made her a little crazy."

"A lot crazy, ask me," Tommy cut in.

"Just so. But there she sits in the mental hospital. And tiny Berthe and Florian Lutz are now together in the hereafter."

"Possibly with some help from Eamon," I admitted. "Though I still hope not."

"You won't give up on one of your singers until they drag him away in irons—and not even then, considering what you've done for Albert, kid."

"And we were right this time."

"But Eamon no longer deserves the benefit of the doubt, and we've been wrong before," Tommy admitted, an oblique reminder of a former employee who had killed Gil's cousin and very nearly me, as well.

"Well, don't be wrong this time." Preston returned to his tart, but not before fixing Tommy with a sharp glare over the dainty pastry. "And make damn sure your pals keep our girl safe tomorrow."

"Anyone who wants her has to come through me," Tommy reminded him.

"All of us."

Of course, they were being old-fashioned and overly protective. But they were still my men, and I loved them. I just smiled into my cocoa.

Chapter 30

A Tense Day for the Company and Friends

I scarcely need tell you I was not alone for so much as a second the next day. Tommy, Preston, and Gil were waiting downstairs when I rose well after eleven. Since I suspected something of the sort, I dressed in a very simple gray-and-violet-striped merino day dress and put my hair up before going downstairs in search of coffee. There was no tray, which was a strong hint that something—or someone—else had drawn Rosa's attention.

Several someones, as it transpired.

The gents had clearly been amusing themselves in some sort of amiable conversation verging on a play fight, apparently over some questionable historical detail in the opera's final battle scene.

"All due respect, Mr. Dare, but she really should be carrying a much larger sword. Medieval weapons weren't designed for fine fencing—"

"Barrister, you tell her, and good luck. Ella chooses her own weapons."

"And uses them," Tommy added with a chuckle.

"Well, a fine morning to you all, as well." I walked into

the parlor, shaking my head. "What, precisely, is wrong with my weapon?"

Gil actually blushed, as he's been known to do on occasion. It's rather appealing, and it quite diluted the impact of whatever critique he was planning to offer. "Well, Shane, I'm sure you're aware . . ."

Preston and Tommy were too well bred to snicker, but it was a close thing.

"That swords in the medieval era were actually much larger and designed for hacking rather than fine dueling?" I asked.

"Just so." Gil poured a cup of coffee and held it out, no doubt as a peace offering.

"Thank you." I took the cup with a smile. "And you are undeniably aware that while we endeavor to provide as much historical authenticity as possible, our first duty is to put on a good show."

"Which you would not be able to do if you just hacked away at Richard."

"No." I sat down in one of the chairs. "And it wouldn't be safe, not for him or me. Which outweighs either authenticity or showmanship."

"And speaking of safety," Preston cut in, "we've got a nice selection of Manhattan's most dangerous boxers providing security tonight."

"Good." I took a sip of my coffee and waited. I knew what was coming.

"One of us will be within arm's length of you all night," Tommy pronounced. "No arguments."

The hard look can be rather intimidating, especially if multiplied by three. But I was a little amused this time, more by the fact that the gentlemen had joined forces than by their efforts to scare me into submission.

"None at all." I drank a bit more coffee. "Friends of the company are always welcome."

"Good. I'm going down to the gym for a bit now that you're up." Tommy nodded to Preston and Gil. "Just have to get through tonight, Heller."

"Just have to get to curtain time . . ." As I said it, the germ of an idea stirred in the back of my head.

"What are you thinking?" All three saw it, but Gil spoke.

"Perhaps just an announcement during vocalization that since Albert is out of jail, he will be joining us in London . . ."

"Which might inspire Eamon to some rash action?" Tommy glared at me.

"Which will surely not involve me, since I will be exceedingly well protected."

"It could work," Preston admitted.

"We'll consider it," Tommy said. "I'm not giving you anything but that right now."

"Fair enough." I smiled. "I know you're going to be watching me like a hawk."

"Not just me."

Tommy headed off, and Preston, surprisingly, did not sit back down with me.

"Is something wrong?" I asked.

"Nothing, er, wrong." Preston suddenly looked very awkward and uncomfortable. "Um, I was planning to take a walk . . ."

When we are in a run, Mrs. G often takes Saturday afternoon off, since there's little for her to do with us out at the theater. A nice walk in the park would be an excellent time to perhaps make one's intentions known.

A muffled thud from the drawing room across the hall reminded me that Rosa was still busily training her little sister Sophia to take over as housemaid in the wake of her promotion to dresser and lady's maid. "You know, I'm quite sure Rosa would be happy to stack books here for a while."

"I don't think you really need a chaperone," Preston said with a little twinkle.

"Not when the fair maiden is so skilled with weapons," Gil agreed, with a conspiratorial nod to me.

"And I would like to get going . . ."

Rosa was more than happy to leave Sophia to dusting the whatnot and to come over to the parlor to bring order to the bookshelves.

Once she had set to work, I looked to Gil. Decently chaperoned, and with entirely legitimate reasons to be together for a while, I wasn't at all certain what we should do.

"Well, Shane. How ever shall we spend this unexpected gift of time?"

We smiled together for a measure or two, just basking in each other's presence. Unfamiliar as it was, the idea of simply being at home with him was quite appealing. I picked up the neglected Hawaiian study. "I believe we had gotten to the chapter on volcanoes."

"Volcanoes."

Our shared smile was not without a certain crackle of attraction, though, of course, one could not in propriety acknowledge the apt symbolism at play.

"Perhaps," Gil began as he took the volume from me, "we shall enjoy our copies of *Volcanoes of the World* together in London."

"That could be lovely," I agreed.

"Perhaps one day we shall need only one copy."

There was, of course, only one way that might happen, and for a breath or two, we watched each other's reaction to the thought. A happy, if unrealistic, idea.

"At any rate," he said finally, "we should really enjoy the book on Hawaii before it must go back to the library."

I sat down on my chaise, and he took the chair beside it, as he'd done before. "You truly are an excellent reader," I told him.

"High compliment from one who should know." He opened the book. "So, volcanoes."

Once again, it was entirely innocent and appropriate. And once again, it felt nothing of the kind. Lava, magma, and the various configurations of volcanic ash are likely exciting only to scientists, but reclining on my chaise, listening to Gil read, was rather amazing. Nor was I the only one enjoying the performance. Every once in a while, I heard a little sigh or giggle from Rosa.

Tommy returned a chapter or two later, to find both Rosa and me blushing like the fair maidens we no doubt are, and Gil diligently keeping his focus on the text as the author outlined the finer points of local religious practice.

"Well, I'm glad to see you're behaving yourself," Toms observed with a chuckle as he walked in. "Did you get to the part where they throw offerings into the volcano?"

"Some time ago, actually." Gil closed the book and carefully handed it to me. "I have another matter to address this afternoon. I hope you can forgive me . . ."

"Of course." I knew this was another of the things I was not going to ask about. "You'll be at the theater tonight?"

"Naturally. My other duties shall never outweigh my role as a friend of the company, Shane."

It was more than a pleasantry, and we all knew it. I caught an approving nod from Tommy and held out my hand to Gil. "I'll see you tonight, then. You'll know we entertain a few friends after the final show . . ."

"I'd be delighted." He kissed my hand and held it for a long moment. "Please do as you're told and stay safe."

I didn't cross the fingers of the other hand, but I also didn't consider a vague response a binding promise. "Of course."

Gil and Tommy exchanged glances and a nod, and then Gil took off, with Rosa sneaking in a good long look at him and giving in to giggles.

"Nursing a crush, Rosa?" Tommy teased. "I'm afraid he's already dead gone on Heller."

"Not even a little, Mr. Tommy. But I sure do like to look at him."

I shrugged. "No harm in a look."

At least not an innocent girlish look like Rosa's.

The rest of the afternoon was uneventful, as was our trip to the theater, Tommy riding along with Rosa and me and entertaining us with a colorful tale of his visit to the boxing gym, where two young fighters had gotten into some sort of foolish argument that led to a real scuffle, several black eyes, and the suggestion that both find another gym.

Ruben appeared in my dressing room before the group vocalization session, looking nervous and concerned.

"Miss Ella, I have an idea, and I wonder if you'd help me."

"Certainly." I glanced back at Tommy, who nodded. "Anything we can do."

"I wonder if you'd like to make this last night a benefit for Albert. I've talked to Ellsworth, the men in the chorus, and a couple of the supernumeraries, and they're ready to throw in."

"I think it's a capital idea. We'll make the announcement at vocalization, and anyone who wants to contribute can do so."

"Good." His face relaxed a little, but his eyes were still troubled. "Thank you. I hate the idea of poor Albert missing his chance because he was accused of something he didn't do."

I knew it was more than that. "You also feel guilty that you got your chance because of it."

"Of course I do."

Tommy gave him a reassuring smile. "Well, don't worry. We've put Henry Gosling on helping Albert make up ground, and if he's still available, you'll both go to London and alternate Richard and Neville."

Ruben nodded. "I would like that."

"And, of course, both of you may find other interesting opportunities flow from that," I pointed out.

"My mother might like Europe for a change . . . ," Ruben mused.

It was likely more than a casual comment. I had heard that the French, especially, are far less concerned with singers' provenance. "Well, perhaps you'll find a start on that in London."

"Right, then," Tommy said briskly, quite reasonably leaving the future to itself. "Let's head out and get to vocalizing."

We three walked out to the stage where the others were waiting, with Louis idly tracing a scale and the cast in various stages of dress and movement.

Tommy stepped to the center of the stage. "Some good news about our friend Albert."

A murmur through the cast. Most had probably not read the *Beacon*, since it's a morning paper, and this late in a run, singers rarely trouble with mornings. Both Tommy and I were watching Eamon, who was maintaining a carefully stony face.

"He's been cleared of any wrongdoing and is free and home."

Eamon blinked. Hard to take much from it, since he had to know Albert's return would mean the end of his run as Neville.

"Unfortunately," Tommy went on, "he's in no shape to perform tonight. But Ruben has an idea to help and encourage him."

Ruben took the floor on Tommy's signal, and I did my best to keep my eyes on Eamon.

"Right. We'll do tonight as a benefit for Albert, and anyone who wants to contribute . . ."

"I'm in," Ellsworth, the tenor, called out first.

"So am I," Marie agreed.

"Add us!" her two young soprano maids-in-waiting chimed in.

"And me," Eamon added quickly. I wasn't sure if I heard a false note in his voice, or if I just thought I did. But his face was definitely flushed, a dead giveaway to anyone who is, or knows, the fish belly–pale Irish.

"Can friends of the company join in?"

Gil, of course, as he walked in from the wings.

"And they are welcome, too." Tommy greeted him with a handshake.

"Then consider me a friend, as well."

Connor Coughlan walked out of the same area of the wings where Gil had been, to a startled blink from Tommy and probably the same from me. What was he doing here? I would have assumed he had somehow got wind of the danger from one of the boxers, except for Tommy's reaction.

"All right, then, we're unanimous," Tommy said quickly, covering his surprise with managerial calm. "Our last night is a benefit for our friend Albert. And we'll see him soon, when we leave for London."

"For Albert!" Ellsworth called.

"Albert!" cheered the rest of us, with applause. Sometime tomorrow, probably quite well into the day, we would round up Ellsworth and some of the others and head over to Albert and his mother's to present the money and, equally important, encourage him with plans for London.

But first, we had a show to do.

"Come along, now," Louis called from the piano. "We've got to get ready and put in one more good night."

"Save the best for last!" Marie proclaimed.

Louis started in on the scales, and I noticed Gil and Connor were already gone from view. I wasn't sure what to make of that, and soon enough, the weight of preparing for the show drove all other thoughts from my mind, at least for the moment.

Chapter 31

A Battlefield Promotion at Bosworth

As that final performance wore on, I admit I was a bit distracted, worried about how we would bring everything to a safe and successful conclusion. Not, I hasten to add, the run. It had been a great success, and very little short of actually burning down the theater would take away from that.

No, my concerns lay in a graver direction. Even though Albert was free, because the district attorney didn't have any trouble believing that the killer was taller than he, thanks to Gil's criminology, we were no closer to our villain; in the eyes of the law, the height argument did no more than clear Albert.

A good defense lawyer would note that in addition to Eamon, the obvious choice, Tommy, Preston, Father Michael, and Booth, the stage manager, were all backstage and tall enough, whether or not they had any motivation. And, of course, the stagehand Rodney Jones, who merited consideration for his height and connections but also seemed to be seriously lacking in motive, not least because he was clearly on the opposite side of the ledger as the unpleasant Mr. Drumm. Not to mention an audience full of potential suspects, any one of whom might have wandered backstage with a knife easily enough in the excitement of premiere night.

Of course, there was still much else hanging fire. I had no trouble believing that Eamon was the killer or that he'd been smart and desperate enough to admit to a few lesser crimes in hopes of covering the most heinous one.

But he was not a good bet for the gunshot at Connor, and I had to rate Jones unlikely for that, too, because he would have been busy with the after-curtain work when it happened. Really, the shooter might even have actually been the unfortunate who ended up in the East River, raising a whole new set of questions. Who knew what else might be lurking out there, just beyond our vision, if Connor was part of this?

His presence tonight certainly suggested he might be. I was quite sure that any number of people might wish to put a bullet in Connor's head on a given day, and probably more than a few would kill for a good role, too. We might, I thought, have more than one plot in play.

No idea how we'd sort out *that* kind of mess.

Still and all, it was my last performance night for a while. After I made my change into my costume for the final battle, I nodded to Toms and slipped out of my dressing room to wander about the wings for a bit. It was perfectly safe, with boxers lurking practically within arm's length, and I was glad for the chance to enjoy just being in a theater, my natural habitat, as one might say of the fauna of the Hawaiian rain forest.

Tommy had already lined up a small but select number of bookings for the weeks between closing and London, benefits mostly, and I would be on a stage again before I had time to miss it. But still.

Marie was singing the short reprise of her vengeance aria, "My Sons' Blood Cries Out," setting up the final battle, and I stopped for a moment to listen to her. Every time she sings, I'm reminded that she is incredibly gifted as well as accomplished in technique. And then there are nights like this, where the virtuoso's skills meet the perfect music and the emotion of the song to produce something amazing.

Sometimes, it just awes me that I share a stage with such an artist.

After a few moments, I took a breath and walked along, pulling my thoughts back to my own performance. I hoped I could send the audience home with a good finish in the final aria. While I don't bring Marie's coloratura fireworks, I have my own impressive instrument, and thanks to Louis's brilliant score, we're both shown to best advantage.

We would be a sensation in London. At the moment, no need to think about what else we, or I, might be while there.

As I walked past Ruben's dressing room, I heard a strange thud and turned. Odd. He should have been taking a moment to rest after his big aria, which had drawn him a huge, nearly showstopping ovation. No one responded to my knock on the half-closed door, so I inched it open a bit farther.

"Ruben?"

He was on the floor, unconscious, his face battered. As I tried to absorb that, I saw two pairs of large male feet, one standing and tense, the other scrabbling and nearly limp. I pushed the door open a little wider, to see Eamon choking Connor with a forearm from the back as Connor struggled to break his grip.

Eamon's eyes flicked to me. "This isn't for you, Miss Ella."

Under other circumstances, I might have argued. But Connor's face was already purple, and he didn't look like he had much fight left, a truly terrifying realization. So I didn't spend too much time contemplating. I just did what I'd done as Tommy's hellcat helper.

I jumped on Eamon's back and pulled his hair.

It was still a great way to finish a fight.

Eamon roared and let go of Connor, and I thumped him on the head with my elbow for good measure. It had always worked in the street, and it did just fine now. As I pushed back from him, Eamon's knees gave way, and he fell on his face, at least as dead to the world as poor Ruben.

Connor staggered over to the dressing-table chair and sagged into it, hanging on to the back and gasping. He managed a rictus of a smile and forced out, "Glad you still fight dirty, Ellen."

The door slammed fully open.

"Shane, what on earth?"

"Heller?"

"Great heavens, kid!"

Gil, Tommy, and Preston filled the doorway, staring at us in absolute shock.

"Are you trying to convince me that women are good at killing, kid?" Trust Preston.

"Street fighting again, Shane?"

I glared at them. "I stopped Eamon."

Tommy laughed. "I can tell that. You got a piece of him."

I followed his eyes to my hand, where I still held a large tuft of orange hair. I threw it down and wiped my hand on my hose. "Ugh!"

They laughed, and Connor let out a rusty noise that was probably a laugh, too. Men.

Ruben groaned just then and struggled to sit up.

"I think Eamon tried to kill him," I put in quickly, moving the gentlemen on to more serious matters. "He's probably going to need a doctor."

Preston, the Gettysburg drummer boy, and veteran of many scraps in taverns, moved to Ruben, then bent down beside him as he opened his eyes. "It's all right, friend. You'll be fine."

Ruben muttered something unintelligible, shaking his head a little.

"Mr. Avila, call for final duel!" Booth knocked on the door and froze when he saw the scene inside. "Good, sweet Lord in heaven. What now?"

The question we must never ask.

"He can't go on." Tommy shook his head. "Send for a doctor, Booth. We need to make sure he's all right."

"Call the police, as well, for that one," Gil added, indicating Eamon, who was breathing but not moving.

Booth nodded. "Do you want me to call the end of the show, too?"

Tommy and I looked at each other.

"I hate to end the run like this," he said.

"He already sang his last aria. There's just the duel . . . and my finale."

"All we need is someone who can fence convincingly," Tommy agreed.

We both knew the answer to that, and as one, we turned to Gil, who had been watching us with dawning horror.

"You will have noticed I am not a basso," Gil started as Tommy took King Richard's cloak from the chair where Ruben had left it.

"It's really fine," I assured him. "You don't need to sing a note. All you have to do is let me vanquish you and sing my triumph aria over your prone form."

"Is that quite all?" His voice was a tad waspish, and his stance tense.

Tommy didn't especially care, and he advanced on Gil. "All right now, let's get that jacket off and this cloak on. You'll look just fine from the dress circle."

"Shane? Really?"

Tommy gave Gil the command stare. "Do you really want anyone else out there with her tonight?"

Gil was silent on that one, but not compliant.

"And," Tommy continued coolly, taking King Richard's crown from the dressing table, "we must, of course, finish the show and the run."

"Must we?"

"Come on, Saint Audrey, be a sport." Connor put in, then finished on a lighter cough. He was probably going to be all right, as long as Gil didn't do what it certainly looked like he wanted to do.

Gil bit back some sharp comment and turned to me.

My turn. I met his eyes with my own version of Toms's force majeure gaze. "Please? For the show?"

I had no idea if my feminine wiles, such as they were, would carry any weight. For a couple of very long measures, I listened to the orchestra playing the martial music that signaled the change of stage for the battle scene.

Finally, Gil sighed. "Oh, all right. I rather fancy the thought of expiring at your feet."

"Excellent." Tommy settled Richard's diadem on Gil's head and handed him the cloak. "Break a leg."

"Break something." Gil seemed resigned. "I'm merely going out there to let her kill me, aren't I?"

"Yes," I said, handing him Ruben's new sword, "but kindly make it look good."

"I hear and obey, My King." He gave me a faint smile as we ran into the wings, the battle music already beginning.

As it turned out, he did indeed make it look good, instinctively following my lead. Ruben and I had moved well together because we'd spent so much time practicing. Gil and I were actually better because we knew each other well enough to anticipate the next move.

It became almost a dance. We matched each other, strike

and thrust, forward and back, the connection and understanding between us guiding our moves. Unlike a waltz,
though, I was leading, and he followed, with absolute care
and respect. In an odd way, it was more intimate than a
dance, because it required such concentration and sympathy to do safely and well.

We made good partners.

Finally, the music reached its peak, and I held his eyes
for a full measure. *Now.*

He came at me with Richard's last, desperate move. I
blocked it with only a little effort and then returned with
the killing thrust, probably a bit more careful than usual
to keep the sword well clear of him, because he was not a
trained stage fighter.

The Latin chant slowed as Gil crumpled to the boards,
then ended in echoing silence.

Now it would be the same as any other night. Except
that his eyes met mine as I bent to take the crown, reminding me that whatever else happened tonight, our connection was real and serious and true. What other man would
take the stage and die for me?

What other man would follow my lead with such respect and understanding?

Bashert. But meant for what?

I wrenched my thoughts back to the performance once
more as I held the diadem, then crowned myself, cueing
the music for my final aria.

As I sang, Gil, God love him, lay patiently at my feet,
clearly trying not to breathe too much and give away the
illusion. I don't know if it was a good finale or not; of
course, I usually have a very strong sense of how I've done
on the given night. This time, though, I was just grateful to
reach the end.

I must have done well enough, though. The audience

was silent for longer than I'd ever heard before bursting into thunderous applause as the curtain fell.

Once it hit the stage floor, I offered a hand up to Gil, as I always did my partner.

He took it, stood, and started to draw me in. For a fraction of a second, as our eyes held with the full intensity of that insane night, I wasn't sure what would happen. We might have fallen into each other's arms and then . . . who knows what?

Not right then, though. The ridiculousness of all that had happened struck us both at the same time, and in unison, we started laughing.

As magical in its way as any embrace.

"You have a promising career in the theater," I teased.

He shook his head, still laughing. "I do not think I wish to pursue that."

"Well, prepare for your first curtain call as a supporting player at least."

The laugh died, and his face turned serious. "I'm sorry. I can't."

"What?"

"I have to take care of an important matter. You are still entertaining everyone back at the town house?"

"Company and friends only tonight."

"I believe I qualify as a member now."

"That you do."

He bent down and kissed me on the top of the head, then stalked off before I could react to the unexpectedly intimate gesture and doffed Richard's cloak in the wings as the curtain rose to a chorus of bravas.

By the time Marie and I took our bows, the houselights were up, and all became clear. Gil, a police officer, and another man, who had that puffy, stuffy look one associates with bureaucrats, were escorting Amelie Van Vleet out of the orchestra. Gil looked back to me for just a moment and smiled faintly.

Of course, I would demand an explanation of all this later. Right now, it was enough that we'd come through to the end.

"What encore shall we give?" I asked Marie.

"Something fast. I want some answers—and a brandy."

"So true."

Chapter 32

In Which the Cast Adjourns to Washington Square

Within two hours or so of the final curtain, the company and friends were gathered in the parlor, sipping various medicinal beverages, with the full expectation of answers and baked goods. The answers might be a few moments in coming, but the refreshments were amazing, a truly magnificent display of Mrs. G's finest efforts. I had no idea what had prompted this; usually, the end of a run meant just Tommy and me and a close friend or two who didn't have a deadline or an early start, celebrating with leftover cookies or even just toast and cheese in the kitchen.

Not this time. There was a fancifully iced opera torte, a large batch of snickerdoodles, a platter of meringues, and an equally generous tray of lemon tarts. Preston's favorite, of course, which perhaps gave a clue as to motive.

The party was larger than usual, as well, despite a few missing faces. Ruben was recovering at home under the care of his worried mother, and Albert likewise, but the mothers had already sent word that both sons would soon be back to full strength and virtuosity, thankfully. And speaking of happy family moments, Louis and Anna had decided firmly in favor of going home to the Morsel, preferring to share the joy of their success with the one they love most.

Cousin Andrew, of course, would be neither enjoying treats nor supplying answers, since he was occupied with Eamon and no doubt settling scores with the Broadway Squad. We would send him a delivery of baked goods and a carefully worded inquiry as to the status of matters with Katie McTeer in the morning.

But for now, I was ensconced on my usual chaise, in a new Parma-violet crepe de chine tea gown—with matching velvet ribbons threaded through the creamy lace at the low collar and bracelet-length sleeves that covered the bandage on my arm—my favorite afghan over my feet. I'd taken inspiration from Marie and settled on a brandy to go with a generous slab of opera torte.

Gil had taken the chair by the chaise, as if it were his natural place, which indeed it was by now, and he was enjoying a drop of whisky while taking great amusement at my enthusiastic demolition of my treat.

"One would think you had been on a desert island where there is no cake."

"I haven't had a scrap in months. No one wants a King Henry who looks like Falstaff."

"There's no risk of that."

"And we'll keep it that way."

"The torte does look quite delicious."

"It is."

"May I?" He reached for my fork.

"Get your own piece."

We were laughing together as Marie and Paul took over the settee closest to us, and Tommy and Father Michael took the other one, bickering over the snickerdoodles.

"Come on, now. Time to tell all." Marie settled into her seat, smoothing her pale blue silk tea gown, a small violation of protocol allowed by the fact that this was a family night in the company, and focused sharply on Gil. "What about Amelie Van Vleet?"

"Yes," Hetty said, putting down her sherry. She, like Yardley, had come straight from the news office—in her case, after dashing off a quick item about two separate arrests at the theater, with more details to come in the next day's edition, and mysteriously describing our last-minute Richard as merely a visiting friend of the company. "Curtain falls on criminals," the *Beacon*'s rather sensational headline writer would say.

Like us, she was more than glad for the medicinal drop. Worse for her, though, she was still in work dress, a suit and shirtwaist, meaning the dreaded stays. "What about that woman?"

"Well," our barrister began, putting down his whisky and settling in to tell the tale, "she was born Annie Hardwick in East London."

"Aha," I said. "With credit to Mr. Holmes."

"I do not believe he ever actually said that," Tommy observed.

"Probably not," I admitted, "but you don't need Conan Doyle's background in criminology or linguistics, to know that woman was not from anywhere in France."

"Just so." Hetty gave me a bitter little smile. "You caught that silly fake voice of hers."

"You knew there was something very wrong about her," I agreed, "but it took an extra pair of ears to figure it out."

"And lovely ears at that," Gil cut in with a warm glance at me before he resumed his barrister face. "At any rate, back to Annie Hardwick?"

"Absolutely," Marie said. "She sounds like a nasty little piece of work."

"Oh, she is. Believed she deserved far better than she came from. That, of course, is no sin . . ."

The company and friends nodded quite resolutely at that.

"The sin, as it were, was the way she went about bettering herself." Gil nodded to me and the rest. "Unlike some ladies I know, born with nothing in their hands and much in their heads, and indeed their throats, Miss Hardwick decided the best way to improve her lot was by charming men. And perhaps harming them."

"Perhaps?" Hetty asked.

"More than perhaps in at least one case. Before Mr. Van Vleet met her, and ultimately his Maker, she rather unexpectedly married a colleague of my friend Joshua's."

Marie's eyes widened. "A bigamist?"

"Would that she were, Madame Marie." Gil shook his head. "Charles—I read law with him—died of a strange and mysterious illness a year or so after the wedding. Not long after he had asked Joshua and myself to see what we might learn about his lovely new wife."

Brows quirked across the room.

"By the time Joshua managed to get a lock of his hair to test, she and much of his money were long gone."

"Test for what?" Yardley asked.

"Mercury. Calomel. Apparently, he started with a bit of dyspepsia, and she just kept increasing the dose. At least moderately creative." His pained expression belied the wry words.

"Her first murder." Father Michael shook his head.

"That we know of," Preston put in with a dark scowl.

"I'm sorry." Marie patted Gil's arm.

A muscle flicked in his jaw as he nodded. "In any event, there the matter lay until a friend sent me Miss Hetty's excellent article about the Van Vleet murder case."

The friend and Miss Hetty both had the grace to blush.

"I couldn't be certain from the sketches, naturally, but

there was a strong possibility that it might be her, once one considered all the evidence. So Joshua asked me to come over here and see what I might see at the trial."

The errand for a friend.

"Of course," Gil said, with a significant smile at me, "there were other compensations to the trip, so it was easy enough to persuade me to come."

"Do you think she killed Van Vleet?" Hetty asked.

"Unless I misunderstand your Constitution, it doesn't much matter. I still doubt she would have stabbed him fourteen times, especially since she was a dab hand with poison."

"I wonder if it really was that nasty Frenchman," Hetty mused. "What happens to her now?"

"Well, we'll sail in the morning, and I suspect it shall be a far less pleasant trip home for her. After that, a trial. I will ask my friend at the consulate to give you an official statement."

"Lovely." Hetty raised her glass to Gil. Visiting friend of the company, indeed.

Yardley shook his head. "She'll just get out of it there, too."

"I would not be so sure, Mr. Stern. We have one great advantage in London."

"Your lawyer friend." Preston nodded. "Nothing like a man who wants justice for a friend."

"Precisely."

"All right," Marie said, "so that's answered. I can guess why Eamon attacked Ruben in his dressing room—but what about Connor Coughlan, of all people?"

I took a sip of my brandy and looked to Tommy. We had some of that answer, but not all.

"Maybe I can help with that, Madame."

Connor stood in the foyer doorway, holding a bouquet

of pansies, a very neutral floral statement (think of me). "I've heard companies often stay up on the last night, and I wanted to thank you."

Gil tensed slightly beside me.

Connor grinned at him. "Relax, Saint Audrey. I know you're the one she's going to marry."

I almost dropped my glass.

"Miss Shane and I have not settled any—" Gil started stiffly.

Connor shook his head. "Right. I know. You won't push her. Good for you." His eyes narrowed a bit. "Just remember. If you ever make her cry, you'll answer to me. Especially after tonight."

"Would you like a whisky?" I cut in quickly. "Or lemon tarts?"

"I won't turn down the whisky." He handed over the flowers as Tommy poured him one. "That was a hell of a thing. Sorry, Ellen, Father."

"That it was." Tommy handed Connor the glass and stood behind the chair as he sat. "You and Eamon didn't even know each other."

"No." Connor took a sip and gave a grateful smile. "I don't think it was about me."

"He's right." I had a small sip of my own drink. "Eamon had no way to know he'd be backstage tonight."

"So . . . ," Marie said.

"I don't know what that was." Connor shook his head. "I had finished my other business at the theater, and I heard a fight in the dressing room. The big redheaded boy was beating the Cuban, just whaling on him. I've got a few Cuban friends, and I don't like an unfair fight."

I smiled a little at Connor. "So you jumped in."

"Not my best decision of the night."

"But why turn on you?" Hetty asked.

"I think he was just trying to kill his way out of it,"

Tommy suggested. "He wanted Ruben as revenge, of course, and if he killed Connor, there would be no witness."

"Ah," Connor said, with a wry note in his voice, "but it's never really possible to kill your way out of things."

We did not want to think too deeply about why he knew that.

"In any case," I said, firmly changing the subject, "this was really all about Richard III."

"Well, it *is* a good part," Marie put in.

"Not worth a life. Or three," I reminded her, registering an approving expression from Gil and the priest. "But it was to him."

"Exactly," Tommy continued. "All he wanted to do—until tonight—was eliminate obstacles to the part. He killed Florian and made it look like Albert did it to move himself up one notch."

"Pretty elaborate—and grisly," Paul observed, no doubt thinking of the closeness of danger to his wife and wee ones. "I wonder if there was some kind of grudge between him and the Lutzes."

"It's possible," Preston allowed, swirling his whisky a bit. "They all grew up together, so there might have been some kind of rivalry."

"Especially since Eamon and Albert would end up competing for some of the same roles." I nodded. "That can breed a lot of bad blood."

"Enough to make people do dangerous and evil things," Marie agreed. She took a sip of her brandy.

"Perhaps it had something to do with Albert's sister, too," Yardley offered. "She married Florian and died, and if Eamon had wanted her . . ."

"As good an explanation as any," Hetty said. Actually *agreeing* with Yardley?

Good heavens.

"At any rate," I cut in, pulling the conversation back to what we definitely knew, "after the killing, Eamon tried to discredit Ruben to eliminate him." No need to go any further than that with this group, all of whom were firmly on Ruben's side. "Failing that, he resorted to some direct sabotage against him."

"Which he admitted when Drumm tried that stunt with the sword," Tommy went on, sliding a moody gaze into his glass. "And when all of that failed, I suppose Eamon broke."

"He would not be the first man to give in to evil," Father Michael said.

"Kill the man who beat you." Connor nodded. "Makes sense."

"Exactly." Gil had clearly been on the sideline of the conversation long enough. "Tonight Eamon no doubt realized that suspicion would fall on him because Albert had been cleared, and that he would soon take his place in gaol."

"So he decided to go out in blood." Tommy took another sip of whisky. "I wonder if that ovation for Ruben's last aria was the last straw."

"It could well have been." Marie shook her head. "Ruben was incredible tonight."

"If Eamon hadn't come after him, we would never have been sure." I put down my plate. Even my notorious appetite for cake couldn't survive this. "He was desperate. Thank God you walked in. I can't imagine what might have happened to Ruben."

"No need for me to imagine." Connor rubbed his neck a little. "If *you* hadn't walked in when you did . . ."

"But I did."

"And you didn't hesitate."

Gil was watching me, and I wondered if it was for signs

of inappropriate affection, an utter impossibility. I ignored him and focused on Connor. "Of course not."

"There are those who'd say you should've let him finish the job. I don't lead the life of a choirboy."

"That's between you and God. I couldn't live with myself if I let someone harm another person in front of me without trying to help."

Connor and Gil both studied me as I spoke. I felt like a china figure in the vitrine. Then they looked at each other.

"And that, Saint Audrey, is all you need to know. Our Ellen's an angel."

"And I treat her as such, Mr. Coughlan."

"Smart man. Put a ring on her hand and a tiara on her head as soon as she'll let you."

Gil and I both laughed. What else could we do?

"Thank you for coming, Connor," I said.

"Thank you, Ellen."

We smiled at each other. Then he turned to Gil with the cold, scary look he'd never given me.

"I assume the Van Vleet woman is on her way to England?"

"In the morning." Gil nodded. "Someone may wish to search her home as soon as possible, but you won't be seeing her again."

"We've already gotten the rest of our interest payment. No one is especially creative about hiding money." Connor's eyes narrowed. "As instructive as it might have been to make an example of her, that's a better ending. Let me know if she hangs."

The two exchanged a grim nod as the rest of the company looked to me, and I responded by shaking my head in confusion and no small amount of dismay.

"What?" I asked.

"Mr. Coughlan and I had a confluence of interests." Gil

nodded coolly to Connor. The other business at the theater.

"Hosmer Van Vleet got himself in some nasty financial trouble," Connor explained, "and he turned to some friends of mine for help."

"Which has been known to happen in shady financial dealings," Gil added, with a little smile to Hetty. "But it became much more problematic when first the stock trader and then his grieving widow decided there was no need to pay all the agreed interest."

"A very poor decision. Especially on her part." Connor's voice was as cool as if he were discussing the weather, but it did nothing to dilute the menace.

"How could anyone be so foolish?" Hetty asked for all of us.

"None of this for the papers," Connor said, his eyes very hard on hers.

"As far as I'm concerned, the story is the unmasking of a British murderess." Not only is my friend no fool, but she also knows the use of having a good source in a very bad place.

They exchanged a small nod, and Connor continued. "He apparently thought this was a matter for negotiation. Rich folk are stupid." He shrugged and looked at Gil. "Some rich folk, anyway. They think their money makes them better and immune to consequences."

"She, at least, should've known better," I said. "Especially after what happened to Hosmer."

"She thought it was the Frenchman," Hetty suggested. "Or at least let herself believe it. Probably figured her lover did it, and that she deserved the extra money for all her trouble."

Father Michael winced at the blunt description of Lescaut but said nothing.

Gil smiled very coldly. "I imagine it went exactly like that, Miss Hetty."

"Well, Saint Audrey here decided he didn't like the idea of her dancing away free any more than we did."

"Hence the confluence of interests." Gil nodded to Connor.

I just stared at the two of them.

"That's enough." Connor held my gaze coolly for a second. "It's not for good women like you to know what would've happened to her if she hadn't chosen to return to England and face a murder charge."

I did my best to hide the shudder. I had no need to know the exact details, but there was no doubt that whatever Connor and his friends might do to make an example of our villainess was far more terrible than anything the hangman might come up with. At least the queen's justice promised a chance of acquittal and, at worst, last rites and a relatively clean death.

Gil would not really have handed her over to Connor, I thought, but there was no way for her to know that. Even with his opposition to capital punishment, he would prefer the law to the lawless.

"Your man was doing right by his friend." Connor turned to me. "Sometimes, that's a very hard job."

I looked to Gil, who merely nodded. Things I can't ask about, perhaps.

Then Connor very carefully took my hand and planted a small, surprisingly gentle kiss on it. "I should go now. You remember, though. I owe you my life, so whatever you need, whenever you need it, no matter what, you call on me."

That, coming from the scourge of Five Points, was very powerful, indeed. It was a marker I hoped I would never need, but knew I would be very glad of, if I did.

I nodded gravely.

He gave Gil one more hard look, as required for any good gangster, nodded to the rest of the ensemble, and walked out.

"Do we want to know what will happen to Eamon?" Yardley finally broke the silence.

"You're not really foolish enough to ask that?" Tommy shook his head. "He signed his death warrant when he put hands on Connor, and even he has to know that by now. He'll be found dead in his cell, one way or another, before the week is out."

"God have mercy on him." From Father Michael, it was a prayer.

"He took one life for no reason other than his own selfish need for glory," Marie said sharply. "Then he tried to ruin two innocent men and finally would have killed twice again if Ella hadn't stopped him. I'm not going to spend much time praying for him."

Paul gazed at his wife, who suddenly looked rather like an avenging angel. "All true, if rather harsh."

"Murder is harsh business." She took a generous sip of her brandy. "And I'm glad we're done with it."

"Well, I suppose that answers it all." Preston's tone suggested he was ready to close the matter.

"Not quite all, Pres." Tommy nodded to him and motioned to the spread of baked goods. "I wonder if there might be something you wish to tell us?"

Preston Dare, dean of the gentleman writers' corps and man of the world, actually blushed and glared at Toms. "Generally, one doesn't make announcements until the banns are posted."

Father Michael smiled and looked down at his whisky.

"The banns?" Yardley asked. "Well, I'll be damned."

"Generally, one *does* tell intimates as soon as one's suit

is accepted," Gil said, joining in, his eyes sparkling like Tommy's.

"And one shouldn't play games one isn't ready to have turned on oneself, Barrister." Preston gave Gil a hard look.

"Well, all right," I said, taking up my cake plate again. "If you don't want to rejoice in happy news with the people who love you most . . ." I cut my eyes to Marie and Hetty. "I'll just content myself with my opera torte."

The others followed my example and prepared to busy themselves with their various treats.

"Oh, fine. If you truly must know." Preston put his hands up in surrender. "She said yes. A wedding in the New Year."

If you think our sportsmen cheer loudly for their teams, you may well imagine how loudly they cheer for a friend's happiness. There were handshakes, hugs, and glasses raised; and the evening, which had started in such tension, dissolved into a sweet, old-fashioned happy ending.

Every good melodrama ends with a wedding, or at least the promise of one, doesn't it?

Chapter 33

Do We Understand Each Other?

Soon enough, there was only one piece of opera torte left, and drawn by the mystical force of layers and icing, Tommy and I both ended up standing at the pedestal.

"Split it with you, Heller."

I laughed, took up the server, and very precisely divided the piece into two thin halves.

"My last cake for a while, Toms. I have to stay trim for London."

"Ah, London. We may soon have another engagement to celebrate."

I looked sharply at him.

"He's already asked my blessing, Heller. I gave it gladly—and told him it's up to you."

"You did?" I put down the cake. "But you and I have such a happy life."

"We still will. With an addition, or two, to the cast."

"I know Marie does it, but I'm not sure I can. And I'm not leaving you."

Tommy patted my arm. "As long as you sing, and you still will, you'll need a manager, and the two of you will need somewhere to live in New York. Our floors have always been far enough apart for privacy. And there's room for more, when there's more."

"You've thought this through."

He smiled. "And perhaps I'll work on a few of my own projects at times you're in London with him. Cabot has some excellent new ideas to encourage poor children to stay in school longer."

"Cabot is a good friend."

"That he is."

I sensed something there, but I knew it was entirely the wrong moment to say anything about it. "You think I can trust Gil?"

"Sooner or later, we all have to trust somebody." Tommy shrugged. "Who better than a man who's willing to die at your feet onstage?"

I smiled at that. Tommy once again knew my thoughts.

My cousin's eyes held mine, loving and serious. "You don't have to say yes tonight, Heller. Just don't say no."

"You don't think . . . ?"

"I don't know." He took a breath. "I told him he'd do better to wait until London and give you time to think it all through."

"Sensible advice." Nobody knows me better than Toms, of course, and the fact that he had not only given Gil his blessing but had also told him how best to go about pressing his suit was the fullest endorsement possible.

"But he may or may not take it." He rested his hand on my arm again for a moment. "See what happens."

I nodded, remembering Marie telling me that men don't ask again. And her wild run to Paul's rooms. I did not think I was the woman for that. "Just don't say no."

"Exactly."

I walked back to my chaise, to find Gil still in the side chair, staring into his nearly empty glass of whisky, not even feigning a minimal interest in Marie, Hetty, and

Paul's speculation on the accuracy of the winter weather predictions from *The Old Farmer's Almanac.*

"Walk me to the door?" he asked with a surprisingly tentative note in his voice.

"Certainly." I just barely noticed Marie and Hetty exchanging glances and Tommy smiling behind me. That last, though, might easily have been because I'd left him the cake.

Gil and I stood in the foyer for a moment, just taking each other in.

"You would not really have handed her over to Connor." I had to clear the worst first.

A very cold gleam came into his eyes. "I surely would have."

I shrank back a bit. What was this man?

"There's something you don't know, Shane."

"All right."

"Charles had a child. A little boy with an impish smile, like my younger son."

"He did?" I wasn't sure I wanted to hear the rest.

"He got very sick soon after the marriage, and if he hadn't been sent to boarding school on the good offices of his mother's family . . ."

"She poisoned him first."

"Just so." Gil's jaw tightened. "Didn't want to share the money, one suspects. But he escaped."

"Well, if she harmed a child, I'd give her to Connor's gang myself."

"I thought perhaps. So you'll forgive me that?"

"Nothing to forgive."

Once again, we stood there assessing each other.

Finally, he smiled a little. "Thank you for trusting me to settle the matter."

"Surely no more than any good friend would do."

"Most women would've spent the past few weeks asking pointed little questions and making acid remarks at odd times. Or, at the very least, would run screaming into the night after this evening's revelations. You just left the matter to me."

"You framed it as a test of trust. I decided to give you a chance."

He nodded. "So I have proven worthy?"

I smiled. "I had no doubt."

"Ah."

"Marie tells me it took her a very long time to believe Paul when he said he wouldn't stand in the way of her singing. And one way she learned to trust him was by watching and seeing him do what he said he would."

"So you are learning to trust me."

"I am."

"And if I tell you that I will find a way for you to keep singing in any future life we might have . . ."

"Well, I'll have to believe you."

Gil very carefully took my hand, and as usual, the electricity crackled between us. "It may take some time to resolve all of this."

"Nothing worth winning is easy."

"So American, sweetheart." He pulled my hand to his lips. "One must work very hard for all good things."

"But true."

"Sometimes, though, life gives a gift." His eyes held mine. "And perhaps one should just say, 'Yes, thank you.' "

"If one can."

For a moment, we watched each other, unsure what to do next, no way to settle the balance between us. Despite Tommy's optimistic plans, marriage is marriage, and once you're a man's property, there are no guarantees. There was simply no good solution here that would not cost me more than I was willing or able to risk. And yet.

Bashert. Meant . . . but meant to give up my vocation

and my happy life? I had obligations and options that my mother had never dreamed of. Walk away from all of that for the sake of a man, even this man? Not a possibility.

"But it's more than you and me," I said finally.

"I know. And I give you my word, I will find a way. *We* will."

I nodded. I might actually be able to believe him. At least right then, as he held my hand and gazed at me with that expression that made me feel like something sacred, or precious.

"Then perhaps we leave this at an understanding."

"An understanding," I repeated slowly.

"I have no need or desire to pursue anyone else, and you've given me no indication that you are doing so . . ."

"No." The whisper was all I could manage.

He took my other hand and just studied me for a couple of breaths, with a faint smile. "Then, while we are not yet in any place to formalize our connection, we agree that in the future, we will settle the terms to do so."

I found a voice. "I can live with that."

"So can I, at least until you bring *The Princes* to London."

"All right, then."

We stood there, silent again, holding hands, the attraction between us practically charging the air.

Finally, Gil let go one of my hands and lightly traced the line of my face. "I am told that while physical expressions of affection are absolutely and rightly forbidden for couples who are not yet engaged, Americans have been known to be a bit less doctrinaire when the situation warrants."

"Possibly." I swallowed an inappropriate giggle at the word *doctrinaire*, one of Montezuma's favorites. Presumably, I would not need *crustacean* or *fortissimo*.

"I have heard, for example, that when one's beau is in peril or facing a long voyage, even a respectable lady might be persuaded to grant him a farewell kiss."

"She might," I allowed, because I wanted that kiss every bit as much as he did. "As long as he understood that it was no reflection on her virtue."

"Of course not. A lady may send her swain to sea with a happy memory without giving the impression that she is anything other than virtuous."

"If we're quite clear on that."

"We surely are." Gil just gazed at me for a second, his eyes almost frighteningly intense. "I would never ask you to anticipate the pleasures of our marriage bed."

For a moment, I was absolutely speechless. It wasn't the shocking bluntness or even the cool assumption that we would one day wed. It was the thought of what pleasures there might be in that marriage bed.

"For now, *mo chridhe*," he said finally, leaning a little closer, "just that farewell kiss."

"Just that."

In my memory, our first—my only—kiss was a blur, an indistinct whirlwind of passion and sensation. This was entirely different, and not just because he was taking the lead. Slow, careful, as much promise as embrace. And I had no doubt he was making sure to give me much to think about during our next weeks apart.

Much indeed. He pulled me closer, his arms tightening around me, as I responded to the kiss. The closeness, the spark between us, the absolute *pleasure* of it, came as a surprise and shock. Good heavens, how do married women maintain focus on anything at all if they're doing this with their men every day? It was the first time in my life that I understood how young girls might lose their heads and get drawn into trouble.

Gil, though, was no cad. Before I found myself entirely swept away, he pulled back carefully and gently, and rested his forehead on mine for a moment, breathless himself.

"We may wish to work out those terms with some speed, Shane."

"No argument."

He nodded and stepped back, then took my hands and kissed one, then the other. "Till *The Princes* comes to London."

"Till London," I managed as he slowly let go and turned to leave.

I leaned on the bannister, trying to cultivate a casual air as he took the last steps across the floor, hoping it wasn't obvious that my knees were wobbling.

At the door, he turned. "You do know that I love you."

"I love you."

As the words hung between us, we stared at each other. He had spoken deliberately, but I had not, and I had utterly no idea what to do. The violation of propriety was enough of a shock, but the dawning realization of what we'd just done with those few words was far more. The Rubicon crossed. Whatever happened now, there was no going back.

Bashert. I still didn't know what it would cost me, or us, but I could no longer deny it, at least to myself. Even if I wasn't going to say the word to him. I'd said quite enough already.

Gil broke the silence, with his hand on the knob. "That is all the understanding we need, then."

"Yes." It felt almost like a vow.

Long after the door closed, I was still standing there, electrified and staring after him, when I heard the first voice.

"So? Do I need to pour you some whisky?"

Marie stood in the drawing-room doorway, chuckling.

"Do I need to post the banns?" Father Michael added.

"Do I need to have a word?" Preston and Toms asked in unintended unison.

"Stop. All of you." I let go of the bannister and took a breath, sorting myself out. "You don't need to do anything. We'll worry about it when we get to London."

Epilogue

For the Festival of Lights

Several weeks later, near the end of Hanukkah, a slim parcel arrived from Britain. Inside, a small cream morocco-bound edition of John Donne's love poems and a note.

> *My Dear Shane,*
> *While Joshua tells me that the Jewish Festival of Lights is in no way as significant a holiday to him as the yuletide is to Christians, I am also given to understand that it is an excellent time for a small token of esteem. Perhaps we can enjoy these poems together in London.*
> *In the meantime, I content myself with imagining you in the light of your candles, your eyes outshining the flames, the glow illuminating your lovely face and hands as you light them one by one. I look forward to kissing those hands again one day soon.*
>
> *Most affectionately and kindly yours,*
> *G*

Though I was a bit discomfited by the lack of a "Love" at the end of the letter, I decided that being a reserved British aristocrat, he might be letting the good Reverend Donne say it for him. And I did recognize the closing as one John Adams used with Abigail. Nonetheless, I took up my pen to write a letter of thanks, determined not to give away too much.

> *Many thanks for a perfect and timely gift. I have always been exceedingly fond of Donne. Perhaps you will read it to me when I come to London. I find myself missing the sound of your voice and looking forward to hearing it again.*
>
> *Yours, as always,*
> *S*

Donne or no Donne, there was still far too much to settle between us for me to believe a happy ending was within easy reach.